Uncle Peretz Takes Off

Uncle Peretz Takes Off

short stories

Yaakov Shabtai

Translated from the Hebrew by Dalya Bilu

OVERLOOK DUCKWORTH
Woodstock • New York • London

First published in the United States in 2004 by
Overlook Duckworth, Peter Mayer Publishers, Inc.
Woodstock, New York, and London

WOODSTOCK:
One Overlook Drive
Woodstock, NY 12498
www.overlookpress.com
[for individual orders, bulk and special sales, contact our Woodstock office]

NEW YORK:
141 Wooster Street
New York, NY 10012

LONDON:
90-93 Cowcross Street
London EC1M 6BF
inquires@duckworth-publishers.co.uk
www.ducknet.co.uk

∞ The paper used in this book meets the requirements for paper
permanence as described in the ANSI Z39.48-1992 standard.

Cataloging-in-Publication Data is available from the Library of Congress
A CIP record for this book is available from the British Library

Type formatting by Bernard Schleifer Company
Manufactured in the United States of America
FIRST EDITION
ISBN 1-58567-340-4 (US)
ISBN 0-7156-3343-0 (UK)
10 9 8 7 6 5 4 3 2 1

Contents

Adoshem

SUMMER WAS DRAWING to a close; as always, mother kept remarking in a surprised tone that it was getting dark early. At the same time, however, she would go on stubbornly with her chores, as the darkness quietly gathered and deepened in the kitchen and the other rooms of the house. Grandmother worked with her, wrapped in her brown woollen shawl. And on one of those late summer days, grandfather raised his bony head from his glass of tea and in one short, interrogative sentence brought up the question of my Bar Mitzvah. No one reacted, but I knew my doom was sealed. Nevertheless, like everyone else, I went on behaving as if nothing had been said.

Then it was autumn. The green cap of the poinsettia tree fell off overnight, leaving the skeleton of its twisted branches, which reached almost to the edge of our balcony. Between the branches the remains of proud crimson blossoms could be seen lying on the grass at its feet, crushed and blackened. From time to time grandmother touched lightly on the subject, cautious, timid, hoping for the best. But as winter approached, her reminders grew more insistent, and evasive discussions took place between her and my parents, sometimes turning into brief and bitter quarrels without anyone wanting that.

My grandfather was silent and so was I. My role in this world was to obey the commands of the grown-ups, honor them, and serve as the object of the great hopes they pinned on me. None of them appealed directly to me, except grandmother, who would steal up on me in the seclusion of the bathroom or the little storeroom, trying to persuade me in hurried whispers to come over to her side, to volunteer of my own free will, thereby averting a terrible disaster.

I felt torn. I was sorry for grandmother; besides, I had no doubt at all that in one way or another I would have to submit to my fate in the end, sacrificing myself to society and my grandfather. But I wanted time. In spite of everything I hoped for a pardon or a miracle.

Grandmother was a clever woman with a big face and a broad nose, whereas grandfather worked zealously in the service of Adoshem,[1] like a fanatic sergeant major in service to the king. The spirit of Adoshem, exuding a smell of old prayer books, medicines, velvet, wool, old suits, synagogue pews, and snuff, dwelt behind the heavy armchair in the corner of the room, while Adoshem himself sat in brown felt slippers in his Egyptian palace in the sky, looking very like my grandfather, only taller, holding a wooden scepter in one hand and in the other a heavy volume of laws bound in leather.

My teacher Mrs. Fuch's Adonaitzvaoth[2] was very different.

Adonaitzvaoth toiled to create the world and parted the sea and sweated with the people of Israel in the wilderness and lost his temper about the poor man's ewe lamb and wept over the destruction of the Temple, and now he was wandering over the face of earth like a Russian monk, all dressed like A.D. Gordon[3] helping the workers and punishing the rich and

raining white bread and fish on the houses of the poor for
Friday nights.

I didn't believe in either of them, but Adoshem filled me
with a terrible fear. Sometimes his wrathful spirit would wander and squat beneath the oval table, or penetrate the brown
wardrobe, lingering in the naphthalene laden air among
grandmother's dark silk and woollen dresses. On gray, rainy
days his spirit would fill our whole room and invade the hall,
where grandfather spent most of his day sitting in the shifting
gloom like an Egyptian mummy on a black, battered chair,
his throne covered with eroded carvings. There he would gulp
watery yellow soup from an enamel dish, stirring his dark tea
with a battered silver teaspoon reserved for his use, sternly
observing the ways of the household.

He was like a sorcerer, like one of the magicians of Egypt.
All night long evil spirits raged in the tunnels of his nostrils
and the cavern of his mouth. In the daytime, wearing a black
hat and an old coat whose frayed collar, like the hairs of his
beard and mustache, was brown and stiff from snuff, he
occupied himself with obscure rites of initiation. For this performance he was assisted by a prayer shawl, a "four fringes,"
little tephillin boxes, leather straps, a hernia strap, a saltcellar,
a silver teaspoon, a red velvet bag, a prayer book, and an
enormous tin mug. In between prayers he was encompassed
by an ancient silence which he never broke except suddenly
to blow his nose, trumpeting like Doomsday, or to utter a few
wrathful sentences if the hint of an infringement of the laws
of Adoshem came to his notice, or to break into the prayers
which poured through his thin lips as indifferently as falling
grain. Then he would make a noise like the crumbling of
rusks in the dim hall.

The terrible rage of his faith withered and yellowed his
face, but he was indefatigable. Sometimes he would burst out

of his chair, snatch from the transgressor's hand a milk uten-
sil erroneously being used for meat or vice versa, bang it on
the table and the door, then rush out to stick it furiously in
the flowerpot on the balcony that had once been full of gera-
niums. On particularly frenzied days the whole flowerpot
was a forest of knives, forks, and spoons gleaming in the sun,
fully visible to all who passed in the street below.

He frightened me, especially when my parents weren't at
home. For then he would lie in wait in the hall and suddenly
grab my neck with his gnarled fingers. He would pull me to
his chair, trapping me in the vise of his legs, covering my head
with his hand, yelling in Yiddish:

"Pray, goy, pray!"

Abjectly I would repeat the whispered words coming out
of his mouth, his face menacingly close to mine: "*Moideyani
lefaneycho melechaivokayam shehechzartabinishmosi bechem-
loraba lemunaseycho seylo.*"[4]

Thus I came under his power and worshipped Adoshem.

Winter deepened and my sentence was passed. Mother, as
usual, tried to sweeten the pill and informed me that I would
take instruction for my Bar Mitzvah in a group with a
modern rabbi. The instruction would take place twice a week
during the afternoons in one of the classrooms at school.
Accordingly, one week later, I put on my Tyrolean trousers,
took my bible and a notebook, and in dejected and embit-
tered spirits I went to the rabbi. Grandmother saw me off
with a look of glad thanksgiving, mumbling a blessing.

The rabbi really was modern: tall, broad shouldered, rosy
cheeked, clean shaven, with only a little square of a mustache
pasted to his lip beneath his nose. He wore a blue and white
silk skullcap with the words JERUSALEM and GOOD BOY
embroidered in gold.

He strolled in front of the blackboard, under the pictures

of Herzl and Ussishkin, lecturing in the voice of an Italian tenor on the priests and the Levites and Temple and God, who emerged from his words as a unique combination of Flash Gordon, the Invisible Man, the High Commissioner, and a magic remedy against every kind of ill. But most of the lesson he devoted to a certain kind of worm that produced a blue dye used to stain a certain thread. Since the destruction of the Temple the worm had disappeared. No one knew where to find it or what it looked like, so they had nothing with which to color the thread.

For four weeks, twice a week every week, the rabbi returned to the subject of the Temple and God and the worm for the sake of every new pupil, and on the fifth week he began to teach us the musical notation of the bible. At this I drew the line. I didn't want to shout in a choir and I was too shy to sing alone, so I stopped going to the Bar Mitzvah classes. I would leave the house in my Tyrolean trousers and slip like a lizard around the corner of the street, through side alleys and strange courtyards to the Muslim cemetery. There, next to the sea, in the salty wilderness ravaged by the winds, dotted here and there with green islands of evening primroses and skimpy lilies, I would hide behind the Arab tombstones. Sometimes I would go down to the beach to sit alone at the foot of the limestone hill, opposite the vast expanse of water, comforting myself with terrible and bitter fantasies.

There I met my classmate, Eli.

If only I could have turned into air or water! I tried to convince him that I had landed there in all innocence by accident, but the lie burst out of my words like the stuffing from a mattress.

Eli was not impressed by my speech. He simply wasn't interested. He was glad to meet someone he knew, that was all. He threw his satchel on the sand, took off his shoes, and bent to look for ticks behind Rudy's ears. Eli expounded on Rudy's virtues and told me that he was a Swiss dog of rare and special breed. One of his female relatives had emigrated to America, where she had appeared in a number of movies; she spoke English as well as the English teacher herself. In fact he was about to sell Rudy within the next few days to a British officer who was already, at this stage, prepared to give him two bottles of Johnny Walker whiskey, several bottles of beer, and ten packets of Three-Three-Three cigarettes.

I pretended to be full of admiration, waiting for the moment when I could beat a retreat. Like my parents, I was afraid of dogs. They were as foreign to me as his stories of whiskey. They belonged to another world, barbaric and inferior, which had to be shunned. It was the world which stretched along the seashore promenade and Yarkon Street, then beyond Allenby Street to Jaffa, and was referred to by my mother as the "Florentine Quarter"; a kind of Tel Aviv-Chicago, populated by hawkers, criminals, cripples, widows, divorcées, Eskimo Pie vendors, poor people, brokers, street urchins swarming with lice, sunflower seed eaters, and kids who went to afternoon shows at the movies and therefore failed school.

I was sure that Eli, the teachers' terror and abomination, must belong there too. Four times a week he would go to the movies; he never missed a performance by Shimon Rudi or Emile Korochenko. Twice he had been held behind in school, and he was always being sent home to fetch his parents, swaggering from the classroom with a defiant smile. Usually his mother came, a big, pink woman in a kind of dressing gown. Once it was his father. His clothes were spotted with whitewash and there was a piece of transparent paper sticking to his cracked lower lip. He looked very shy, almost sad, but Miss Fuchs seemed alarmed by his appearance, perhaps because of the whip he held in his hand.

I asked Eli if he had already learned "Be Comforted My People" by heart.

"No," he said shortly and let Rudy off his leash.

He took an orange out of his satchel and peeled it with a little penknife that had a silver handle.

"I won't learn anything for her. She's a whore," he said firmly and offered me half the orange. "She fucks the art teacher and Mr. Green and all the British soldiers."

The dry eastern wind brushed my face and my heart fluttered.

"Are you sure that's what she's like?" I asked in a hollow voice.

"A hundred percent," said Eli and wiped the blade of the penknife on his shirt. "Haven't you seen the art teacher sticking his hands up her dress?"

"Oh yes," I lied, the orange juice dripping off my chin.

"She walks around without panties on, the whore. I know she does. I looked with a mirror and saw everything. But I'll get her one day, you'll see."

My face blazed and my mouth was full of saliva. Eli took off his clothes, threw them on a heap in the sand, and stood in his wide underpants, from which a pair of skinny, very sunburnt legs emerged with knees as knobby as a camel's.

"Come on, let's go for a swim."

"I can't," I said. "I've got a Bar Mitzvah class."

"Rubbish," said Eli. He hitched up his falling pants, tightening the elastic and tying it in a knot. "The sea's very healthy. Come on," and he ran into the water.

Rudy bounded after him, happily scattering sand.

I was left alone with my bible and the notebook in which I had written all the details about the Temple, God, and the worm. The beach was deserted and the sea was calm, a turquoise colour, with a broad path like a blurry broken mirror, along which Eli and Rudy gaily advanced. On the left, in the distance, was Jaffa with all its spires floating in an orange-gray mist, like a fairy-tale Baghdad. How beautiful it all was,

but only apparently. Because the world was really full of
chasms and mysterious underground tunnels.

As in a nightmare I wanted to run but stayed where I was.
Curious and frightened, I waited for Eli. I had to ask him
again about Miss Fuchs. What did it mean that she was a
whore going to bed with the art teacher and Mr. Green, and,
especially, the British soldiers? I wanted to ask him about the
gym teacher and Ziva Birnbaum too, and maybe also about
our neighbor whose husband worked at the port. Twice I had
been drawn with an anxiously beating heart to peep through
the keyhole when she was in the shower, and I had seen the
enormous navel on the soft whiteness of her belly, and her
black pubic hair, and she stroked it lightly with her fingers.
Now it seemed almost certain that she too was not pure.

Eli emerged from the sea, his lips purple, his skin bumpy
with gooseflesh.

He beat his chest, dried himself with his vest, wrapped his
underpants in it, bundled them both into his satchel, and
combed his hair. Then he took a piece of bamboo from his
pocket, lit it and started smoking.

"Want a puff?"

I shook my head, then said, "So you're sure that's what
she's like?"

"Who?"

"Miss Fuchs."

"Sure. That's what all girls are like," he said dismissively.
Then he added, "Come on, I'll show you something." With
Rudy lying between his legs, he rummaged in his satchel and
took out something whitish. He stretched it a bit, asking me if
I knew what it was. Yes I knew more or less, but in the embar-
rassment of the moment for some reason I shook my head.

In any case Eli took no notice of my reaction. He spread
the object out on his knee and told me that it was called a
condom. The word rang in my ears, stopping my throat like

a cork in a bottle. Then he explained what the purpose of the thing was and exactly how it was used. In conclusion he said, "This one's used, but you can use it again. You only have to wash it with soap and water and see there aren't any holes."

We stood up. Eli picked up his satchel and together we climbed the path to the Muslim cemetery. A cold shadow had already covered the whole beach, where the sea lay heavy and leaden at our feet, gleaming dully. Clouds came up on the horizon, fencing in the sea like a hedge around a broad, deserted field. Eli sat on one of the tombstones and put on his shoes.

"Do you think that the dead can rise again?"

"No," replied Eli firmly. "When people die their bodies turn to earth and their souls go to heaven, getting mixed up together. But I think that the whole world's going to blow up soon and we're going to fall into the abyss. The Turk from the vegetable shop thinks so too. That'll be the end."

He spoke with absolute confidence, almost indifferently, and I felt a sudden elation. However far-fetched his words, there was something persuasive and very frightening about them. The fear was full of wonder and it even had a kind of appeal. For a moment I thought of my teachers, my parents, my grandfather, and my Bar Mitzvah, and I wanted to break into a loud shout. How ridiculous and pathetic they all were in comparison to the truths that Eli had revealed to me without a trace of calculation or conceit. I was grateful; I wanted to propose that if the explosion should take place we should both hang on a tree trunk together.

We emerged into Yarkon Street. Eli carried the terrible thing in his satchel. I was full of secrets and sweated inside my Tyrolean trousers. Two English policemen advanced toward us.

I dropped my eyes but Eli walked right up to them and said in English, "Good morning."

When we had passed he said, "May they rot in hell."

On the corner of Frishman Street I stopped and said that I had to go home.

"Come with me," urged Eli, "we'll go to Gentilla."

"I can't," I replied, but continued to stand on the pavement.

"You won't be sorry," said Eli. "Come on."

"I have to go to the rabbi," I lied with a heavy heart. "My parents will kill me."

"To hell with them," said Eli, who had evidently given up on me already. "They're making a fool of you. Making you get up and sing for them in a synagogue like a goat. I'd never let anyone make a fool of me like that."

"I can't," I said, "some other time," like the coward I was, still waiting for some hint of understanding from him.

Eli shrugged and started walking down the street, which was bordered on both sides by the clubs and cafes of the British soldiers. As he walked he whistled loudly, "Kiss Me Goodnight Sergeant Major."

I didn't wait for him to disappear from view. I shook the sand off my clothes, straightened my hair, and hurried home. Two days later I went with him to Gentilla.

We met next to the green public baths. The sea was stormy. A whitish mist floated in the air, which was oily and sticky. The cafes along the promenade were deserted and the iron shutters of the gaming alleys were down. Everything was damp and desolate. We crossed Herbert Samuel Street, penetrating deeper and deeper into foreign, dangerous territory: gloomy housed, peeling walls, shadowy entrances, neglected yards, colored panes in high windows with ornamental borders, arches, all kinds of towers and turrets and bits and pieces of palaces ransacked from the four corners of Europe, laundry tubs on balconies whose rusty balustrades were ornamented with flat, metal flowers.

"That's where the Turk lives," said Eli respectfully, pointing to one of the houses. "He's got two wives and a vegetable shop." I nodded my head but my heart filled with a growing distress. I felt strange and helpless and I waited for the journey to end. Sure enough, Eli stopped, put two fingers into his mouth, whistled, and a moment later Gentilla's head appeared at a third story window, then immediately vanished again.

We went up to the roof.

Gentilla was already sitting there on a box in the corner with her hands clasping her knees. She was wearing a yellow skirt and a green sweater. At first sight she looked like a frightened wild cat bedraggled by the rain.

Eli introduced me, held out a packet of chewing gum, and sat down on the whitewashed tar. Gentilla put one arm around his neck, glancing briefly in my direction. Her eyes were as black as fresh soot. I hid the bible and notebooks behind my back but stood where I was.

Eli took a packet of sunflower seeds out of his pocket. He cracked seeds for her, then for himself, and invited me to join in. Hardly a word was said. Afterwards he asked me to go into the laundry room and wait until he called. I did as he told me, but I peeped through a crack in the door.

Gentilla stroked him gently on the neck then slipped her hand underneath his shirt. She appeared to be massaging his back. Eli, for his part, cupped her hair in one hand and fondled her gold locket, very slowly and dreamily, with the other. Suddenly he drew her to him and they kissed.

"You can come now," he called, wiping his mouth with his hand.

The damp afternoon sky darkened but far away in the west the edges of the blue-gray clouds were stained a pale tentative crimson. A chill wind blew, bringing with it the smell of rust and burning tar. I felt exhausted and I wanted it all to be over. Eli took a crumpled Player's cigarette and two Simon Arzt stubs out of his pocket. He gave the Player's to Gentilla and offered me one of the stubs.

"Go on," he said, "no one will know."

I filled my mouth with smoke and coughed. Eli patted my back and he also coughed, light, suppressed coughs. Only Gentilla smoked comfortably. She rested her head on Eli's shoulder, chewing the gum and blowing out spirals of whitish smoke. Suddenly, without saying a word, she took his hand and burned it with her cigarette, looking right into his eyes.

Eli bit his lips, twisting his face into a smile; I averted my eyes.

"Why don't you look?" cried Gentilla mockingly, pulling his hand to her lips and licking the burn.

Eli accompanied me as far as Allenby Steet. Before we parted he bought me a waffle and told me that Gentilla worked in a cafe and that he and Gentilla were going to get married soon; her father had a garage.

Pursued by my sins and full of fear, I hurried home. I threw the waffle away immediately and walked with my mouth open, breathing the fresh evening air. I felt hatred for Gentilla and swore to myself that from now on I would never go near Eli. In the yard I washed my face and mouth, gargled, and breathed into the palm of my hand. It seemed to me that I would never get rid of the smell of cigarettes.

For two weeks I kept my oath, two weeks of modesty and penitence, humbleness and good deeds. Eli appeared not to notice the change, while my mother thought at first that I was sickening for something and later concluded in consultation with Grandmother that I was excited because of my Bar Mitzvah.

Indeed the days flew. In the meantime they began drawing up a list of guests, calculating the cost, and planning the arrangement of tables in the flat. Aunt Rifka and Aunt Zipporah came to offer their assistance by baking the cakes. Then Leibshu Krup, that laughing, sunburned old man, came to pay us a visit. He drank a glass of tea, announcing that he had already bought me a prayer shawl, tephillin, and a velvet bag. He made this announcement in the usual mixture of solemnity and mockery with which he spoke of women, religion, or synagogue affairs, and for which my grandmother detested him. He pulled me toward him, banged his fist on the table, made his announcement, and burst into rude laughter, looking at us with great enjoyment and a hint of malice in his blue eyes, smoothing his thick mustache with his fingers.

I lost my appetite and spent sleepless nights. Every day I would make up my mind to tell my mother the truth, every day I would put it off to the next. Between these postponements and endless expectations of a sudden miracle, I made desperate plans; I thought of running away, getting sick, or even drowning myself in the sea. Before I drowned myself, I thought, I would write a letter putting all the blame on my grandfather, who went on sitting silently in his chair, all-knowing, waiting.

Then I went back to Eli. I followed him around like a dog, eager and abject. I stole cigarettes for him and money to buy chewing gum or sunflower seeds. I smoked and ran messages for him. I hardly ever saw Gentilla, then when I did we never exchanged a single word.

Ten days before the date of my Bar Mitzvah the rabbi finally noticed my absence. As soon as the bell rang for recess, David the Long came up and said the rabbi asked about me. He was going to send an urgent letter to my parents. The circle was closed.

That day Eli didn't come to school. I wanted to ask his advice, even though I knew that the game was already up. In the afternoon I ran all over town looking for him until I arrived at Gentilla's house.

I whistled for her. She was on the roof and beckoned me to come up. When I went to her she said Eli had gone to the Eden Cinema and would be back in about an hour.

I stood on the threshold but I didn't know what to do. I was in despair. From where I was standing I could see the boundless sea, all hills and valleys full of movement, roaring with a heavy muffled roar.

"You can wait for him here," said Gentilla, and she sat down on the box. "He'll be back." She beckoned me to sit down next to her. There was no warmth or sympathy in her voice. I went up to her and leaned against the balustrade. I paged through the bible with cold fingers until Gentilla snatched it from my hand, threw it onto the tar, saying, "Sit down. Are you afraid of getting dirty?" When I sat down she added, as if she were stating a fact, "You're like a king. You'll never get dirty." She passed her hand caressingly over my head and the nape of my neck. "You've got pretty curls and you smell nice, of lemons."

I said nothing. Something quivered in me and tensed. I turned my head away.

"What's the matter?"

I was stubbornly silent and she went on stroking my head with sure, greedy fingers. She was close to me; her living smell, the smell of wet wool and sweat, surrounded me. Suddenly, almost unconsciously, I opened my mouth, telling her everything with a feeling of release and tears in my eyes.

Gentilla listened attentively but without expression. When I was finished she asked what my grandfather's name was and how old he was. I told her.

"An old man," she said, and after a short pause she added in a different voice, "We could cast a spell on him."

"Cast a spell on him?"

"Yes," whispered Gentilla with her mouth close to my face, looking at me strangely. "If you want me to I can cast a spell on him and make him die. He's too old anyway."

For a moment her eyes had a hollow look, as if they were wandering in some other place, either very near or very far or perhaps they were turned around and looking inside herself. Her warm breath blew into my face.

I didn't believe her.

"Yes," I said in a fragile voice, "I want you to."

Gentilla pressed her body to mine, leaning her head against the wall, closing her eyes. The wind ruffled her hair, a slight flush appeared on her face as she took my hand and began stroking it slowly, hypnotically, as if she were falling into a trance, then pushing it further between her legs, at first gently, then violently with her mouth wide open.

I did not stir. Silence filled the world to overflowing, everything came to a stop.

Gentilla shuddered.

"He'll die today a week," she said languidly and let go of my hand. Afterwards she tidied her hair a bit and went back to chewing her gum.

I hurried home as fast as I could. There was someone pursuing me like a shadow, hiding in the entrances to buildings, peeping out of courtyards. The pavement slipped under my feet. Everything was in chaos.

I went into the yard of our house but hid between the bushes. A yellow light was shining in the bedroom and kitchen windows. I waited until it was already late, then went upstairs, quiet and drifting like a leaf. At home everything was as usual: father was sleeping in his clothes with the newspaper over his face, mother was ironing in the kitchen, grandmother was writing a letter, grandfather was sitting on his chair, wearing a black magician's hat, with bleary eyes wide open. I slipped past him with downcast eyes.

I didn't really believe it but still, somehow he was already dead, or if not, he soon would be. It was horrifying. All night long I waited for the angel of death to appear between the slats of the shutters to take one of us away. Then at dawn Gentilla rose from the depths, looking very pale. She wrapped her skinny arms around my neck with terrible strength, as if she wanted to strangle me, saying "You'll never get dirty. No, you'll never get dirty," and I couldn't suffocate her. The next day the letter came from the rabbi and there was a terrible scene. My father banged the table in a towering rage, shouted at the top of his voice, "Liar! Liar!" His face was contorted with fury.

The Bar Mitzvah came and went. I received presents and compliments on the way I read my portion in a breaking voice. The rabbi had composed a homily for me and I read it with emotion, promising solemnly to be a dutiful son and student, loyal to my people. I promised to walk in the ways of righteousness, the ways of the Lord. Now for the space of an hour or so, I felt free and at peace with the world.

My grandfather went on sitting in his chair, terrorizing us. But not for long. He died a year later, on a day when the light was soft and pleasant. A few months before, Adoshem began robbing him of his memory from time to time. When this happened, on his way home from synagogue for example, he would sometimes wander, lost in the streets like a helpless, brown beetle. Whenever I saw him in this state, I hid. My parents would go out to look for him, take him by the hand, and lead him home. Now he was a child with wrinkled parchment cheeks, a wispy grey beard, empty eyes—the blind staff of Adoshem. One day, toward evening, he lost his memory again, and two days later he was dead.

Dead he terrified me more than alive. His body lay on the cold floor of the room next door with legs pointing at the door, wrapped in a white sheet with a few candles flickering at the head, while his lean brown spirit prowled the house.

All that day and the night after it, and the morning after the night, I waited for them to take him away, to throw his chair out after him, then his worn silver skullcap, his enamel dish, his tephillin, his hernia strap, and the big mug he had used for the ritual washing of his hands.

In the morning the house began to fill with relatives and friends dressed in their best. In the afternoon the people from the burial society came, picked him up, took him down the steps, and the house grew empty, quiet. From the balcony I saw them putting him into the black hearse. The convoy moved slowly off to the tune of a march being played by a British military band that happened to be passing down one of the nearby streets.

For four days I stayed away from school, four carefree days that I spent hanging about in empty lots or next to the stables on Gordon Street. I went back to school on Thursday and everyone spoke to me in low, gentle voices as if I were sick. Outwardly I was sad, resigned; inwardly I felt glad and proud. My grandfather was dead.

Grandfather's secret ritual objects soon disappeared. In the spring, which came early that year, the house filled with light. The poinsetta tree grew a fresh green cap and flaming red flowers like fiery birds. In the youth movement that I joined I learned that the world had never been created but had simply always been there from the beginning. This idea seemed completely reasonable. Day by day I grew cleverer in my own eyes. No many months later I was a scientific social-ist full of a sense of mission, constantly trying to drag my grandmother into arguments in order to prove to her that God did not exist, to show her how false and harmful it was to believe in him. This made her very cross, but she would control herself, then send me about my business with a few perfunctory words. Her God needed no proofs.

I started avoiding Eli right after my Bar Mitzvah. In the last analysis he belonged to a different world, inferior, barbaric. When the long vacation came around, the class scattered and I never saw him again. I never saw Gentilla either, though she had gone on existing in the darkness of my fearful desires that whole year long until my grandfather died.

NOTES

1. A term used by the very pious in order to refer to the divinity without pronouncing the word "God": it is composed of the first part of the Hebrew word "Adonai"—meaning the Lord God, and the Hebrew word "shem"—meaning "name" i.e., the name of God.

2. Tzvaoth—the Lord of Hosts.

3. 1856–1922, ideologist of the early labor Zionist movement, he preached the "religion of labor," a mystical, Tolstoyan form of socialism.

4. The child's morning prayer, spoken by the grandfather in a Yiddish-accented Hebrew.

Model

TAMARA BELL LAY sprawled in the courtyard of the building, most of her body in the flower bed and only her legs resting on the narrow pavement. It was early, and the balconies, the flame trees and the lilac, the bushes and the dewy lawns were still shrouded in a soft, cool shade, full of the serenity of a summer morning.

At the sound of the thud some of the people living in the building woke up. One after the other they appeared at the windows and on the balconies, sleepy and dishevelled, looking rather perturbed. They glanced around them to see what had caused the noise.

Suddenly, from different directions, alarmed cries for help went up, and immediately afterwards the first of the people began arriving in the courtyard at a run. They stopped at a distance, frightened and helpless, without daring to go any closer. Someone suggested running to fetch a doctor, and the greengrocer, who was on his way to open the shop, ran from one person to another mumbling "Water, water." Up on the roof, Tamara's dog Rex began to bark.

Gabriel Riebach emerged from the entrance next to the cypresses and directed his footsteps toward Tamara. He walked rapidly and without pausing. Everybody stood still and watched him. He reached her, bent down, and stretched out his hand, as if he wanted to touch her face.

Tamara Bell's right hand was stretched out at her side. It lay gently on the brown soil with its fingers touching and not touching the silvery shoots. The tall sunflowers stood around her head and shoulders.

"Here's some water," cried Gabriel Riebach's wife, appearing in the courtyard with a cup of water in her hands. She held the cup of water out in front of her and called again: "Here's some water." But Gabriel Riebach did not turn around. He knelt on the ground, carefully picked up Tamara's hand and held it in his, close to the wrist, while passing his other hand over her forehead and face and even shaking them a bit. A few of the people who had gathered in the courtyard came and stood next to him.

Silence fell, and only Mr. Schwartz shouted from the balcony of his apartment:

"We have to call the police! We have to call the police!"

"Dead," said Gabriel Riebach in a dull voice and rose to his feet.

He went and stood next to his wife, who was standing stock still under the Persian lilac, wrapped in a wide bathrobe and mumbling ceaselessly to herself: "So young. How can it be possible? So young."

"Enough!" said Gabriel Riebach, taking the cup out of her hands and pouring the water onto the ground.

In the meantime the courtyard had filled up with people and movement. People went up to Tamara and looked her over, murmuring words of sorrow, pity, and shock as they did so. Afterwards they huddled together in excited, agitated groups. They all exclaimed over and over again at the terrible thing which had just happened right in front of their eyes, and someone remarked in surprise that there wasn't a drop of blood on her. At this the greengrocer approached the body again and examined it closely. He noticed a thin trickle of blood coming out of the corner of her mouth and staining her cheek, which was half-buried in the loose earth and hidden by the grass. For some reason, however, he preferred to ignore the evidence of his eyes and kept repeating in amazement to everyone he came across that there wasn't the faintest trace of blood on her body.

The sun rose quickly. Now it was on the balustrade of the roof. The heads of the sunflowers flamed, and after a few minutes the upper half of Tamara Bell's body was also alight. The hem of her orange dress was drawn up slightly, revealing her legs to above the knee. They were as beautiful as they had been when she was alive.

She was about twenty-nine years old, and whenever any of the neighbors spoke to her, they continued to address her as "Mrs. Proiss." There was something nasty and provocative in this, but she ignored it. Her face remained as blank and expressionless as ever.

Proiss was Michael's surname. He was a few years younger than she was, and they lived together on the roof, in the room which had previously been used as a laundry. Very little was known about them. They kept to themselves and lived in a world of their own. For a year and a half they lived together, until one day he left her. The gardener's wife claimed he had told her he was going out to paint on the banks of the Yarkon River, and sailed for Paris. None of the people in the building was surprised or sorry. On the contrary. They were all of the opinion that the whole affair was sordid and immoral from the beginning, and the end was only to be expected, like the end of anything else conceived in sin and continued in sin and beyond the pale of common decency from the word go.

All of them except the gardener, who dismissed the whole thing in one sentence, which he never tired of repeating: "Life is confusion and chaos." He pronounced this sentence in a philosophical tone, full of sorrow and resignation, but he was talking mainly about himself. He repeated it now too, and averted his eyes from Tamara's body.

She worked as an artist's model in the studio in the courtyard, where Michael painted. It was there that they met, and from her modeling, apparently, that they lived. She would sit motionless for hours on end in the little room, which was full of the smell of oil paint and turpentine and clay. She sat on an old chair, with her legs crossed, her long-fingered hands on her knee, always in a simple, tight-fitting dress that showed off her figure, and with a scarf around her neck. She never spoke to anyone when she came or when she left, and she did not mix with the artists. She was a combination of passionate sensuality and proud and tormented refinement.

One day her mother showed up. It was winter. Laboriously she bore her heavy body up to the roof on her slender legs, and then the sound of voices was heard, the voices of Tamara and her mother. Mrs. Bell demanded that her daughter leave Michael, return to Jerusalem, and complete her education. Her father refused to come. He refused to even send her his regards. He would have nothing to do with her until she came home.

A long time later Mrs. Bell could be seen emerging into the street. She stood still for a moment, as if confused, and then she walked off and disappeared around the corner in her black fur coat.

The baby was born some time after Michael left. Tamara was now more beautiful than ever. Something painful and anxious etched itself on her pale face, and her breasts grew full. She would walk down the street with her head held high and her body swaying ever so slightly. "The bastard's mother," some of the residents called her among themselves and sniggered.

A few months later a man arrived on the scene and then disappeared. After him another one, and after him one with a tanned, muscular body and a scar running across his face. The gardener's wife claimed he was a gangster. Others said he was a boxer. Not long afterward he too disappeared.

The child, who was pale and sickly from birth, grew slowly in the intervals between one sickness and the next. Tamara earned a living from typing and translating from German and English and looked after the child. She cooked for him, carried him to the doctor, and took him out for short walks, with big sunglasses hiding her eyes. The child cried a lot, especially at night, and she sang to him to soothe him and put him to sleep. Some of the residents complained about the noise, which disturbed their rest.

A year later, at the beginning of spring, the child died. It was impossible to save him, and he died. Nobody knew what he died of, and nobody asked. Suddenly it was quiet.

That summer Tamara removed the dark glasses from her eyes and wore light clothes. Now she burst into bloom, wildly and splendidly, with all her strength, and only her lips betrayed something bitter and tired. At about this time heavy curtains were hung on the studio windows and the panes were blocked with cardboard. Something new was happening in there.

The residents expressed their disapproval, which in the course of time grew into constant tension accompanied by outbursts of anger and threats of violence. Mr. Schwartz spoke to the head of the residents committee several times. He declared angrily that there was still some law and order left in the world, and that they had to put a stop to this abomination, which was having a harmful influence, especially on the children. In this he was expressing the opinion of all the residents, who demanded active measures to end the outrage. Everybody thought that the studio should be shut down, and in any case Tamara should be made to leave the building whether she liked it or not. The head of the committee said that he was taking steps but that it wasn't so simple from the legal point of view. He promised to take further steps and asked everyone to keep their tempers in the meantime.

The long vacation arrived. The yard filled up with the dry smell of summer flowers and cut grass and the buzzing of bees and insects. The poinciana tree burst into wild, scarlet bloom and cast a heavy shade. The children would gather underneath it and stare at the locked doors and blank windows of the studio. They were curious and excited, they used dirty words and told rude jokes and giggled. Some of the older ones made repeated attempts to steal up and peep through the cracks, but the artists chased them away. Occasionally fights broke out and curses and blows were exchanged.

The vacation drew to a close. And on one of those empty days one of the children, a swarthy lad, succeeded in breaking through and witnessing the mystery. He crept up by himself, from behind the building, climbed up the drainpipe, hung onto the bars of the skylight, and looked through the glass.

Down below, inside the studio, the painters stood in a semicircle in front of their easels and painted. And in the center, on a low, round platform covered with a carpet, was Tamara. She was kneeling completely naked, the upper half of her body erect, leaning slightly backwards, with her black hair falling onto her shoulders. She had both hands on the back of her neck, and her face was raised to the skylight.

He remained hanging there, excited and afraid. The naked body bowled him over, the pure whiteness of the skin, the breasts, the armpits, the stomach, the black pubic hair. He couldn't take his eyes off her, and suddenly they met her own, gazing at him in utter, icy calm. He let go of the bars in a panic, slid down the drainpipe, and ran back to his friends, who immediately surrounded him.

Now they all stood in the harsh sunlight, in their short gym pants and their tricot vests and waited impatiently.

The door opened and Tamara emerged from the darkness. The glaring light hit her in the eyes and for a moment she paused, as if she didn't know which way to turn. The children stared at her and retreated. Most of them hid in the entrances and behind the bushes, and only a few remained standing boldly on the grass, in the light.

Tamara took no notice of them. She straightened the scarf on her head and walked away. There was a silence, but suddenly, after she had taken a few steps, someone whistled shrilly from behind the oleander bushes, after which silence fell again, but this time it was more tense. Tamara did not stop or turn her head. And then the swarthy boy called out:

"Hey, you, what's that black stuff you've got between your legs?" And all restraints broke loose.

"Whore!" the children shrieked jubilantly, "Whore! Whore! Whore!"

In the shade of the poinciana tree they caught up with her. They rolled about under her feet, they jumped up in front of her, they shoved each other against her, they pulled at her dress, pushed her and laughed at the tops of their voices.

The police had not yet arrived and Tamara Bell lay spread out in the pleasant morning sunshine, as if she were resting. Some of the people dispersed, but others remained huddled in little groups. They had not yet tired of discussing all the known and unknown details of Tamara's life and death, and at the same time they were hoping to hear some new, hitherto unrevealed secret, and waiting for something else to happen. The gardener walked to and fro, holding a pair of large shears in his hand, and trying to stop people from trampling the flowers and damaging the trees and bushes. He was angry, and when Mr. Katz accosted him and said gravely that life was sacred and belonged to God, and that only pride and insolence could have brought Tamara Bell to do something that was forbidden to human beings even if they were in despair, his anger broke out and he replied furiously that only fools and God knew what was permitted and what was forbidden, and that in the last analysis all she had done was to bring forward a little what was in any case fated, and in his opinion death was only a continuation of life and perhaps a far more agreeable one at that, and in any case more comfortable. He wanted to add something, but at that moment Mr. Schwartz came up to them and said:

"We should keep the children away. It's bad for them."

And indeed, some of them were already in the courtyard, washed and combed and fresh from their sleep, and they were cautiously advancing.

The gardener ignored Mr. Schwartz's contribution, but Mrs. Riebach, who was standing next to them, hurried to the edge of the courtyard, pulled a large tablecloth down from where it was hanging on the railing of the balcony of her ground floor apartment, and covered the body with it.

Now Tamara Bell lay covered with the tablecloth, upon which were brightly printed a blue sea, streets, tall buildings, green parks, bridges, a river, the Statue of Liberty, and a message in big English letters:

"Welcome to New York."

True Tenderness

ELISHEVA GIPPIUS WAS not at home when her husband died. It was the eve of the first of May, and she was out of town at a May Day meeting, where she was reading something by Alexander Blok and something by Mayakovsky to conclude the program, when it happened. She came home at one A.M. and found him dead. The cause of death was a sudden heart attack.

The day after the holiday, which was surprisingly cold and gray, the house committee hung a mourning notice in the stairwell. The time of the funeral was printed on the notice, and the residents were called upon to come and pay their last respects to the departed. Our neighbor, Noah Fine, undertook to deliver the eulogy. He worked for the General Labor Federation, and saw it as an act of kindness and reconciliation to make up for his coldness toward the deceased when he was alive.

In his eulogy he extolled the virtues of "Comrade Gippius" and described him as a quiet and noble man, a man of erudition and high moral standards, faithful to the ideals of the

Labor Movement. He also noted that he had died as he deserved to—instantly and painlessly, and holding onto his hat to prevent it blowing away he concluded with the words: "Your memory will always be with us on the first of May." At that moment it began to rain, and the cold wind blew the rain into the mourners' faces. They shrank into their coats, raised their collars, huddled together, and shuffled their feet. Only Elisheva Gippius stood still on her short, skinny legs, like an indifferent partridge, and the wisps of gray hair peeping out of her fancy hat stuck to her broad face like seaweed. Next to her stood the dead man's brother, who did not resemble him in the least. But she seemed oblivious to his presence and to everything that was happening around her.

The sky grew dark and lowering, and a faint white light, the light before nightfall, which seemed to be coming from the cold ground, illuminated the tombstones. When the ceremony was over people threw wet bunches of flowers down without any order and hurried to the two buses, which were waiting at the gate. Someone rattled a tin collection box and cried: "Charity will save from death. Charity will save from death." The next day the eulogy was printed in the Labor Party newspaper, *Davar*, with an old photograph of Gershon Gippius above it. This gave Noah Fine great satisfaction, and several times during the course of the day his eyes rested nonchalantly on the fine words he had composed in honor of the deceased and on his own name printed at the bottom of the text.

Suddenly a strange silence descended on the courtyard of the building. Only the voice of the cantor, who lived in the opposite entrance, went on trilling as usual. Now it was like an orphaned bird wheeling at its pleasure in the vast empty spaces. But three days later, first thing in the morning, Elisheva Gippius's voice joined in, and the void was filled again.

She was at it again, repeating the poems and trying out different inflections until she found the right way of stressing the words. The possibilities were endless, and she would keep practicing the same few poems over and over again without ever being finally satisfied. It was a stubborn, tireless battle, full of fierce exultant cries, exclamations of despair and supplication, of anger and contempt and passion interrupted by short bursts of laughter and groans.

"Listen!

If the stars shine—

Surely someone must want them? . . ." cried Elisheva Gippius as in days gone by.

That evening Noah Fine and his wife dropped in.

"*Nu*, what do you say to our *artistka*?" said Mrs. Fine the moment she appeared in the kitchen door, and burst out laughing. She laughed with her whole body, loud, full laughter.

Noah Fine's pale face took on a stern expression. He stretched out his hand and took a piece of Matjes herring and said that he would never have believed that she would ever go back to reciting after the tragedy that had overtaken her; at any rate, not before the flowers had even faded on the dead man's grave. In his humble opinion, he said, chewing the herring with enjoyment, her behavior showed a lack of feeling and also of tact. The dead should be respected, he said, first of all for our own sakes, for the sake of the living. And he helped himself to another piece of herring.

"But he was dead even when he was still alive," cried Mrs. Fine and regarded the company with laughing eyes in anticipation of their agreement. And then, without any obvious connection to what had gone before, she added that if she, in other words Elisheva Gippius, had had any children, she would probably not be behaving this way, but she was apparently happy without any, and now perhaps she was happy to be without a husband too, and she shot a glance at Noah Fine, who cleared his throat and removed the herring bone from his mouth, placed it on his plate, wiped his oily fingers on a kitchen towel, and said that it was a long time since he had tasted such a fine Matjes herring. The kettle boiled and my mother served tea and cake.

"A thousand times would I rather
Look at the stars
Than sign a death sentence. . . ." cried Elisheva Gippius from below.

A soft light, as if filtered through a number of veils, shone out of her window leaving a faint stain in the air and illuminating the tangled branches of the poinciana tree, which sketched marvelous arabesques in the darkness.

". . . a thousand times would I rather
Listen to the voices of the flowers,
Whispering: 'It's him!'
As I pass through the garden,
Than see the barrels of guns,
Killing those who wish
To kill me. . . ."

She went on living as she always had, with only one change evident in her way of life. Every day, toward evening, she would stand in the corner of the balcony of her first floor flat and look out into the street. She always stood in the same corner and looked in the same direction, wearing an old-fashioned silk dress with a floral print and one of her elegant old hats on her head. Usually a broad-brimmed hat banded with a velvet ribbon tied in a big, floppy bow, and embellished with a bunch of brightly colored felt flowers. Even when I came toward her, directly in her line of vision, and greeted her, she never acknowledged my greeting, not even by a hint, but went on gazing with calm concentration, as if into veiled distances inside her head. And then, suddenly, she would tear herself away, go back inside, switch on the light, and begin reciting again.

In the past she used to greet me heartily, in a broad Russian accent, and even stroke my head affectionately and exchange a few words with me. But her husband, Gershon Gippius, would walk past me in total indifference, or avert his heavy horse-face and grunt angrily in reply to my greeting. I decided that he must be a minor clerk in the Anglo-Palestine bank. Unlike my father, he always wore a black suit, albeit an old-fashioned one, and a hat, and carried a shabby leather case, it too black, in his hand.

It seemed that in his leisure time he was busy writing a book, the first volume of which had been published soon before he died. This was a big, thick book brought out with no expense spared. The first seven pages were devoted to an introduction and acknowledgments to all kinds of people who had assisted him in his work on the book. All the other pages were covered with photographs of graves and gates from cemeteries all over Russia, accompanied by a few lines of explanation. Here and there, for ornamental purposes, were prints of pen and charcoal drawings by Russian artists, showing fields, woods, and country houses.

They had no children, but they did have a few friends who came to visit them regularly. In the summer, on Friday nights, they would all sit on the balcony and conduct peaceful conversations in Russian. Sometimes Elisheva Gippius would read something, or sing Russian songs, songs pregnant with longing, which would sail out into the dark courtyard, where bats soared and swooped soundlessly, and I would toss and turn in bed and listen to her singing, and afterwards she would sometimes appear in my dreams: a small woman wearing an enormous hat crowned with a mountain of flowers.

Several times a year she would read poetry in halls and

workers' clubs. Her recitations would provide the conclusion
to lectures and speeches, like a kind of artistic dessert. But
after Passover, when the scent of the Persian lilac and the
mown grass filled the yard, Elisheva Gippius would be swept
up in a fit of feverish activity, full of excitement and tension.
The first of May was approaching, and this was her big day.

My father would come home early from work, like on
Fridays, sunburned and sweating. After taking off his heavy
boots and his shirt, he would sit down at the table and glance
through *Davar*. Mother would give him a late lunch, and I
would sit next to him, looking at his strong hands, breathing
in the smell of his sweat, and waiting impatiently, but with
complete confidence, for the moment when he would climb
the ladder to the entresol and bring down the flags.

After taking a shower and putting on a white shirt and
pressed khaki pants, he would take them down. There were
four flags: two red and two blue-and-white, all of them made
of silk. He would shake the dust off them and hang them up
on the two balconies that faced the street, and I would gaze
at them greedily, waiting to see them flutter in the holiday
breeze.

All the balconies were festooned with flags, in addition to
the two enormous ones hung by the committee at the entrance
to the house, and Noah Fine's were edged with fringes and
tassels and attached to long poles with pointed tops. Only
Mr. Kolton did not put out a flag, and as if on purpose to
annoy he would seat himself on his balcony, his legs crossed,
wearing an elegant suit made of English cloth, a gold cigarette
holder between his long fingers, leisurely puffing out clouds
of smoke and reading the independent liberal daily, *Haaretz*.
He always looked to me like the scion of an aristocratic
English family who for some mysterious reason had landed in
Tel Aviv.

"A General Zionist," said Noah Fine to my father in disgust and glanced furiously at Mr. Kolton, "something should be done about it."

In the evening friends and acquaintances, very festive and high spirited, would gather at our house, from where they would set out together for the demonstration, leaving behind them peels, cake crumbs, empty glasses, and me and Grandmother, sitting in an armchair and reading the *Amerikaner*.

Some years later I too saw Elisheva Gippius perform.

The last of the speakers concluded his address, the emcee announced her name, and she emerged from the wings and stood in the middle of the platform. With the string of white beads around her neck and the long, gathered gown she was wearing, she looked to me very aristocratic and foreign to the flags and signs and slogans festooning the hall. She suppressed a nervous smile and glanced around the audience. I hung my head until I heard her voice.

She began quietly, her hands clasped and her head slightly inclined, like the head of a bird. But little by little her voice grew stronger, and something like a combination of childish glee and proud majesty radiated from her person.

"We will light the old world's pyre,
Fling the boorzhooy to the fire.
We will loose a flood of blood:
Bless us, Lord God!"[1]

When she came to the words "Lord God!" she stood erect and lifted her slender hands high in the air, until it seemed that she was about to take off and fly. But then she left them fall and for a moment she was still.

A year after her husband's death Elisheva Gippius remarried, and a few months later she and her new husband were separated. Her marriage made Noah Fine angry, but her divorce made him even angrier. He never stopped complain-

ing about it, and he even thought of going down and telling
Elisheva Gippius to her face what he thought of her, but his
wife stopped him. Three years later she married again, and
was separated again, and from then on she lived by herself.

Her public appearances became few and far between, but
her voice, which had grown hoarse in the meantime, was still
heard in the courtyard. Now it bit and scratched at the voice
of the young singer who had moved into the apartment next
to the cantor's. The cantor himself had gone to America.

"Que sera, sera, Whatever will be, will be. . . ." she would
croon in her warm, wheedling voice.

From the balcony or the window I would watch her pin-
ning up her brown hair and fixing her face in front of the mirror, stretching herself out on the bed, or wandering around
the room scantily dressed, sometimes in a bathing costume,
tanned, supple, and carefree, like a magazine model, singing
over and over again:

"Que sera, sera,
Whatever will be, will be,
The future's not ours to see,
Que sera, sera,
Whatever will be, will be."

On the tenth anniversary of Gershon Gippius's death the
eulogy Noah Fine had delivered in his honor was printed in
Davar once more, but for some reason everything had got
mixed up: his own name appeared in place of the dead man's,
while the name of the dead man appeared in place of that of
the composer of the eulogy. Noah Fine fumed. He claimed
that someone had done it on purpose and announced that he
would demand a clarification at the Labor Federation. His
wife was alarmed. Although she didn't actually admit it, she
was afraid of the evil eye.

That evening I met Elisheva Gippius standing in front of

the door to her apartment and rummaging in her bag. She seemed at her wit's end. I greeted her and she replied that she couldn't get into her house because she couldn't find her key. Perhaps it was lost, she said, or she might have left it inside. I climbed the drain pipe onto the kitchen balcony and opened the door for her. She showered me with thanks as profusely as if I had saved her life, but suddenly she stopped, looked me up and down, said: "Ah! It's you!" and invited me in.

Against my better judgement I followed her inside.

She led me into the big room, apologizing for not recognizing me immediately as she did so. After putting her bag down and taking off her hat, she hurried into the kitchen, where she remained for some time, repeatedly calling out:

"I'll be with you in a moment, I'll be with you in a moment!"

I sat and waited.

It was the first time I had been inside her flat. It resembled ours, except for the air of emptiness which is sometimes to be found in childless homes. Apart from which, it seemed darker, perhaps because of the furniture. Four straight-backed, brown, leather-upholstered chairs stood around a heavy table, beneath whose glass top lay old photographs and white doilies. On the sideboard, one of whose shelves was full of cardboard files, stood two dark busts, a large copper candlestick, and a vase. The other candlestick stood among the books in the bookcase. There were a few pictures on the walls, among them dim landscapes and portraits. The room smelled of books and wilted leaves.

Elisheva Gippius came in holding a tray. She was extremely flustered and kept apologizing for taking so long. She put the tray down on the table, removed from it two glasses of tea, two saucers of preserves, sugar and cookies, and sat down. But she immediately got up again, hurried into the kitchen and returned with teaspoons and slices of lemon.

"So, it's you?" she said again, and offered me the cookies. "I didn't recognize you."

Now I noticed the faint mustache growing on her lip and her eyebrows, which were plucked to a thin line and painted a purplish brown. Earrings set with green stones dangled from her ear lobes, looking very out of place on her heavy face.

"That's Grisha," said Elisheva Gippius, pointing to one of the photographs under the glass tabletop. "That's what he looked like when I met him. Exactly. A head full of curls. Do you remember Grisha?"

How tenderly she pronounced his name.

I nodded and glanced at the photograph again.

"Thirty five years, gone in a moment," she said and looked at me.

The youth with the black curls in the photograph gave rise in me to astonishment, together with a shade of ridicule. He did not look in the least like her husband, at any rate, not as far as I could remember him.

She seemed to have read my thoughts, for she looked at the photograph again and said:

"Yes, he changed greatly." And after sipping her tea she added, "He grew so silent and withdrawn that sometimes he didn't say a word for days on end. I don't know why. I never asked him. I was afraid to. Today I'm sorry that I didn't ask him, but then I thought it best to hold my tongue," and she fell silent.

I sipped my tea and tasted the preserves, while she played reflectively with a teaspoon. I racked my brains for something to say.

"Actually, there was no need for me to ask," she said suddenly. "I knew the truth, but I didn't want to hear him say it in so many words. I loved Grisha, but he loved Vera. The old story. You know. He fell in love with her here, in Eretz Yisrael.

And what could I do? She was beautiful. Very beautiful, with a lot of temperament. Her brother used to come here to visit us. You may have seen him. He worked in the Labor Federation. After a few years she went back to Russia. She was a Communist and she wanted to change the world. For years we didn't hear from her, and then, about a year after the war, the news came that she was dead. Before that we still used to go down to the Yarkon river on Saturdays. We even went as far as the Seven Mills. And sometimes we went to Sharona. There was a eucalyptus glade there that Grisha was very fond of. But after her death everything died."

She fell silent and helped herself to the preserves. If there was any bitterness in her words, it was not directed at anyone in particular.

"Do you remember Sharona?" she suddenly asked me.

I nodded and said that I had once heard her reciting Alexander Blok's *The Twelve* in the basement of the Moghrabi Hall.

For a moment she looked confused, and as if she had not taken in a word I said. But then she smiled and said in an animated tone:

"Ah, Blok," and she began reciting: "Black night. / White snow. / The wind, the wind! / It will not let you go. . . ."[3] Ho, I remember it all," and she stood up. She went over to the book case and took out a book with a red-brown cover.

"He was married to Mendeleyev's daughter. I forget her name. The Mendeleyev who composed the Periodic Table. They didn't live like a pair of turtle doves, she and Blok," she said and giggled.

She held the book and turned its pages with a kind of restrained joy and intimacy.

"First edition," said Elisheva Gippius proudly and raised the book slightly to her face, "It has a wonderful smell. The smell of old books," and she smiled. "I found it here, in a little bookshop on Ben Yehuda Street," and she held out the book to me.

"And have you already heard 'The Scythians'?" she asked.

"No."

"What a pity. This year perhaps? If they ask me, of course. In any case, I'm preparing. I always prepare. It would be terrible to miss an opportunity just because I wasn't ready."

The flush of old age had already spread over her puffy cheeks and her chin sagged like a withered crop.

The singer's voice rose languidly from the courtyard:

"Que sera, sera,

"Whatever will be, will be. . . ." and for a moment I saw her in my imagination standing in her room in her scanty attire and singing for me, and this vision, together with her voice, filled me with desire.

"Listen to her," said Elisheva Gippius and shut the window.

I praised the preserves and so doing I stood up and apologized for having to leave so soon. She smiled absentmindedly and expressed her regret at the shortness of the visit and accompanied me to the door. I placed my hand on the doorknob and apologized again. She expressed her regret again and asked if she hadn't bored me with her talk. I said, not in the least. She shook her head slightly and said with a kind of hesitant frankness that she loved Russian poetry, especially the nature poetry and the lyrical poetry, a small part of which had appeared a few years before in Hebrew translation, and that she would have been delighted to recite some of the poems from this collection in public but she had never been given an opportunity to do so. "Beautiful poems," she said, and asked if I would like to hear something before I left.

"Yes," I said. "With pleasure," and reluctantly retraced my steps.

Her face lit up. Her movements filled with animation. She excused herself and left the room, returning a few minutes later with a string of white beads around her neck and a black woollen shawl around her shoulders. Unhurriedly she crossed the room and took up her position next to the sideboard. For a moment she paused, her eyes gliding over me and coming to rest at some point in the corner.

I didn't know where to look, and the voice of the singer caressed the dark window pane and seeped in through the walls.

"'True Tenderness,' by Anna Akhmatova," I heard the hoarse, tired voice of Elisheva Gippius announce. And after a short pause:

> "True tenderness there's no aping,
> It tells, though it hardly stirs.
> No use your carefully draping
> My shoulders and breast in furs.
> And no use your abjectly serving
> First-love talk which reassures.
> How well I know these unswerving,
> These ravenous looks of yours!"[4]

There was a silence. I didn't know what I was supposed to do. I raised my head. For a moment our eyes met and I saw a smile of sad triumph, sober and full of undisguised despair, cross her weary face in the shadow of the yellow lamplight. I told myself that I should compliment her, or at least nod my head in thanks, but I did nothing.

Outside summer reigned. It was in the warm air and the light breeze, in the smells of the flowers and the asphalt, and in the lit-up balconies where women in dressing gowns and men in undershirts sat looking into the street. I walked aimlessly. I was angry, and I hoped that walking would dispel my anger. Up above, in the clear sky, the moon was surrounded by a misty white aureole that presaged a *hamsin*.

It came the next day, the eve of the first of May, and lasted for three days. It was a very heavy *hamsin*, which hung suffocatingly over the town and dazzled it with its arid glare. There were no flags to be seen on the balconies. Our own flags had disintegrated long ago, and had been thrown out about a year after my grandmother's death, when the entresol had been cleared out, and the Passover dishes had been discarded together with various other things for which we no longer had any use. Only the house committee had draped the entrance to the building, as they did every year, with two vast silk flags. And there, under the faded blue sky, in the deserted street visited by occasional gusts of scorching wind, they hung limply all day long, until night fell.

NOTES

1. Translation by Babette Deutsch and Avrahm Yarmolinsky, *Russian Literature Since the Revolution*, Ed. Joshua Kunitz, Boni and Gaer, New York, 1948.

2. Tranlated by Walter Arndt, in *Anna Akhmatova, Selected Poems*, Ardis Books, Ann Arbor, Michigan, 1976.

3. *Ibid.*

Uncle Shmuel

IN THE OLD COUNTRY Uncle Shmuel was a member of the Zionist-socialist youth movement, *Hashomer Hatzair*. In a brown snapshot in the photograph album he could be seen sitting upright, wearing the movement uniform and a peaked cap made of leather, his arms crossed on his chest. Surrounding him, rank above rank, sat his charges of the "Young Judea" brigade, expressions of exalted gravity on their little faces.

He was the founder and leader of the local chapter, reviewing parades, making speeches, editing newspapers and directing plays that he himself had written. In addition to the above, he was also the goalie in the Zionist Youth soccer team.

When he immigrated to Palestine he joined the Jewish workers' party, *Hashomer Hatzair*. But for some mysterious reason, precisely after the murder of the labor leader Arlosoroff he became a disciple of Jabotinsky, and suddenly switched his allegiance to the Revisionists. He had a violent argument with my father and for several years they weren't on speaking terms.

Later on Uncle Shmuel abandoned the Revisionists and gave his support to other parties, but he never joined any of them. The truth of the matter is that he became a one-man party, alone in his opposition to all the rest.

Whenever he came to visit us loud and bitter arguments would break out between my father and himself, all because of the fact that Uncle Shmuel liked arguing, and my father didn't like being beaten. My mother and my aunt, Uncle Shmuel's wife, would try to change the subject or negotiate a compromise, but in vain.

His attitude toward places resembled his attitude toward political parties. At first he lived in Haifa, and later he moved to Nesher, and from there to Tiberias, and from Tiberias to Jerusalem. From Jerusalem he moved to Tel Aviv, where he remained for a long time, constantly changing his address. First he lived in Jaffa, and then he built himself a shack in the Nordiyah quarter, after which he rented an apartment in Sheinkin Street, moving on from there to Ranack, Basle, Gordon, and Reines Streets. All his wife's pleas and demands that he stop this wandering were to no avail.

"Settle down, for God's sake," she would attack him with cold fury. "Where are you running? Look at yourself, a grown man in short pants. You've got nothing in your hands."

"What should I have in my hands?" Uncle Shmuel would answer with an ironic smile and shrug his shoulders. But when he saw her hard face he would soften and add, "It'll be all right, Zipporah, it'll be all right," and wriggle out of it.

In one thing, however, Uncle Shmuel showed absolute consistency: his trade. He stuck to the building trade, where thanks to his energy, imagination, and skill he was a great success, and rose to the rank of a foreman and "almost an engineer."

Within the space of a few years he became responsible for executing large-scale, complex building projects, during the course of which he invented all kinds of things that made the work easier, more efficient, and more economical. In addition to these inventions, some of that came to him in a sudden flash of illumination, he had other brainwaves too, such as a house composed of parts that could be changed from time to time, or a house that could be transported from place to place without any difficulty.

And there were other inventions too, which were more in the realm of fantasy: all kinds of imaginative ideas for houses and machines that his restless spirit would track down feverishly and in the full confidence that tomorrow or the next day they would put on flesh and become practical possibilities. All he was looking for in these inventions was practical, day-to-day usefulness, as well as the possibility of achieving, one day in the foreseeable future, and in a single swoop, economic security and a certain modest wealth.

"His imagination will be the death of him," his wife would say in a dry, bitter voice.

She hated the brown cardboard files in which her husband kept hundreds of pages covered with drawings and calculations. The files stood in the bookcase, dusty and neglected, multiplying from year to year.

"Get rid of them," she would scold, "What do we need them for?"

Suddenly Uncle Shmuel decided to move to a *moshav*.[1]

One Saturday evening he called on us with Aunt Zipporah to tell my parents the news. My mother served tea and cheesecake, and my father, wearing slippers and short khaki trousers, listened coldly. Then he voiced his doubts.

The idea had nothing whatever to recommend it, he said. It made no sense at all. The building trade was booming, and Uncle Shmuel had established a position for himself that enabled him to put his gifts to good use as well as giving him social security and a measure of material well-being. If he gave up his job now he was liable to lose everything. Apart from which, he had never had anything to do with agriculture in his life and didn't know the first thing about it, so what on earth was the point of burying himself in some godforsaken place miles away from his family? And what about the children? Where would they go to school? And what would Zipporah do?

Uncle Shmuel interrupted from time to time, contradicting him and putting forward all kinds of arguments of his own, passing from businesslike seriousness to unrestrained enthusiasm, and then, all of a sudden, to a kind of frivolous, mischievous irony that undercut everything. From time to time he made some bitter joke aimed against himself and smiled with all the wrinkles of his brown face. Aunt Zipporah looked at him sternly and maintained a proud silence.

She was a big, tall woman, with a smooth, fair, rather frozen face, and a hairdo that resembled a cake turned upside down. She was invariably elegant and well groomed, with a string of beads around her neck and a large silver brooch on her bosom. Her appearance and the restraint of her manners made an aristocratic impression. In any case, it was impossible to imagine her trudging through the mud in boots, hoeing the land, or feeding chickens.

The date of the move to the country was set for the beginning of spring. But even before Uncle Shmuel set foot on the *moshav* soil, his head was swarming with plans. He would sit in our kitchen and hold forth on them to my father, and they would expand and multiply and bear fruit as he talked. My father would listen, playing with the breadcrumbs scattered over the oilcloth, and ask questions. Uncle Shmuel would answer and sail on. A few days later he would return with new plans. Sometimes they would move into the big room and sit there for hours, making calculations on pieces of paper and newspaper margins.

Spring arrived. Uncle Shmuel and Aunt Zipporah took possession of their plot at the edge of the *moshav*. Next to it virgin fields stretched broad and peaceful. Everything was covered with fresh, green growth. Farther off there were a few small eucalyptus glades, and after them, in the distance, the deep, dark patches of the citrus groves. There was a faint mist rising from them and toward evening they looked like dark lakes.

For the time being, the *moshav* put an empty house at their disposal. The house was far away from the plot but this did not bother Uncle Shmuel. In any case, he intended building a house to suit his own requirements as soon as possible.

He set to work with a will, the sight of the empty virgin fields adding fuel to the flames of his usual energy and imagination. The other farmers sowed two dunams of potatoes—he sowed three. They cultivated half a dunam of peppers, one of tomatoes, and one of cabbages, and he—twice as much. From the minute he got up in the morning he would run around his fields in his heavy work boots, his skin sunburned, his lips chapped, his nails black, and his neck a shriveled net of wrinkles. And in the evening, after grabbing a bite to eat, he would pore over books about agriculture and ponder his plans.

The next thing on the agenda was the henhouse.

He decided to build a henhouse for two hundred brood hens. The *moshav* members chuckled affectionately. They called him "Mister Cock-a-doodle-doo." Some of them tried to dissuade him from this rash project. They proved to him that he would never be able to cope with so many chickens on his own, and that in the end the henhouse would bury him under its ruins.

Uncle Shmuel argued and smiled. He observed the neighbors' chicken coops and devised the semi-automatic henhouse in his head.

First he built a hatchery. This was a very low structure, long and narrow as a corridor, which was divided into three compartments, with a concrete floor and walls, a tin roof, and a front consisting entirely of one large, netted window.

When the hatchery was ready and filled with yellow chicks, Uncle Shmuel brought wooden planks, sheets of tin, and rolls of netting, and set about constructing the first semi-automatic henhouse on an experimental basis.

The experiment was a success. The henhouse was convenient and economical and came up to all his expectations. The *moshav* members clustered around it, looking, touching, and admiring. Uncle Shmuel joked and answered all their questions enthusiastically. He was elated. He bought his wife a new necklace and decided to establish a small plant for the production of semi-automatic henhouses. And he set about persuading Uncle Israel to leave the city and come and work in the plant.

Uncle Israel hesitated. An ironworker by trade, he had recently been promoted to the permanent staff at his place of employment. But in the end he wound up his affairs in town and with a heavy heart moved with his family to the *moshav*.

The only one to remember that a year had passed since they had arrived on the *moshav* was Aunt Zipporah, for she was the only one to count the days as she waited, full of animosity, for this adventure to come to an end. During the entire year she had not known a single day of happiness, but only anger and bitterness and a feeling of failure and shame. Nevertheless, she threw a modest party, to which she invited the whole family, in honor of the occasion.

The table, which was covered with a white tablecloth, was formally laid with the old silver cutlery, china plates, and cups with gold rims, napkins, crystal wine glasses, and two copper candlesticks. Aunt Zipporah wore her big silver brooch and her new necklace and looked welcoming. Outside, as if just beyond the walls of the house, frogs croaked.

The party began with a mild altercation. Even before the company sat down at the table Uncle Shmuel stretched out his hand and took the black olive that was stuck in the middle of the chopped liver as a decoration.

"Shmuel!" said Aunt Zipporah sternly, and her husband immediately put the olive back and wiped his fingers inside his trouser pocket.

"Shmuel!" repeated his wife, her eyes reddening in rage, "Here!" and she pulled a handkerchief out of his other trouser pocket.

Toward the end of the party Uncle Shmuel told my father that he would soon begin building his house. He had considered the matter and decided to build himself a cottage.

The idea of this cottage, including a special study for himself, enthralled him to such an extent that it gave him no rest. He pored over architecture journals, took notes, made calculations, sketched plans on pieces of paper, book covers, and the oilcloth on the kitchen table, argued with Aunt Zipporah, and made frequent trips to see my father. The two of them would sit bowed over the papers, their heads almost touching. Uncle Shmuel would explain that they were only crude sketches, and my father would pass a sunburned finger over them and make his comments.

Gradually the plans took shape, but before they were ready the *moshav* committee demanded the house back, the time allocated for their occupancy having long since past. Uncle Shmuel did not ask for an extension. He packed his belongings and moved into the hatchery with his family.

He crowded the chicks into one compartment, put the children into the second, and moved into the third with Aunt Zipporah. The toolshed now served as kitchen and dining room. A warm smell of chickens and feed and a faint murmur perpetually filled the low chambers, upon whose walls the kerosene lamps made heavy shadows flicker at night, and which by day were flooded with a great, glaring light, pouring through the glass façade together with the sight of the trees and earth and sky. They were so close, it seemed there was nothing separating the outside from the inside.

Aunt Zipporah did her best to made the place look like home. She spread white embroidered cloths on the cushions and the table, hung pictures on the wall, and waged a tireless battle against the dust and grains of sand, the stalks and thorns and chicken droppings which every little breeze blew into the rooms. She spent most of the day wandering round the hatchery with her head crowned by the upside-down cake hairdo, bowed, as if she were perpetually searching for something which she had lost on the floor. She consoled herself with the delightful "rural tranquility" but her face was exceedingly glum.

Uncle Shmuel took no notice of these irritations. The plans for the cottage were complete, and all that was left was to execute them. For the time being, so as not to miss the season, he planted two dunams of fruit trees around the plot on which the house was to stand, opposite the entrance and the big veranda. This was one of his great dreams—an orchard of fruit trees next to the house.

The house itself he decided to build with his own hands, with the help of my father, who was a builder and scaffold maker. My father took time off from work and set out to help his brother.

Two months later the foundations were laid. Six months later the walls were standing, and a month after that the partitions between the rooms were up as well. On Saturday afternoons the family would arrive to tour the building site. They would wander around the empty rooms, stroke the walls, peer through the window holes, get their clothes dirty with the dust from the concrete and the whitewash and exclaim admiringly. At the same time Uncle Shmuel would describe to them how the house and the rooms would look when everything was finished.

Three days after the roof was laid Father was brought home badly bruised. He had climbed up to work on the roof and it had caved in, taking him with it.

Uncle Shmuel came to visit. He was embarrassed and apologetic, but took comfort in the fact that nothing worse had happened. It was simply a mistake in the calculations, he said, and he had already discovered it. Now they would be able to finish the job without any problems.

Two months later they laid the roof again.

That whole year Uncle Shmuel and Aunt Zipporah lived in the hatchery and worked the land to the best of their ability. A blight had broken out in the potatoes, and the yield was poor. But the peppers and other vegetables had done well. Likewise the vetch, except that Uncle Shmuel had sown so much of it that he had to call on the entire family—brothers and brothers-in-law and cousins—to help him cut and stack it on time.

And on Friday night, when the work was done, everyone lay on the fragrant haystack with the transparent night sky spread out overhead and the soft air full of the sounds of giggling and dogs barking and jackals howling in the distance. The dew wet their hair and stuck their shirts to their skin, and they sang old songs of Zion, beautiful songs full of yearning, and scratched themselves, until everything suddenly sank into the still, heavy darkness before dawn.

But most successful of all was the semi-automatic henhouse plant. The henhouses were snatched up, people bought them even before they were ready, and Uncle Shmuel decided to increase his scope. Soon big piles of planks and tin and rolls of netting filled the yard and production became feverish, on the principle of the conveyor belt. From early in the morning until after the sun went down the air rang with the sounds of hammering, clattering, sawing, and scraping.

Aunt Zipporah was like a madwoman. Not a trace of her "rural tranquility" remained. All day long she stalked about with a stony face, sending hostile looks at the whole world, especially her husband. She prayed for something to happen to suddenly change the course of events and uproot them from this dreadful "agricultural adventure." Her hands grew hard and cracked, her fine clothes hung in the closet growing shabby with disuse, and her jewels gathered dust in a drawer. Even her aristocratic manners now gave rise to nothing but rage in her heart.

At the beginning of the third year Uncle Shmuel was elected to the *moshav* committee. In honor of this event his wife bought him an elegant new hat. He wore it that whole evening and then put it away in the closet for special occasions.

His committee membership changed nothing in Uncle Shmuel's life. His head and heart were absorbed in the development of his farm, in the henhouse plant, in the building of the cottage, and in his repeated attempts to persuade Uncle Josef to leave Tel Aviv and move to the *moshav*.

Uncle Josef was a tall man, very deliberate in his behavior and withdrawn into himself. He rarely spoke, and it was even rarer for a wise, modest smile to appear on his heavy face. He spent his leisure hours after work reading or arranging his large stamp collection. He too worked in the building trade and was far removed from agriculture and *moshav* life.

Suddenly, and completely unpredictably, the sales of the semi-automatic henhouses fell steeply, and dozens of henhouses in various stages of construction piled up in the yard without anyone to buy them.

Uncle Shmuel did not despair. Again and again he analysed the reasons for the drop in sales to my father and concluded that it was a temporary setback that would be over in a few weeks time. All they had to do was be patient and wait.

He believed in his predictions, but the situation went from bad to worse, and after a few months he had no alternative but to close down the plant for the time being, and also stop work on the cottage. My father went back to his old job, Uncle Israel began to grow vegetables on the plot in front of his house and Uncle Shmuel, who went on cultivating his land, occupied his thoughts with designing the furniture for the cottage and deciding where each piece would stand.

The days grew shorter and clouds began coming up from the sea. And in the meantime the henhouses buckled in and fell apart and were overturned by the fierce autumn winds, which carried stinging grains of sand and gravel from the abandoned piles next to the cottage and kicked up clouds of dust and cement. Broken bits of wood and pieces of tin and netting lay scattered about, and Aunt Zipporah would stumble into them as she came and went, and her face froze in despair. Afterward the rains came, clattering deafeningly on the tin roof, and harsh, bitter quarrels broke out in the dank gloom of the hatchery, where they were now imprisoned for days on end. Aunt Zipporah would talk while he muttered under his breath, shook his head, and looked outside. And outside, right next to the glass with its wire netting, was the low, gray sky and the shell of the building rising like a somber vision from a lake of water.

Gradually spring returned. The light turned yellow, the air grew warm and caressing, and a dry skin covered the earth. The little fruit trees, some of them spattered with whitewash and cement, put out their first, pale green leaves. At the same time, the henhouse market began to show signs of reviving, and the henhouses started selling again, although not as well as they had at first. Even Aunt Zipporah's bitterness of spirit thawed somewhat. She aired the winter bedding and urged Uncle Shmuel to finish building the cottage. She appeared to have resigned herself to life on the *moshav* and to have settled for improving it as far as possible. In the middle of summer work was resumed on the cottage, and they began to plaster the walls. And then, out of the blue, Uncle Shmuel sold the farm, took leave of Uncle Josef and Uncle Israel, and went to live on a kibbutz. A year later he bought a house on the outskirts of a small country town and went to live there.

He got a job as technical advisor to a building contractor at a good salary that provided him with a respectable living. But after coming home from work and bolting down a late lunch, he would get busy on the house. He changed the rooms around and added on to them, enlarged the kitchen, built a big veranda, broke down walls to open doors, and heightened windows. The house was always in the process of construction. In front of the house and in the yard he planted ornamental bushes and flowers and a little orchard.

One day he came to our house with Aunt Zipporah. It was the day after my grandfather died, and they had come for the funeral.

There was something confused in the atmosphere, something at once frightening and festive. Grandfather's body lay embalmed on the floor of the room, covered with a white sheet. The windows and shutters were closed, and at a glance it was possible to imagine that he was floating lightly in the dark, with white candles flickering at his head. Grandmother was sitting with him, and there were another three or four people there now too. Others—relatives, friends, and people from the same town in the old country would go in for a minute and come out again. Everyone was dressed in their best and looked as if they were on holiday.

Uncle Shmuel too was festively attired: a starched white shirt, a dark blue suit, tie, and the elegant new hat his wife had bought him on the day he was elected to the *moshav* committee, only now it looked a little old-fashioned and seemed a little too big for him.

He sat with my father at the kitchen table, from where it was possible, with a slight inclination of the head, to peep into the dead man's room, and they conversed and ate the lunch my mother had prepared: fish, soup, and chicken. Head to head they sat, so alike, even in their movements, except that Uncle Shmuel's face was longer and thinner and furrowed with wrinkles, and now also exhausted. Uncle Shmuel said that Ben-Gurion and the government were being mean and petty in their refusal to bring Jabotinsky's bones to the country for a ceremonious official burial. To this my father replied that Ben-Gurion was right and that Jabotinsky didn't deserve any official government ceremony, since he was nothing but the leader of a bunch of Revisionist schismatics who had made more than a little trouble for the Jewish population of Eretz Yisrael. But Uncle Shmuel held his ground and said that most of the trouble had been caused not by the Revisionists but by the Labor Party and the corrupt Labor Federation, who had turned the state into their own private shop. My father interrupted him by saying that it was thanks to the Labor Party and the Labor Federation that the state had come into being, and he began listing the sins of the Revisionists from their inception to the murder of Arlosoroff. But Uncle Shmuel did not let him finish and said that it wasn't the Revisionists who had murdered him but his own friends. My father's face turned red with rage. He said that he remembered the murder vividly and everyone knew who the murderers were. In this connection he mentioned the death of the

Revisionist Avraham Stavsky, who had been killed on the beach in the same place as Arlosoroff, and appeared to be hinting that he had been executed by the hand of fate. The argument grew more and more heated, until my mother and Aunt Zipporah and a few of the other people present intervened and reminded them of the dead man lying in the room next door. A silence fell, broken only by the shuffle of feet, the clatter of cutlery, and the soft murmur of the prayers coming from the dead man's room. Suddenly Uncle Shmuel raised his head from his plate and said irrelevantly:

"Yes, people die." And after a moment he added good humoredly, "*Nu*, we might as well finish the chicken," and smiled a sardonic smile.

Father was placated. He smiled back, said something, and went on struggling with the chicken bones, cracking them with his teeth and sucking out the marrow, and as he did so they resumed their former peaceful conversation, close to each other and set apart from everyone around them.

After the meal was over Aunt Zipporah put her hand in her husband's pocket and took out a handkerchief, which she held out to him, and he wiped his fingers and his mouth and rose to his feet. She straightened his tie and stood there talking to my mother. A faint smile of satisfaction played constantly on her fresh complexioned face, which was once more shining, as in the past, with its cold light.

Afterwards Uncle Shmuel died too. It happened a few years later, and it was quite unexpected. The house was already finished, white and gleaming, and the fruit trees were already bearing fruit. One night my father climbed the stairs laughing a terrible, high-pitched laugh. He was crying.

The next day we traveled to the funeral.

It was winter and it was a beautiful day. The sky was blue, a rich blue, and the sun was yellow as an egg yolk and gave off a pleasant warmth. The earth was brown and the citrus groves were green and the fields were covered with an abundance of wild flowers and fresh grass, and there was a fragrant smell in the air.

Next to Uncle Shmuel's house a large crowd had gathered. The white house was too small to hold them all, and they clustered around it, trampling the plants. Afterward the funeral procession moved off, proceeding at a leisurely pace in the pleasant sunshine, along the fields and citrus groves, like a procession of celebrants, and at its head, erect and proud, walked Aunt Zipporah, supported by her sons, and apparently weeping bitterly under the black scarf covering her face. They put the body down on the brink of the pit and everyone gathered around. The great cypress trees hedging the place in cast a cool, heavy shade. Here and there groans, sounds of stifled weeping and nose-blowing rose into the air.

Afterward a man stepped forward and delivered a eulogy. He pointed a thick finger at Uncle Shmuel's body and spoke to him in the second person, as if he were still alive and could hear him. He reminded him enthusiastically of how he had been a Revisionist and how much he had hated the red Labor Federation and how all his life all he had ever wanted was to own a home and a piece of land of his own, and when he gained his wish—he died.

Everyone listened passively. And then there was a shout, a black, despairing shout. It was my father.

He burst forward shouting that it was a lie, it was all a lie. That nobody had known his brother.

"It's a lie!" he cried, his face wild, "a lie!" and there was something threatening and terrible in this cry, which burst out and rose into the heights of the sky, something not of this world, but torn at the end of its tether from the dark depths into which it wished to plunge and merge again.

Uncle Josef and Uncle Israel had to hold him down, and Mother stood next to him embarrassed and ashamed.

I bowed my head and took cover in the cypresses.

Father stopped shouting. A strange silence fell on the mourners, a silence of shame and discomfiture, even annoyance. Nobody was crying any more. They filled in the grave and the son said *kaddish* and everyone hurried to disperse.

I waited a while and slipped away.

Beyond the cypresses the day was fine and sunny and clear again. I was alone and I strode off quickly over the loose red soil. When I had covered a little ground I looked back for a moment. In the distance I saw my father. He was striding alone through a field of groundsel and feverfew. My mother followed him at a distance of a few paces. I thought I heard her calling him, but he did not reply or even favor her with a glance, but went on walking straight ahead.

I stole like a thief through a thorny acacia hedge, and then down a low hillside. When I turned my head, he was no longer there. I stretched out on the hillside, on the damp soil, and looked up at the sky, which was full of movement.

NOTE

1. *Moshav*—cooperative agricultural village

A Marriage Proposal

HIRSH MOISHE STRAIGHTENED the black hat slightly on his head and entered the dark stairwell, which smelled of a fresh coat of whitewash. He pressed the electric light button, took two or three steps, stopped, and after a belated hesitation began climbing up the stairs. He climbed slowly and heavily, his handsomely carved, silver-knobbed walking stick tapping with every step he took. He had to climb three flights of stairs, which gave him a bitter feeling of grievance in addition to the resentment that he had been nursing without giving it a chance to die down and disappear ever since leaving the house that morning. From time to time he stopped and leaned on the railing in order to get his breath, and as he did so he reviewed the situation and considered his chances and prospects, which seemed to him good and delightful from every point of view. But it was no use. Something angry and morose accompanied him and his thoughts, and twice between the second and third floors he decided to turn back. When he reached the top at last, he paused in front of the door to calm his spirits and steady his breath. He drew himself up slightly, smoothed down his broad beard, and straightened his hat again. It bothered him, and once more he wondered if he hadn't dressed too grandly. The light went off and he was left standing for a moment in total darkness. Then he pressed the electric light button and rang the bell.

Grandmother opened the door. Even though he had made up his mind to wait for her to greet him first, he greeted her first and she replied and led him to her room. The fact that he had not held firm to his resolution darkened his mood again, but he consoled himself with the kindly smile with which the old lady had welcomed him and also with the fact that there was nobody else at home.

Hirsh Moishe sat down in the plump armchair with its coarse floral cover and leaned his cane against his leg. Then he took off his hat, but immediately put it on again. All his movements were very slow, and in his opinion, dignified. Grandmother sat down in the chair next to the oval table and asked him how he was. He inclined his head and mumbled something, passed his hand over his beard, and asked her how she was. She replied that old age didn't make life any easier, as he probably knew, and asked him how his sons were and what they were doing. He replied with a wave of his hand and a kind of suppressed groan, which were apparently meant to imply that there was nothing new there, and after that there was a silence. A ray of sunshine trembled between the folds of the curtains, slightly staining the wall. The rest of the room was already in darkness. Both of them, both Grandmother and Hirsh Moishe, knew that the other knew exactly what the purpose of this visit was, but for the time being they preferred to ignore it, albeit each of them for different reasons. The silence dragged on until Grandmother asked him if he would drink a glass of tea, and he accepted gladly. The offer, although routine, pleased him and gave rise in him to a certain feeling of complacency. Grandmother stood up and went into the kitchen and Hirsh Moishe was left alone in the room.

The sunspot on the wall faded and in the stillness of the room the only sound was the harsh ticking of the tin clock standing on the bedside table, and a few noises coming from the street. Hirsh Moishe sat without moving. His pale, set face, the face of a cold pancake, was somewhat tense. Apart from that, its only expression was one of wretched pride, and the expectation that everyone around him, and in fact the whole world, would treat him with respect. He went back to stroking his magnificent beard and thought for a moment about his hat, and then about his black silk waistcoat, and then about his jacket and his cuff links. Yes, this time he had definitely overdone it, and the thought upset him considerably. At the same time, he hoped that Grandmother would know how to appreciate the splendor of his attire, testifying as it did to solid virtues, prestige, and an exalted position in society. And indeed, judging by his appearance, anyone might have thought that Hirsh Moishe was a highly respected businessman with a network of flourishing financial concerns, which is exactly how he saw himself in his imagination, if not as something much grander than that. The truth was, however, that he worked for the burial society, in which capacity he accompanied the dead from their homes to their final resting place. He did not like talking about it, or having it mentioned in his presence, since in his heart he saw his current place of employment as one of temporary exile and banishment from grace, in which he was obliged, for the time being, to hide his light under a bushel. In the same way he turned his back on his entire past life, disowning it all apart from one short visit he had paid to Berlin at the beginning of the century, where he had even had the good fortune to see the Kaiser driving past in his carriage.

Grandmother brought in two glasses of tea and a saucer full of sugar cubes. He drew the glass toward him, dipped a sugar cube into it, sucked it, and took a sip of tea. Grandmother did not like him, because of what she regarded as his arrogance and because of the contempt with which he treated the dead. She dropped two cubes of sugar into her tea, stirred it, and asked him about an acquaintance of theirs who owned a handbag factory and his wife, who had suddenly fallen ill with diabetes. Afterward she told him about the letter she had recently received from her sister in America, remarking by the way that life was hard there too, and that even there, it seemed, you couldn't pick up gold in the streets. He shook his head, raising his eyebrows and saying with profound importance, "Ah, yes, it's exactly the same in Berlin." This sentence, which he never missed the opportunity to repeat, annoyed Grandmother, but she restrained herself and told him that two days before, in other words, on the thirtieth day after her husband's death, she had donated a sum of money to the synagogue and an additional sum to an orphanage. Hirsh Moishe nodded approvingly, tipped his hat slightly backwards, said complacently, "We gave him a fine funeral, every Jew should have such a funeral," and finished drinking his tea. Grandmother said nothing, while he took a silver cigarette holder and a silver cigarette case out of his pocket, extracted a cigarette from the latter, broke it in half, replaced one half in the cigarette case, inserted the other half into the cigarette holder, and lit it. The funeral had been absolutely ordinary, but in a certain sense he was right. For this was the one and only time when he had performed his duties at the burial society wholeheartedly, conscientiously, and with a sense of exaltation. He had treated her husband royally, because they were boyhood friends and he felt a special closeness and responsibility toward him. Hirsh Moishe blew out a cloud of smoke and tapped his fingers lightly on the arm of the chair, and both of them, he and Grandmother, sensed that the inescapable moment was rapidly approaching.

Grandmother pushed an ashtray toward him, and he tipped his ash into it, shifted his cane from one side to the other, touched his beard, and then opened his mouth as if to say something, but said nothing. A ray of hope awoke in Grandmother's heart, and she asked him if he didn't think she should close the window. He did not reply, but blew out another cloud of smoke and said, "Yes, we gave him a fine funeral," and after a short silence added, "Everyone dies, it's God's will," and the faint ray of hope that had awoken in the old woman's heart faded, since she immediately realized where his words were leading. He went on talking about the way death was coming closer all the time, and then he started talking about the miseries of old age and loneliness. Grandmother said nothing, but only nodded her head from time to time in agreement. Hirsh Moishe put out his cigarette and began to speak of the weakness of the body and the depression of the spirit and how fortunate was the man who had someone to succor him and bring him a glass of tea when he needed it. Suddenly he stopped and looked as if he were waiting for something. But since the thing he was waiting for did not occur, he began talking again, continuing in the same vein as before and at the same time debating whether to propose in so many words, or just drop a hint, and whether it might not be better to wait and let the hint come from her. He decided to postpone the decision for the time being, and in the meantime he alluded to Adam and Eve, and the fact that the Lord in his wisdom had created them male and female.

Grandmother felt very uncomfortable. She did not have the least desire to marry for the third time, and it was clear that she would have to turn him down. But she did not want to hurt his feelings, and so she smiled slightly, as if to hint that she had grasped his intentions, and that it was obvious to her that he was only joking. She hoped that this smile would save them both embarrassment. But Hirsh Moishe did not understand her smile as she wished it to be understood, and he went on elaborating on the theme of Adam and Eve and advancing his case by means of their example. Grandmother did not know what to do. She sighed enigmatically, stood up, and switched on the light. The sudden light embarrassed and angered Hirsh Moishe, but he soon recovered and began to speak in praise of himself.

He started off indirectly, by praising Grandmother's previous husband, but very quickly came around to himself and declared that he was a healthy man, thank God, and that apart from mild chills and occasional pains in his legs, there was nothing wrong with him. Good health was a blessing, he said, and he guarded it jealously by never allowing anything fatty, spicy, roasted, or fried to pass his lips, or anything that had been left out in the sun either. Likewise, he was scrupulous about cleanliness. And in general, everybody knew that he was an uncommonly neat and tidy man who never made any dirt or left a mess behind him or took snuff like her late husband, God rest his soul, whose beard and cuffs and collars were always covered with ugly brown tobacco stains and gave off a bad smell. Grandmother said nothing, but after he referred to the tobacco stains another couple of times, she remarked quietly that it wasn't nice to speak ill of the dead. Hirsh Moishe was embarrassed and said that nothing could have been further from his mind than to insult the memory of the departed, who was a decent, honest man and also his best friend. But it was evident that her remark had lowered his spirits and thrown him off balance, and for the next few minutes he fumbled for words, until he found the thread again and told her that he had a steady income from his job, in addition to a monthly allowance from his three sons, all of which together added up to a tidy sum on which two people could live comfortably. He said this in a magnanimous, emphatic tone, while carefully avoiding any mention of the sum itself, watching Grandmother closely to see the impression his words were making on her, and perhaps even expecting her to ask. Grandmother smoothed the velvet tablecloth with the palm of her thick hand and Hirsh Moishe, speaking with great animation, inserted another half cigarette into his cigarette holder and listed all his property—sheets, pillow cases, blankets, suits, furniture, kitchen utensils, the wall clock, the radio—he remembered everything except the two dunam plot in Holon his first wife had left him in her will. He also mentioned the apartment in which he resided that would be at their disposal for as long as they lived, remarking obscurely and irrelevantly that the apartment belonged to his son in Canada, even though to tell the truth it was his own private property and registered under his name. After this he fell silent and looked at Grandmother expectantly. She rolled a scrap of paper between her fingers and said something about the rocketing cost of living, and in the tense silence that fell after this remark the only sound to be heard was the ticking of the tin clock.

Hirsh Moishe, without taking his eyes off her, shifted his weight in his chair. The old lady's stubbornness and ingratitude gave rise in him to a fury such as he had never known before, and made his earlobes burn. He drew the ashtray toward him, and Grandmother asked him if he would drink another glass of tea, but he did not reply. He made up his mind not to say another word until she asked him to marry her. But the urgent desire for her to do so, together with the dread that she never would, put him into such a panic that, gripping the handle of his cane, he opened his mouth and began to praise himself again, but this time with increasing impatience. He uttered a few sentences in this vein and then suddenly began calling down fire and brimstone on the head of her late husband, who unlike himself, he said, had been a coarse and ignorant fellow, who snored at night and fell asleep during prayers, was quarrelsome to a fault and so short-tempered that he had once beat up the synagogue treasurer in front of the entire congregation. This event had taken place more than forty years before, but Hirsh Moishe, who could barely restrain himself any longer, described it in detail, without, however, mentioning Grandmother's husband by name even once, and referring to him throughout as the "bad-tempered goat."

Grandmother did not say a word. She sat and listened to him with her head slightly on one side, and Hirsh Moishe, sensing at last that he had gone too far, suddenly fell silent. Now he wanted to make haste and repair the damage done by his last remarks, but in his panic and despair he could not find the way to do so. And then, all of a sudden and without any preliminaries, he asked her to marry him. He did this so clumsily and awkwardly that as soon as he heard the words coming out of his mouth he wanted to get up and run away. But he went on sitting where he was, and his eyes, after wandering blindly around the room, finally came to rest on Grandmother's face.

A light breeze ruffled the curtains. Grandmother, who found the chill disagreeable, thought of getting up to close the window but did not do so. She smoothed the tablecloth repeatedly with her thick hand and after a long, thoughtful silence, said in a quiet, conciliatory tone that they were both already old and their days were numbered and that in her opinion there was no point in the blind leading the lame. She wanted to go on, but at this stage Hirsh Moishe lost what little self-control he had left, and his face yellow with rage, he yelled:

"And *kiddush*—that means nothing to you?" And with this he rose, snatched up his cane, and left the house, slamming the door behind him, while Grandmother went on sitting where she was, letting her eyes rest for a moment on the empty armchair in front of her.

Past Continuous

IT WAS ALREADY almost eight o'clock and there were still two customers left in the shop. Akiva felt a great weariness in all his limbs and wanted to be rid of the customers and go home.

He started slicing 200 grams of cheese for Mrs. Kaminke who was standing and talking to Mr. Gabriel Slep. They were talking about the Breuer's youngest son, who had been killed in the Jordan Valley. Mrs. Kaminke kept exclaiming about what a wonderful boy Meir Breuer had been, so gifted and good looking too, and she said that this war was a terrible thing, and the most terrible thing about it was that there was no end in sight. Gabriel Slep agreed with everything she said, but remarked that we had no alternative but to go on fighting, because they wanted to kill us and we had to get them before they got us first. He looked at Akiva standing in front of the scales and weighing the cheese as he spoke, as if he was waiting behind the thick lenses of his glasses for his support. Akiva shook his head and said, "This death of Meir's is certainly a shocking business," and put the cheese, wrapped in wax paper, down on the counter. The cheese weighed 220 grams, and he wondered if he should credit Mrs. Kaminke's account with the extra twenty grams. He decided against it, put a bottle of mayonnaise, a packet of butter, yogurt, a jar of jam, and a loaf of rye bread down next to the cheese, and went to get her black olives. He took a nylon bag and wondered if he hadn't make a mistake in letting her have the extra twenty grams of cheese for nothing. Gabriel Slep mentioned Hanan Avni and Baruch Friedman, who had been killed in the War of Independence, but Mrs. Kaminke kept on talking about Meir Breuer and what a tragedy it was for his parents. Akiva bent over the barrel with the good, pungent smell of the olives rising from it and heard what they were saying, and for a moment he even saw the mourning notices that the residents of the apartment block had had printed with Meir Breuer's name in big letters in the middle, and for a second he felt a sense of relief and satisfaction at not having missed the funeral. But apart from this fleeting sensation he felt nothing, not even a stirring of sadness or a twinge of pain. Something else was bothering him, but he didn't know what it was. He put the olives on the scale and Mrs. Kaminke said, addressing herself to him as well, that for four days now she had not been able to stop thinking about Meir Breuer and the horrifying fact that he had died by accident and for nothing. Akiva watched the pointer on the scale and felt anger against himself for not making her pay for the extra twenty grams of cheese, because after all he had no obligation to make her a present of slices of cheese.

Gabriel Slep responded to her last remarks by saying that everyone who was killed in the war died for something, and that there was no avoiding errors and accidents in wartime and, in any case, he continued, it was a well known fact that in Israel more people were killed in traffic accidents than in battle. You can't make an omelet without breaking eggs, he said in the end and looked smugly at Akiva and Mrs.

Kaminke, who squeezed and kneaded the bread with her fingers and said that she knew all that as well as he did, but it was no consolation. Then she turned to Akiva and said that she wasn't going to take the bread because it was stale and no good. The tone of her voice and the way she pushed the bread away aroused Akiva's anger, but he restrained himself and said that he didn't have any other bread and that was all the bread there was. But Mrs. Kaminke kept on and asked him why the grocer on Sirkin Street had a different brand of bread that was much better. He wanted to tell her to go to hell and take her business to the other grocer and leave him alone, but he didn't say anything and put her purchases in her basket, added up the items, and wrote the total down in his ledger.

After she had left Gabriel Slep said, "A land that eats up its inhabitants," and Akiva nodded his head, although he didn't know what he meant. He took Gabriel Slep's list and gave him the groceries that were written on it, except for lox, which was out of stock. At the same time he tried again to discover what it was that was bothering him and oppressing his thoughts, but without success. Gabriel Slep went on talking about traffic accidents and told him about an accident in which his brother's son had been involved, and Akiva looked at him and shook his head slightly and waited for him to take his change and purchases and leave. After he left the shop was empty. Akiva went on standing still for a moment, smoothing his face with his hand, and then he took the salami to hang it up on its hook. On no account could he remember whatever it was that he was trying to remember, but once again he felt a sense of satisfaction at having participated in Meir Breuer's funeral. Suddenly it seemed to him that he had made a mistake in Gabriel Slep's account. He hung up the salami and examined the account and discovered that he had indeed made a mistake. So he took one lira and seventy-five agurot out of the till and hurried after Gabriel Slep and gave him the money and apologized. Then he returned to the shop and leaned on the counter to get his breath back. He looked around him and saw the worn floors and the dirt and the crack in the wall stretching from the corner of the ceiling to the little window, and again he thought that he should really get hold of some plaster of Paris or plastic cement and fix it. He hated the shop, which was dark and gloomy all day long and illuminated in the evening by two dusty electric bulbs that spread a yellow light over the bottles and tins and boxes and crates and shelves and socks, which were always in a bit of a mess and which always gave him the feeling of being trapped. There were years when he had thought of selling the shop and investing the money in something different, with more class, like an outfitters or a shoe shop. Afterward he had decided that at least he would change the tiles and the counter and shelves and whitewash the walls. But up to now he had done nothing, and he knew that he never would do anything and the shop would stay exactly as it was. He told himself that it would involve him in a lot of trouble and unnecessary expense, and that life was passing anyway and in the end he would die.

He straightened up and went out onto the pavement and started bringing in the crates of vegetables and sacks of potatoes. After his heart attack he had been told not to exert himself, but he took no notice of the doctors' warnings. Only sometimes, when he felt pressure on his chest or shortness of breath, he would pause for a moment and feel what he had felt right after the attack—that death was standing at his shoulder and had entered his body and might take him by surprise at any moment. To some extent this feeling was not different from what any man might be expected to feel, he thought, and leaned against the door-post to straighten his back a little. In the last analysis, he said to himself, Meir Breuer too must have felt that death was close at hand, and at the same time a minute before his death he never knew that in another minute he would be dead.

He looked at the street, which was sunk in darkness, and for a moment he pictured Meir Breuer and tried to imagine the boy's accidental death. He saw him lying lifeless on the ground, his face blackened by smoke. "Ah well, that's life," he said meaninglessly to himself and felt a great weariness in his back and legs. He moved away from the doorpost and started carrying the crates again, and while he did so Gabriel Slep's words—"A land that eats up its inhabitants"—came back to him and started rolling around in his head, like a collection of words that had lost all meaning and become separated into sounds. After he had brought everything in he lowered the shutter and took the money and ledger and receipt book out of the till and got ready to go.

He switched off the light and put his hand on the door handle and then he stood still in the darkness and tried to remember whatever it was that he had to remember and that was hanging over his head like a cloud because of his inability to remember it.

Zipporah, his wife, who had finished working in the shop about an hour before him, was standing in the kitchen making supper for them both and for their younger son who had come home on a two-day visit from the kibbutz. Their older son was studying at the Technion in Haifa and hardly ever came home. Akiva put the money and ledger and the receipts on the sideboard in the hall and went into the bathroom to wash. The face reflected in the mirror was gray and exhausted and unshaven. His eyes were bloodshot. He passed his hand over his chin and cheek and decided to put off shaving until the following morning. "What a bitch that Mrs. Kaminke is," he said to himself as he was changing his clothes, and then he went into the kitchen and sat down at the table. The presence of his son oppressed him.

He felt obliged to talk to him, but he was very tired and besides, he couldn't think of any subject or question to start off with. In the end he asked him if he wouldn't stay another day and if he needed a little money. His son said no, and he went on eating in silence, while he made a mental list of the goods he had to order for the shop and at the same time tried to remember the thing that was bothering him. He knew that it was something important and urgent, which concerned him closely. He stole a glance at Zipporah and asked her if they needed barley. She replied in the negative, but he decided to make sure for himself straight after supper, and for a split second he saw the shop and the place where the barley sack stood in his mind's eye. Zipporah served tea and asked their son if he had been to see Meir Breuer's parents, and the boy said that he might do it the next morning before he returned to the kibbutz. "Yes, yes, you should do it," Zipporah urged, and put a slice of lemon into Akiva's tea. Her words, which he imagined were directed at him, darkened his spirits because for the past three days he had been intending to go up to the Breuers' and putting it off, and all because of a quarrel he had had about a month before with Ephraim Breuer, Meir's father, about the upkeep of the lobby and the stairs. The whole thing was silly and unimportant, but it had filled him with such terrible rage that he felt quite capable of killing Ephraim Breuer with his bare hands. But he controlled himself and didn't even reply to the latter's accusations. He sipped his tea and soothed his conscience by reminding himself that he had attended the funeral and even contributed toward the printing of the mourning notices in honor of Meir Breuer, who a week or ten days before the accident had come into the shop to buy cigarettes. He was on leave from the army and came in with his girlfriend, who remained standing in the doorway, a little embarrassed, and smiled at him.

He bought a packet of Time, and when he left he said, "Come on Ruhama, we're off," and off they went. He felt nothing at all for Meir Breuer, neither affection nor pity nor longing, but neither did he feel anything for his younger son, who stood up and said "Shalom," and went out of the front door, and only his older son gave rise in him to a painful embarrassment and uneasiness and made him helpless and miserable with his demonstrative reserve. He could not understand why the boy treated him with such coldness and contempt. He had entertained such high hopes for him, more than for the younger son, and never denied him anything—food or clothes or money—and when he was a child he had taken him for little walks, and sometimes, on Saturdays, he had taken him to the sea, even though he himself hated the sea intensely.

He sipped his tea and looked at the empty chair where his younger son had been sitting a moment before, and said to himself, "A land that eats up its inhabitants," but he didn't have anything in mind when he said it, not even the words themselves, because he was thinking of something else entirely.

He pushed the tea away and picked his teeth, and then he stood up and went back to the shop to examine the barley stock. While he was doing so he noticed that they were running short of flour, and he felt annoyance at Zipporah for not telling him. He stood and surveyed the shop in order to see if there was anything else they were running out of, and he saw the shelves with the paint peeling off them and the old shutters, the cobwebs, the dust marks on the windows, the crack in the wall, the rusty hook with the bunch of bananas hanging from it. "It's falling to pieces," he said to himself, in a tone that included a certain malicious satisfaction, and then he went back home and sat down at the table to add up the accounts and make up the orders for the next day. He drew up the ledger and receipts and picked up the banknotes, and at the same moment he remembered that in five days' time it was Zipporah's birthday. This was the thing that had been bothering him so much and that he could on no account remember, and now that he remembered it he felt relief and even happiness. He looked at Zipporah as she left the kitchen and went into the room. Then he counted the money, wrote down the total, recounted it, and then opened the ledger and started copying the figures from the receipts into it, and at the same time he wondered what he would get her. At first he thought of a new dress or suit, or a fur coat. Once, when they had first met, she had been wearing a kind of black fur coat, which had been very flattering then, but he wondered if it would look so good on her today. If only he could be sure that she would enjoy it and wear it he would buy her a fur coat in spite of the expense. He stopped writing and abandoned himself to these deliberations and felt himself sinking from one moment to the next into irritation and depression. The more he thought about it the more he realized that he didn't know what to buy her because apart from the first two or three years of their married life he had never once bought her a present and ever since then he had also stopped taking an interest in her taste or the things she lacked and would be glad to have. If it was up to him he would have let the day go by this time too without taking any notice of it, but this time it was her fiftieth birthday and he felt an obligation to buy her something. He abandoned the idea of a fur coat and thought of a nice handbag, or a necklace, but not like the one that Ruhama, Meir's girlfriend, had been wearing. Yes, there was something attractive about the girl, but the beads she had been wearing were a young girl's beads, and he wanted something different, something more expensive, maybe pearls. The idea of a pearl necklace pleased him and he tried to work out how much a necklace like that would cost. In the meantime he remembered the headscarf he had once bought for Sarah Krauze. As always, this memory made him feel mildly surprised, because many years had passed since then and Sarah Krauze had disappeared from his thoughts as well as his life. He smiled with the surprise, and because of a sensation of being slightly ridiculous that came over him whenever he remembered the scarf. It was only by straining himself that he could find any connection between himself and the woman called Sarah Krauze, or between himself and the man who had bought her the scarf. He remembered that it was a green silk scarf and that he had bought it for her on her birthday, which fell on the Feast of Weeks, but that he had never given her the present because he was afraid of declaring his love and committing himself to her. In addition to this, he had been waiting for Sarah Krauze to make some kind of gesture of this kind first. If he had given her the scarf and gone on seeing her, he thought, everything might have turned out differently. This notion oppressed him and he quickly dismissed it. He sniggered to himself, saying that the truth was that he had never wanted to marry her but only to go to bed with her. And once he really had gone to bed with her, in Jerusalem. He wanted to go on thinking about this, but Zipporah called him from the other room to come and help her move the table. He said "coming," and stood up and went into the room.

Zipporah was already wearing her limp nightdress and he tried to avert his eyes so as not to see her arms and throat and heavy legs. They moved the table and she reminded him that they had to order halva and pickled herrings, and then she got into bed. He nodded his head and went out of the room and sat down by the kitchen table again and picked up his pen to go on with the accounts, but before doing so he paused because he wanted to go on thinking about Sarah Krauze for a little longer. No matter how hard he tried his recollection of her appearance remained very hazy, but he knew that she had been pretty and had had big green eyes and black hair. He pointed this out to himself and felt pride at having gone to bed with such a pretty girl. He worked out the number of years that had passed since then and discovered that it was already thirty years, because it had happened in exactly the same week that Hitler had invaded Poland. He looked at the column of figures in front of him and asked himself why he had never gone to bed with her again, even if he didn't want to marry her. This question led nowhere and dejected him, because it was always accompanied by a feeling of helplessness, and especially by the tormenting sensation of an opportunity that had been missed and would never return again. He decided to turn his mind away from the whole affair, but instead he closed his eyes and tried to reconstruct the act in all its details—how they had met in the street by chance and how she had invited him to come up to her room and how they drank tea from jam jars and how she sat next to him and took his fingers and played with them. The sunlight filtered in through the slats of the blinds, and stripes of light and shade fell on her face and breasts and arms. She took his hand and drew it up her thigh and then lay back on the bed and pulled him after her and he bent down and pushed himself against her with his eyes closed. These remote and clouded pictures afforded him no more than a faint pleasure. He kept on trying but the more stubbornly he clung to it and the harder he tried to bring it closer, even this faint pleasure dissipated, until in the end he felt nothing but anger and disappointment. It was dead and irritating. He brushed his face with his hand and started adding up the figures, muttering them aloud to himself. In the meantime he was reminded of Mrs. Freund. In the early evening she had bought some things on account and it seemed to him that Zipporah had forgotten to write the sum down in the ledger. He finished adding up the figures and went into the other room to ask her, but she was already sleeping, with the night light casting a yellow light on her heavy face. He stood looking at her for a moment and thought that if he had returned to Sarah Krauze he would certainly never have married her, only he never did return. He moved to Tel Aviv and kept on putting off getting in touch with her until one day, about four years later, he suddenly heard that Sarah Krauze had died of leukemia. After her death he felt an intense desire to be with her again and he even forgave her for not having tried to see him even once in all those four years. But after a short time his desire faded and died away.

He switched off the night light and went into the kitchen and poured himself a glass of grapefruit juice and drank it, and said to himself that it really was lucky for him that he had not married Sarah Krauze, and that Zipporah too had once been a beautiful woman, and especially vivacious and full of life. If only his elder son would come, he thought, he would be able to consult him about the birthday present, but he hardly ever came home. He washed the glass and put it back in its place and then he went back to the table and sat down and took a piece of paper and began writing on it, "one sack of flour, halva, pickled herring, lox," and at the same time it occurred to him that he could have consulted his younger son too, but now they probably would not see each other until after the birthday was over, unless he delayed his departure on account of the visit to Meir Breuer's parents. There was no chance that the boy would bring the subject up himself, because he didn't even know the date of his mother's birthday. The word "lox" floated in front of his eyes and he stared at it for some time, and suddenly he felt dissatisfied with the way he had written it. He crossed it out and wrote it again, thinking that even if he had had a quarrel with Ephraim Breuer and even if the latter had offended him without cause, it was his duty to go up and pay them a condolence call. He decided to do it the next day in the evening, and he saw himself climbing the stairs and ringing the bell, and then going into the big room and sitting with Ephraim Breuer and

Gertie Breuer and Naomi, Meir Breuer's sister, who had come all the way from London. And maybe Meir Breuer's girl Ruhama would be there too, and he remembered how Meir Breuer had lain covered with the national flag and how his eyes had rested on him curiously and then passed over the large crowd of mourners, when suddenly he saw Ruhama, who was standing on the other side of the open grave, withdrawn into herself, her brown eyes wide open and staring, and there was something so appealing and touching about her that he dropped his eyes and let them rest for a moment on her tanned legs, which disappeared beneath the hem of her skirt, moving slightly in the breeze and clinging to her thighs.

From the side the sound of the falling clods of earth reached his ears and he felt a slight constriction in his chest and a tremor of weakness in his legs, and at the same time he heard the voice of the cantor intoning, "Oh God full of mercy / Who dwelleth on high / Grant him rightful repose / Beneath the wings of the Divine Spirit . . ." and afterwards he heard three shots and he closed his eyes and saw an empty summer sky, full of sunlight, and when he opened them all the people were beginning to move toward the exit.

He looked around for Ruhama and when he did not see her he pushed his way through the crowd, looking for her so that he could walk by her side, but she had disappeared from view and all his efforts to find her were in vain. But when he reached the cemetery gates he turned his head around once more and suddenly he saw her walking a little distance behind him. He thought of waiting for her or even turning back and retracing his steps, but instead he only slowed down a little and then climbed into the bus and sat down with a feeling of disappointment and despair, and these feelings too faded away and disappeared when the bus stopped in the city and the mourners dispersed.

Cordoba

1

I'M SITTING ON THE hotel patio surrounded by a Saturday morning atmosphere. The light is still soft and a leisurely tourist bustle stirs in the crisp air. The Spanish waiter sets my breakfast before me on the white tablecloth: rolls, butter, jam, and a china jug full of black coffee. I thank him with a nod but don't start eating. I'm waiting for the little American, and in the meantime my eyes wander indifferently over the map of the city.

Two weeks ago I arrived here on the train from Madrid. I left my suitcase in the Hotel Simon, Grand Capitan Street, and set out to tour the town. Two days later I said to myself that I'd seen all the places recommended by the guide and I was now free to continue my trip. Toward evening I began my preparations. I went to the information office at the railway station, bought a few trinkets to give my friends as presents, sent off a couple of picture postcards, and sat down to write a letter.

Four days went by in this way. But one week later I was still staying in the Hotel Simon, room number 43. I still hadn't finished the letter. The greenish pages are still lying on the heavy wooden table and next to them, under the ashtray, the train ticket to Seville, as well as the notebook in which I had jotted down the details of trains between Cordoba and Seville, Grananda, Malaga, Algericas, Valencia, Barcelona, and Ciudad Real. The price of the tickets is written there too. From time to time I look into the notebook with renewed energy and a feeling that this time something's going to happen.

It all begins in the morning, while I'm still floating in the shallows of sleep, but already conscious of the disagreeable smell of the strange bed-linen, and the foreignness of the place. Names of towns and times-of-departure run around in my head as if I've never, not even in my sleep, stopped thinking exclusively about them. Through the window looms the dark cypress tree and the gray, pre-morning strip of sky. I turn my face to the wall, lay my head on my arm, and despairing of sleep decide to finalize my affairs. With this end in view I go back to the beginning and explain to myself, almost aloud, that Cordoba is only one station on the way, a temporary station. Now that I've seen it, I have to go on to Seville, in accordance with my plans. But from then on everything gets complicated. After all, I never had one real reason for deciding to go on to Seville, just as I never had a reason for coming to Cordoba. But Cordoba is where I am, and I'm already sick of traveling. And what good will it do me to see a whole lot of new faces and ancient churches?

"A person has to make up his mind," the little American said to me yesterday with a cute expression of gravity on her face.

"Yes, Nancy," I said with a smile and selected a walnut cake.

She was definitely right. After all, I wasn't going to stay here for the rest of my life, and as a draftsman living on his salary, I couldn't even afford to extend my stay too much longer. Maybe I should go back to Madrid and take a train from there to see the palaces of El Escorial?

"A person has to make up his mind."

She was right. But even if she wasn't, I wasn't about to contradict her and confuse her clear world for her. On the contrary. With all my heart I wanted her to stay exactly the way she was forever: something clear and fresh, like a kind of lithe, simple-hearted tennis player on a spring day bathed in green foliage and covered with a blue sky.

On my way to the patio I stopped outside her door for a minute and listened. Then I bounded down the stairs and sat down at the table.

2

Nancy appears at the bottom of the stairs in dark blue slacks and a light blue shirt, and I take a bite out of a roll and watch her from behind the map. She pauses, glances around with her frank, almond-shaped eyes, smiles, and walks up to me gaily swinging the bag hanging on a strap from her shoulder. No, she no longer suspects me of intending to do her any harm, or planning to abduct her and selling her to the Emir of Kuwait or the King of Saudia Arabia.

"Hello," says Nancy.

"Good morning," I reply, pretending to be surprised, and quickly put the map down.

Her pretty arms are bare and also her straight neck, ending in the clear and sensual line of her jaw. All the sunny beaches and fresh air in the world have been soaked up by her smooth skin, which gives off a delicate fragrance of young bodies and soap.

I met her three days ago.

It was early in the evening and a desolate, dusty sky hung over the town. I wandered aimlessly in the hot, dirty air around the railway station, and let myself be picked up by someone who looked like a bank clerk.

There were four women sitting in the room watching television. When I came in, three of them got up and went behind the curtain into the next room. The big bed was covered with a red velvet spread, embroidered with stylized gold flowers. On the television screen the bicycle race was almost over and the crowd roared. Then the winner crossed the finishing line and a number of people burst onto the track waving their arms. She wouldn't even let me touch her hair in case I spoiled the spray. Now the winner was smiling a tired, happy smile and panting heavily. A girl gave him a bunch of flowers and kissed him. Afterwards someone in a fancy suit supported him and some others made a ring round him until he disappeared from view, except for his hand waving to and fro.

Outside Cordoba was drearier than ever and sickeningly dull, sinking into a long-drawn-out desert dusk with all its hordes of clerks, cab drivers, porters, policemen, hotel doormen in generals' hats, hawkers, and men sitting in cafes wearing business suits.

Nancy was standing on the corner of Avenida del Generalisimo and Avenida del Grand Capitan, outside the door of the Tourist Office, in a striped spring dress and sandals. She took hold of the door handle and shook it slightly, pressed her face against the window pane, retreated to the middle of the sidewalk, pushed her hand through her hair, glanced at her watch, and looked up and down. I crossed the road and turned in her direction. She stopped me and asked, somewhat embarrassed, if I happened to know when they would open the office. I said that today they weren't going to open it, because it was a holiday, but maybe I could help.

"Oh, thank you," she said quickly, smiling politely, "but it isn't urgent, really, thank you," and walked off. I remained standing in the dull dusk light, one hand in my pocket, in the other a cigarette, on my lips the lingering shadow of a sweet smile, and tried to put her figure together again from the disintegrating fragments: the soft chestnut-colored hair, the lovely cheek, the clean-cut lips, the clear look, the line of the throat, and the tender protuberance of the collarbone, and the shapely leg with the delicate tendon at the ankle, as I had glimpsed them from behind.

The whole of the next day I walked around the streets, but it was already evening when I met her again, standing in front of a shoe shop window. Yes, she said after a moment's bewilderment, she remembered me. From yesterday. On the corner of Avenida del Generalisimo and Avenida del Grand Capitan.

I invited her to have a cup of coffee with me.

"Oh, thank you. I'm in a hurry. My boyfriend's waiting for me. I'm awfully sorry." A slight cloud of embarrassment darkened her face. "Some other time, perhaps," she said after turning away.

Cordoba's a small town, so yesterday, at about noon, we met in the Post Office and I helped her to buy stamps, and during lunch, which we ate in one of the restaurants in the center, it turned out that we were staying next door to each other in the same hotel. Nancy laughed out loud, showing two rows of even white teeth, while I contented myself with a smile and went on cutting my meat. I was thinking about the evening.

In the evening we sat at a cafe in Avenida del Generalisimo.

"Let's order wine," I suggested gaily and beckoned the waiter.

"I don't drink," said Nancy. "Could I have something else?"

Later on, while she was licking her ice cream, she admitted

what I had already half-guessed, in other words, that she had been lying about her boyfriend.

"You see, I didn't know you," she said and gave me an apologetic look.

"That's okay, Nancy. You have to be careful," I said heartily and touched her arm with a sudden feeling of relief.

When we got back to the hotel it was already late. Nancy went up the stairs one step ahead of me, but every few steps she paused, bent down and said something in my ear, almost in a whisper. Two or three times I could feel the fluttering touch of her hair, and even the film of warm air covering her face. She was that close to me.

In front of the door to her room we stopped. Nancy put her hand on the door handle while I stood there with my hands in my pockets. The night light shed a mean, institutional light over the narrow, deserted corridor. For a moment we stood there side by side, and then I blurted out an abrupt "good night" and went into my room.

On the other side of the wall, very close, I heard her locking the door, walking around, moving a chair, opening the closet, opening the tap, and in the end flopping down on the bed. For a moment I thought of going to her, and I even took a few careful steps toward the door, but then I changed my mind and went up to the window and looked outside. Suddenly the light in her room went out and the cypress tree together with the roof of the house next door sank into darkness.

It's time to get out of here, I said to myself, and flipped impatiently through my train time-table.

I smoke a cigarette and Nancy sips her coffee while her finger glides over Cordoba. She's busy planning our sight seeing for the day. First, she says, we'll go to the mosque.

It's all the same to me.

3

We stop in the shade of the stone wall of the mosque. Nancy gazes at the sight with a look of eager expectancy, opens the guide and reads aloud: "This vast edifice takes us back to the eighth century, to the days of Abd el-Rahman the Great. . . ."

Then we go in.

Like a child in a magician's cave Nancy wanders through the dim forest of arches. Her eyes are wide and her lips parted. She gingerly touches the walls, points her finger, tries to count the pillars, tugs my sleeve, and whispers something in my ear. A wave of happiness engulfs her when she discovers signs of the Baroque and the Renaissance, or when she finds that the real tower is exactly the same as the one in the photograph in the guide, and likewise the gateway and the courtyard with its slender-stemmed citrus trees.

When we emerge into the dusty street flooded with harsh sunlight and noise, she is still breathing a different, visionary air. But after a few steps she is walking by my side again, lithe and light-footed, admiringly but uncovetously examining the objects in the shop windows, peeping into the patios, and dropping a few coins, with a serious expression, into the cap of the organ-grinder, who bows to us while his wife, presumably, goes on laboriously turning the big handle.

"Listen to the music," cries Nancy, gripping my arm, "Isn't it wonderful?"

"Yes," I reply and put my hand on her shoulder.

"You know, only poor people are truly happy. Don't you think so?"

"Maybe. I've never been poor."

"What do you do?"

"I'm an architect."

"An architect?" Nancy repeats and stares at me admiringly, while I turn her attention to a little funeral procession crossing the alley far ahead of us.

By now I know that she was born in a medium sized town in the state of Michigan. Her father is a successful lawyer and horse lover, who is seeking election to congress as a representative of the Republican Party. He is opposed to racial segregation and is a great fan of Sammy Davis Junior. Her mother is a beautiful woman and the chairlady of a local charitable organization. They live well. One of her uncles is a road engineer and the other is a press photographer. She has two younger brothers. She graduated from college with honors, and excelled in sports too, especially swimming. She loves philosophy and the theater and riding horses. Now that she has completed her first year at university, she's come on a two-month trip to Europe, paid for out of her own savings, to "learn something about life." Her parents, for their part, contributed the plane ticket. She feels quite homesick. She's happy at home, whereas over here, although it's so interesting, everything's different and the strangeness makes her feel uneasy, especially early in the evening.

A woman dressed in black, kneeling in a wooden box and scrubbing the cobblestones, directs us to the synagogue. For a few moments we stand still in the modest, empty room whose heavy air is steeped in damp and full of an ancient chill. We look at the crude walls with the plaster peeling here and there, at the simple arabesques and the fragments of Hebrew inscriptions. There's a kind of combination of joy and anxiety in Nancy as she looks into my face and listens as I read the mysterious words to her. When I finish she asks me to translate for her and I do the best I can. And then, with a wonderful seriousness, she asks:

"What's it like to be a Jew?"

"Nice," I reply without thinking and smile. But I immediately grow serious and say: "Tiring."

Nancy doesn't understand. The word "tiring" confuses her. She wants an explanation, and her face shows an expression of interest together with a willingness to help, if need be. Very gently, barely touching, I pass my hand over her hair and neck, and for a moment I feel something like regret.

Outside, in the great light, invisible church bells are chiming, drawing circles of festive gold in the empty sky. Nancy stands looking up and I, behind her, at her legs. Suddenly she swings her bag and starts running and skipping down the white alley.

4

Choking with laughter and short of breath we go into a restaurant. Nancy orders a salad, steak, and chips. When I get my oxtail in sauce a merry cry of admiration breaks from her lips, and I announce that the owner of the tail was slain in the ring by the sword of El Cordobes himself, which is a great honor.

Nancy utters a peal of laughter, but it subsides immediately, and she says:

"Don't you think that killing bulls for entertainment is cruel and ungodly?"

"How about not for entertainment, but for steaks?" I retort with sudden anger.

Nancy cuts the meat in silence and eats without raising her head from her plate.

"What's the Corrida like?" she asks in the end, trying to appease me.

"Fantastic."

While we're drinking our coffee she wonders why she hasn't had a letter from her boyfriend yet. I reassure her and put the blame on the Spanish postal services. Later on, after we pay and leave, she tells me about him.

His name is Stephen Bagritzky. He's a good-looking Catholic boy, whose parents are of Polish descent. In his spare time he takes photographs. He's serious and honest. Blond. And he really wants to be a movie director, but first he's going to finish his studies as a railway engineer. In two years time. And then they're going to get married.

I listen without taking anything in. The deserted street lies supine in the heavy heat and the ugly desolation. The rich meal makes my legs heavy and fills my head with a drowsy fog. My eyes, straining dully to stay open in the glare, see without seeing. I separate from myself. My wakeful self floats above me and examines me in weary perplexity. No, I haven't the least idea what I'm doing here in this ghost town, abandoned by its inhabitants. It's all so senseless, a mirage where nothing is connected to anything else: me, Nancy, the street corner, the scrubbing woman, the Hotel Simon, the rest of the journey, the Municipal Museum, the word Jew, going back to Israel, Stephen Bagritzky, the American tourist who took a photograph of us in the courtyard of the mosque. He was sure we were lovers, maybe newlyweds, and he asked us to stand with our arms around each other in front of the gate and smile.

I drag my feet to the Plaza de Colon. We sit down to rest on a stone bench. A few dusty palms and other trees whose names I don't know cast a suffocating shade. Nancy's tired. Her bag is on the ground, her hands lie on her lap. I don't move, but gradually a terrible desire engulfs me for this innocent body, so abandoned in its lassitude and seductive in the swooning afternoon, and Nancy talks and says that there's nothing as wonderful as love and that she and Stephen will love each other for ever, while my hand gropes over the cool stone backrest and my head buzzes with schemes for getting her back to the hotel right now, at this very minute.

My eyes are full of a seaside glare, dizzy and blurred

with a hallucinatory haze. The false, shimmering light goes round in circles. All I can see are her two knees and her thighs, very close indeed and disappearing under the hem of her skirt sinking limply between them, and her tanned skin gives off a warm smell of sweat, and I wait full of suspense for the slightest sign from her, while she goes on talking, and suddenly I hear her say that a girl has to take care of herself and get married a virgin.

In the hollow silence invading my head and surrounding me like a bubble, it seems to me that the palm is tilting further and further and in a moment it will keel over and cover us with its fronds.

"Yes, Nancy," I say in a hostile tone and withdraw my hand.

Opposite us, in the middle of the park, stands a parched marble fountain. I want to get up and walk away, but I go on sitting there, feeling as if I've been sitting in the same place for years and I'll go on sitting there years longer.

Light as a leaf drifting from a tree, with a gesture full of trust, she lays her head against my shoulder. I keep absolutely still but look at her out of the corner of my eye and see how a single sunbeam, very bright, filters through the branches and illuminates her hair and temple.

Nancy is asleep and I'm awake.

5

The more the day declines and the heat lifts the gloomier I grow.

After dinner we go to Victoria Park to visit the carnival set up there in honor of some local festival. Nancy is radiant. Her cherry-colored man's shirt emphasizes her tan and adds a bewitching sensuousness to her appearance. She chatters and giggles, but I don't open my mouth all the way there.

From a few blocks away we can already hear the Spanish tunes blaring deafeningly from the loudspeakers, and see the haze of light floating in the night sky. Then we can hear the noise of the crowd too.

When we cross the street and mingle with the milling crowd, she takes my hand, and her eyes dart around, trying to take in all the sights at once.

Slowly the Ferris wheel begins to turn. We sit jammed into the narrow seat, and Nancy looks dreamy. But when we rise into the air and the wheel increases its speed she panics. She clutches my arm and presses her head against my chest with a dazed, frozen smile on her pale face.

"Isn't it fantastic," she says with an effort and points down.

I look down indifferently and see the tops of the trees and the roofs of the booths and stalls with crowds of people milling around them.

After a few turns the wheel stops. Nancy stands up and gets off heavily, but I suddenly sit down again to go on spinning around by myself. Nancy, her face yellow, looks at me for a moment, confused and at a loss. "I'll wait for you here," she calls when the wheel begins to turn and points to one of the nearby booths.

I say nothing, I don't even take the trouble to nod, but when I reach the top I look down carefully and see her standing there and gazing upward in a kind of mute appeal.

When the wheel stops again, I stumble off, pause for a moment, and then work my way toward the booth, which is surrounded by a closely packed crowd.

Nancy is nowhere to be seen. I push and shove a bit, stretch my neck and turn my head until I catch a glimpse of her among the dozens of shoulders and heads separating us. She's standing at the counter with a rifle in her hands. Deftly she sets it against her shoulder and aims it at the figures running past in a row on a conveyor belt. There's the sound of a shot and she disappears from sight and reappears again, her eyes searching the crowd, disappears and reappears again, loading the rifle while the man behind the counter says something to her, smiling and waving his hands and patting her on the shoulder.

Little by little I move away, stop, turn my head, take a few more steps and stop again, hesitate, and in the end I cross the street and stride rapidly down the deserted alleys until the noise and the lights vanish into the distance behind me. The alleys wind this way and that in the pale moonlight. Until the bus station looms up again, and the Plaza de Colon and the Avenida del Generalisimo and the Avenida del Grand Capitan and the environs of the railway station and the gloomy building with the seedy restaurant, illuminated by a dim brown light. I rush up the steps, knock on the door, and go inside.

A little while later I emerge. Outside Cordoba slumbers, tired but appeased, like a town granted a short respite from its troubles. A clear sky covers it, full of stars, and the coolness of the night consoles its streets until the sun rises.

I stroll empty of everything and smoke. I stand on the Puente Romano bridging the Rio Guadalquivir, lean on the railing, throw my cigarette butt into the water and contemplate the point of light flickering for a moment and going out in the fathomless depths. Tomorrow I'll leave. Early in the morning. I don't owe anyone a thing. Not even a good-bye. I'm a free man and all I have to do is pack up my bags and leave.

The receptionist looks at me with sleepy eyes and gives me the key. Nancy's room is dark and silent. I go into my room, take off my shirt, wash my face and hands, and sit down to study my train time-table. Then I hear her door opening, and afterward light steps in the corridor and a cautious knock at my door. I go on poring over my time-table, and only after the third knock I say, "Yes."

"I looked for you," she says and comes up to me. "Did something happen?"

6

All day long I run around the streets with Nancy, light hearted and happy as a boy forgiven his trespasses. In the early evening she drags me to a church. Santa Marina, or maybe it was Santa Maria. In the white alleys, already invaded by the quiet cool of twilight, she swings her handbag, shakes her head, skips from the curb to the street and laughs. But as soon as the church appears she puts on a grave, solemn, almost sad expression.

There are a few people sitting in the church and a heavy smell of incense and burning candles fills the air. It seems as if a giant eye, a concentration of black air, is spying on you, always from the back. I lower my voice and speak to Nancy, but she only shakes her head, since she is totally absorbed by the act of worship being carried out next to the altar.

The head priest sings in a voice full of reverence and the two priests by his side murmur in response as if spellbound. Their broad backs, turned toward the congregation, are brightly illuminated. Behind them, a little to the side, stand two slender boys. In their hands are silver candlesticks taller than they are, covered with engravings of leaves and flowers, with white candles burning in them. Like bored schoolboys they raise and lower the candlesticks, step to and fro and get entangled in their long, trailing robes.

I turn my head and examine the oppressively elaborate gilded woodwork covering the gates-of-Paradise leading into the adjacent alcove, in whose depths stands a statue of the Madonna. Her marble head is bowed in utter submission, her whole attitude bespeaks a supreme humility and purity, of which she herself is not unconscious. No, on no account does she remind me of my mother or my grandmother. A huge garland of white flowers lies at her feet, but she will never bend down to pluck one of the flowers and smell it. I look at the flowers, expecting to see a bowl of semolina and honey next to them.

The voice of the head priest drops and a low murmur spreads through the church, like the buzzing of a swarm of bees. Nancy stands still, heartbreakingly innocent and entranced. I draw cautiously closer to her and wonder whether to put my hand on her shoulder.

The head priest makes signs with his hands, kisses the altar cloth and kneels with his head bowed, and the other two priests kneel with him, except that the one on the left is apparently lame, since he has difficulty in kneeling and even more so in standing up again, and so he falls farther and farther behind the others as they kneel and rise.

Nancy turns to me with an amused smile on her face. As she does so she leans on me with her whole body. For a moment our mouths are almost touching and our breath mingles warmly. The floor moves gently under my feet and my eyes cloud over drunkenly, and somewhere a marble crucifix gleams and grows blurred, and out of the corner of my eye I see one of the altar boys pinching his friend behind the priests' backs, and receiving a kick for his pains. They have a hard time suppressing their laughter, and the two candlesticks sway in their hands like sticks. I smile and place my hand on Nancy's nape and take a step backward and lean against the stone pillar.

The rites are concluded. We emerge into the street and Nancy walks by my side as silent and withdrawn as if she has just been to a funeral. A last, sharp light clings to the crests of the trees and bursts out between the houses. We wander aimlessly through the maze of alleys, which are calm now and already steeped in evening shade.

"People have to believe in God," says Nancy without disturbing the silence. We come out of one of the alleys and walk along the Guadalquivir. In the broad, abandoned street stretching along the river bank there is hardly a soul to be seen. The gloomy buildings lining one side of the street cast shadows which merge with the greenish-brown dusk coming from the empty spaces on the other side of the river and bringing with it a smell of water and plants and turds and garbage and dust.

After the abandoned water mill, not far from the Puente Romano, we stop and lean on the stone balustrade. The water, stagnant as swamp water, is getting blacker and blacker. Down below, to the side, two Spaniards are standing with their backs to the street and pissing into the river, conducting a conversation as they do so.

"People have to believe in God," repeats Nancy, and this time she gives me a stare, while I can't take my eyes off the pissing Spaniards.

She believes in Him, just as her parents believe in Him. And in fact, she says, everyone believes in Him, even those who're sure they don't. Isn't that so?

I nod my head but my eyes remain stubbornly fixed on the two Spaniards, who walk slowly away and recede into the distance until they vanish into the dusk forever. And here, not far away, a group of children are still kicking a ball against the wall, and a horse-drawn garbage cart passes through the desolate street like an empty death wagon, and the creaking of its huge wooden wheels mingles with their gleeful, birdlike cries. And with increasing pain I know in my heart just how false and separate and hopeless everything is. In other words, the children's happiness, which depresses me, and Nancy too, leaning on my shoulder with such friendliness, whereas I know that we are only bound to each other for a moment by chains of unbreakable strangeness, just as I am bound for some reason to these children, to this street, and to this town.

So, her parents believe in God, she tells me. They go to church, confess their sins, donate money, observe the rites and rituals, and pray to Him every night before they go to bed. But her father gets angry with her mother for bothering Him with nonsense.

"What nonsense?" I ask without interest, wondering about parents who let their daughters go on trips around the world by themselves.

"All kinds of nonsense," replies Nancy with animation. "For instance, if there's going to be a party the next day and Mom's had her hair done for it, she'll pray to God not to let her hairdo get spoiled until after the party's over."

"And your father?" I ask.

"My father?" says Nancy, and we move off and continue walking, "He prays to God to help him win some lawsuit or to advance him in his career. And to help him stop smoking."

"Really?" I say, and smile.

"Really," says Nancy, and she smiles too. "He prays a lot about smoking. He's scared to death but he keeps right on smoking and right on praying. He's even doubled his donations to the church in order to stop smoking."

"What brand does he smoke?" I ask.

"Marlboro."

I feel like bursting out laughing and kissing her, without any lust but out of the inexplicable happiness which suddenly seizes hold of me. And I really do hug her close to me, and as we turn into a street full of people and flooded with lights I imagine, without mockery, her parents kneeling next to their beds in white nightgowns, folding their hands on their chests, closing their eyes, and praying: "Oh Lord our Savior, who took upon yourself all our sins and suffering, please bestow your grace upon me and make me stop smoking Marlboro cigarettes."

I look at Nancy and the smile doesn't leave my face. Somehow I suddenly feel fond of them too. They are close to my heart. I am at one with them and with all these people milling round me, buying things in the shops, sitting in the cafes, or passing by and vanishing from sight.

"They must be having supper now and watching television," she says.

The sound of singing suddenly bursts out of a shop selling electrical appliances.

"The Beatles!" cries Nancy, and she slips out from under my arm and begins dancing in the middle of the street.

7

On Sunday gray summer clouds cover the sky. A silvery haze settles over the town and the air is heavy and very still. A white light, seeming to burst out of the bowels of the earth, illuminates the walls of the whitewashed houses.

In the afternoon we go to the Corrida. Nancy is very tense. On the way she suddenly asks me why I don't leave Cordoba.

"I don't know," I reply.

A low buzz hangs over the packed stands of the bullring. And while the last of the spectators hurry to take their places the trumpets blare and the performers enter the arena in a formal parade and are received with applause.

Nancy claps with the rest of the crowd and even waves her hand. Her face is very animated. The former tenseness is still there, but it has been joined by a kind of elation. After the last of the performers disappears she looks around expectantly, and then the first bull bursts into the ring.

"Look at him," says Nancy in excitement and points to the bull running to and fro, its black hide sleek and shining, its muscles quivering, its strong legs trampling the ground and its horns goring the air. Suddenly it stops and raises its head proudly and stands still for a moment, threatening and full of grandeur and beauty.

"He is beautiful, but he will die," our Portugese neighbor explains to us in his stilted English, "That is how it is," and he takes a drag on his cigarette.

Down below the bullfight proceeds in elaborate costumes and according to a division of roles and set of rules laid down in advance. Only the bull, of course, does not know its role, and at this stage it doesn't even know that it's fighting for its life. It charges around the ring and tries to gore the banderilleros, who try for their part to enrage the bull by waving their capes at it. Then it charges the mounted picador, who sticks the point of his lance again and again into its withers, until blood streams down its magnificent neck. From time to time cries of sympathy rise from the crowd, uniting for a moment into a kind of deep sigh.

"He is good," says the Portuguese admiringly, meaning the bull, in whose bulging black eyes a terrified bewilderment is crystallizing in the face of the blurred, cheering crowd and the men dancing and dodging round him, flashing their capes and sticking their barbed colored sticks into him. Now it seems that all he wants is to get away.

Nancy is quite still. Her eyes are fixed on the bull and there is an expression of fear and pity on her face.

"That one is from Barcelona. So-so," remarks the Portuguese of the matador who steps proudly into the ring to the applause of the audience. He strides over to the box, bows humbly to the Presidente, and turns to face the bull.

In total, ritual concentration he performs his role, playing a deadly double game against his own fear and against the bull, and leading it slowly and reverently, with the precise and graceful movements of a dancer, toward its death. With exquisite skill and self-control, but never swerving from his goal, the matador executes pass after pass while the excited crowd roars "Ole!" in appreciation and encouragement, until a silence falls in which the bull and the matador, isolated and apart, stand quite still concentrating intently on each other, enemies bound together by a terrible force, like the two halves of a single whole. And then—the straightening of the sword, the lunge, the charge, the thrust, the blade sinking in to the hilt, the sigh of the crowd, the bull sagging and swaying on its feet, the exhausted smile but still tense expression of the panting matador, the heavy sinking of the bull that seems to combine a pleasurable feeling of release with sudden breakdown and resignation, the relaxed stance of the matador watching now without desire, and the cries of relief and admiration spreading through the stands while crowds of spotless handkerchiefs flutter like excited doves.

Nancy does not cheer. In absolute silence she watches as the defeated bull is deftly chained to a plough shaft harnessed to three mules. The whip cracks and the bull is quickly dragged out of the ring, while a group of men in red operetta coats run around it, and others rake away the broad swathe left behind on the brown sand. When the carcass of the bull goes past us the Portuguese applauds in its honor. Afterward he leans over Nancy and offers me a cigarette.

"How is it in America?" he asks her.

I stop applauding, wipe the sweat off my face, and take a cigarette.

"Good," says Nancy, staring at some invisible point in the empty arena.

"Five hundred and twenty kilos," the Portuguese reads aloud from the notice that appears the moment the new bull charges into the ring.

"Five hundred and twenty kilos," I repeat after him, and down below, in the ring, the toreros begin to enrage the bull with their capes again.

"Look, he is fighting hard," says the Portuguese and tugs at my sleeve. And indeed, at that moment the bull succeeds in throwing the horse off balance and it teeters and falls over like a rocking horse with the picador stuck on its back, and both of them lie sprawled on the ground, frightened and ridiculous. The crowd roars and the toreros rush around like a panic-stricken flock of chickens, flashing their capes and stamping their feet, and Nancy grabs my arm, a flicker of anxious hope on her intent face.

During the round of applause which greets the appearance of the new matador in the arena, she suddenly turns to face me and asks if there is a chance of one of the bulls at least coming out of the ring alive.

"No," I reply and go on clapping.

Once more the bull runs around the ring, trying to escape and forced to fight, and there is the same look of frightened bewilderment in his huge eyes. And then once more the stillness and suspense, the straightening of the sword, the charging of the one toward the other, the thrust, the quivering, the sagging, and in the end the heavy sinking to the ground.

I cheer and see them surrounding the vanquished bull in their colorful uniforms, its amputated ear waved aloft in the hand of the victor, the eyes and faces of the crowd, the handkerchiefs, the shouts, the Portuguese's gaping mouth next to Nancy's face. And the three mules appear and the black carcass is tied up and dragged out, the back of its magnificent neck turned toward us, and Nancy watches and her slender fingers twist the ticket around, and afterward she throws it away and looks helplessly from side to side as if she doesn't understand what's happening in front of her eyes, and something takes fright inside me and I put my sweating hand on her shoulder and draw her gently toward me. Suddenly all I want is to bury her head in my chest, to encompass her like a protective wall, and to get her away from the strange crowd and the Portuguese, the heat, the cruel spectacle, the applause that never stops, from the whole world.

"It'll be all right, Nancy," I say, "it'll be all right," and a new bull bursts into the ring.

"Four hundred and eighty kilos," announces the Portuguese.

"Let's get out of here."

"No," says Nancy," I want to see."

I no longer take any interest in what's happening in the ring. I'm preoccupied with a concern that depresses and purifies my spirits. Again and again I stroke her head and arm, with a growing feeling that the world is a sly, vicious place, lying in wait to corrupt her innocence and hurt her with pitiless cruelty.

When the last fight is over she gets up slowly, claps a few times in honor of the matador, and looks grave. We leave with the rest of the crowd, and at the same time the clouds disperse a little and an orange sunset mingles with the evening shade and illuminates the street and the walls of the buildings. I lead her aimlessly about, and in the end we go into a restaurant not far from Victoria Park and sit down.

"Coffee?"

"I'm hungry," says Nancy. "I'm dying of hunger."

I order asparagus soup, artichokes in mayonnaise, clams, fish, baked vegetables, and chicken chasseur with mushrooms, stuffed spleen, and Andalusian rice.

"Wine too," Nancy puts in quickly, "red wine."

The waiter brings the first course and pours wine into our glasses. Nancy raises her glass to mine, takes a careful sip and smiles. Afterward we eat.

Nancy eats heartily and without affectation. Occasionally she takes a sip of wine and refills her glass. As we eat she tells me about the dishes they eat at home and her parents', especially her mother's, tiresome insistence on elaborate rituals and table manners. Afterward she describes their friends and relations, and how they spend hours on meaningless small talk and bridge games, and the ostentatious affection displayed by her mother and father, who actually feel bored, discontented, and estranged from one another. There isn't a trace of bitterness in her words, or even of mockery, only a kind of frank, humorous appraisal.

To round off our meal we order ice cream and coffee.

"The wine deceived me," she says when we emerge into the street and leans happily against me. "We ate too much. Let's go for a walk."

We walk through Victoria Park and land up next to the Guadalquivir and the labyrinth of quiet alleys again.

"It's wonderful to be a stranger, an absolute stranger," she says suddenly and nestles up to me.

Late at night we return to the hotel.

"You know, I haven't said anything to you about the Corrida yet."

"Tomorrow, Nancy," I say and open the door of her room with the big bronze key.

Her body clings to mine, very relaxed and complaisant, her head rests in the hollow of my neck, and the smell of her hair filling my face is like the smell of a child's hair rinsed in lemon juice.

"It was great, really, the wine, and everything. All of it, the bulls, the matadors, everything. But that moment when they drag them out of the ring—it's ghastly. And there's really no chance at all of it ever ending any other way?"

"No, Nancy," I say and gently loosen the grip of her hands around my neck.

"Are you going?"

"It's late. Good night. I'll see you in the morning," and I beat a hasty retreat into my room.

The strange room doesn't bother me, neither does the rest of the trip. It's all the same to me if I'm in Corboda or some other place. I stretch out on the bed in my clothes, very proud of myself, and the purity of my concern fills me with serenity and elation. I could lie like this—I think to myself—exactly like this, for years, listening to Nancy on the other side of the wall closing the door, walking around, moving a chair, opening the tap. It's cold tonight, I say to myself, maybe I should go in and tell her to shut the window.

Afterward I hear her stretching out on the bed, and again it occurs to me to go in to her and sit down beside her and warn her against all the dangers lying in wait for her, in other words, against the heat of the sun and the chill of the night and stormy seas and pits in the ground and snakes and automobiles, and especially against people, both bad and good, against friends and relations and strangers, and even against myself.

One by one I repeat the dangers to myself and think of getting up and going to her, and at the same time I listen alertly for the sound of her footsteps in the corridor and the sound of her knocking lightly on my door.

Nothing happens, only an empty silence going on and on forever, as if the world has died and disappeared beyond the high ceiling and four bare walls between which I am lying on my back in a treacherous expectation which does not subside but grows more intense and takes me over and turns into a feeling of humiliation at being treated with ingratitude, which arouses my anger against her and then against myself, until I get up and put out the light and lie down on the bed again in a state of angry distraction and apathy and try to calm down.

Suddenly I am seized by panic. I think I hear footsteps in the corridor. I sit on the edge of the bed and listen. The numbers on the face of my watch glitter like little cats' eyes. The time is ten to three. There isn't a sound from Nancy's room or from the corridor. The train to Algeciras leaves at a quarter past three. I grab my suitcase, collect the papers scattered over the table, hurry down the stairs, pay my bill, and run to the railway station.

At ten o'clock in the morning the train arrives in Algeciras, where my tired, burning eyes are greeted by the sight of the sea, and a cool breeze, saturated with moisture and the smell of fish and seaweed and rust, caresses my face and fills me with relief.

8

From Algeciras I go to Cadiz and from Cadiz to Seville and from Seville to Jerez and two weeks later I return to Cordoba.

I leave Cordoba early in the morning and go to Jaen and from Jaen to Granada and from Granada back to Seville and Jerez and from Jerez to Malaga. There I bathe in the sea and return to Cordoba.

I don't sleep at the Hotel Simon. I don't sleep anywhere. I check my suitcase in at the railway station and go out to prowl the town empty-handed. Hour after hour I wander through the austere white streets and alleys, which are steeped in a chilly stillness, stroll along the Guadalquivir, go into the mosque, pause for a moment next to Santa Marina or Santa Maria, lean on the iron railing at the corner of Avenida del Generalisimo and Avenida del Grand Capitan in front of the Tourist Office, observe the passersby, and go back to the railway station. Once or twice I peep into the Hotel Simon. I do this without any hope, of course. The receptionist remembers me but his only reply to my few questions is a shrug.

Sometimes I regret not knowing her family name or the name of the medium-sized town in the state of Michigan from which she came, since it never occurred to me to ask her. Even though by now, only five months later, I can't even conjure her up in my imagination, except in fragmentary glimpses of strangers in the street, or the faint trace of a smell suddenly accosting me and instantly swallowed up again in the infinite void of the air.

Twilight

ALFRED'S IN THE WHITE bed in the corner, near the window, very thin already, his face a pale yellowish color. But all of a sudden, at twilight, an hour of grace: with his eyes shut he begins to sing an aria from *Rigoletto* in a hoarse but pleasant tenor voice, and the woman, on her hefty legs, smiles at everybody with a wondering, grateful smile, as if they had saved him and sent the Angel of Death away. Very cautiously she asks him to sing something else, and he sings a passage of cantorial music, and there's something mischievous in his expression as he sings. The woman watches with bated breath, and Abraham, in the next bed, says to her, incredulously, sharing in her happiness: "God is great," and she, overjoyed, nods her head in whole-hearted agreement. "Haha," says the Austrian to nobody in particular, "how willingly human beings consent to be taken in," and he returns to his newspaper.

A week later the situation deteriorates again, and at twilight Alfred does not sing, but lies stretched out in his white bed, his eyes closed and his lips pursed, breathing heavily, or groaning in pain, and once more the woman's face is full of anxiety, and once more she is beside herself with worry. "There are no miracles," says the Austrian to Abraham unconcernedly. "You can never tell," says Abraham, who doesn't believe it himself.

One morning, a few days later, they put Alfred in the corridor, his facial skin stretched over a skull, its color grayish-white, his hands emaciated. It's hard to look at him. At first the woman tries half-heartedly to protest, but then she resigns herself and wipes away her tears, averting her face. She's frightened and she's tired. Nevertheless, and even more than before, she tries to ingratiate herself with the nurses and the doctors, and with the patients too, perhaps, who knows, one of them might have it in his power to save her. She smiles at this one and that one, brings flowers to the ward, pulls a photograph of Alfred out of her black handbag and shows it around, going from bed to bed and actually forcing people to look at it, pointing a thick finger and saying: "Look, that's him. Only three months ago. On the Sabbath, in Independence Park, next to the Sheraton." The way she repeats these words over and over again is a little strange, as if she's trying to amaze the viewer and at the same time convince him of the truth of what she's saying. In the snapshot Alfred is standing in a summer suit, with the sea stretching out behind him, and a Sabbath smile spread over his full face.

From day to day his condition deteriorates. His hands lie in front of him like two dry bones, and his bony nose sticks up between eyes sunk deep in their sockets and covered with big lids. The woman, however, goes on bringing him, every day or two, a jar of the pickled herring he likes. But Alfred doesn't touch the fish. Ceaselessly he complains of his pain and pleads for his life in a hoarse voice and with great cries rising to roof of the gloomy corridor. He calls on God, sometimes in Hebrew and sometimes in Yiddish, and the woman takes the jar of herring and puts it disappointedly away in her bag.

"He's got two more days," pronounces Abraham.

The Austrian says nothing, whereas Alfred, like some jokester, behaves as if the laws of nature have no more dominion over him, and four days later his cries are still filling the corridor and invading the rooms, and Abraham, embarrassed, says to the Austrian: "Two more days, at most." Some of the patients try to ignore the screams, while others ask the nurse to give him something for the pain, out of pity or because the screaming frightens and disturbs them, and in some of them it even arouses hostility.

"He's under sedation," says the nurse. "He doesn't feel anything."

Now the scream appears to have separated from the body, breaking of its own accord out of the thin, threadlike lips. And thus he burns away. Not dead. Drying up like a piece of wood. And the woman, with her fat, plain face, sitting opposite him and looking at him dry-eyed and almost motionless. She doesn't even try to tighten the strap of the watch hanging loosely on his wrist. But she can't sit there for long, and from time to time she gets up and walks up and down, holding the snapshot showing Alfred with a Sabbath smile spread over his full face and the sea stretching out behind him.

"He had a wonderful tenor voice," she says wearily, "and only four months ago he was as fit as a fiddle. Here, this is him. In Independence Park, next to the Sheraton." And she raises her eyes from the picture to the person looking at it.

The Voyage to Mauritius

1

CHAIM BARUCH WAS BORN in the village of L. Until the age of thirteen he never ventured further afield than the villages around his own, with the exception of two trips to Lodz.

His mother died while giving birth to him, and his sister Leah brought him up. His father, who was a timber merchant, claimed that the week before the baby was born he had seen a black bird on the roof of the house, but no one else could confirm the story, and he himself changed the description of the bird from time to time. On the other hand, his uncle averred that since the birth had taken place in the seventh month—he had been born under a lucky star.

Chaim Baruch was silent and withdrawn from birth. He had thick lips and broad cheekbones, and it was impossible to take anything he wanted out of his hands except by force. But his eyes were blue and dreamy, a fact that never ceased to astonish his father.

He liked hiding away in cramped, forgotten corners in the house and the yard, and he also liked looking through the slits in the shutters, especially when it was raining, at the low houses and the wretched cobbled square, at the end of which stood gloomy warehouses. He thought of his mother only rarely and fleetingly, and she appeared to him in the light of something pure.

After his Bar Mitzvah a stubborn independence became increasingly apparent in his character. He began to make friends with the village children and to go with them, or alone, to the river, to bring home forbidden books and to absent himself from the synagogue whenever he felt like it, without asking permission or telling anyone where he was going. His father, who displayed a warm and sensuous affection for him, which would rapidly give way, for no apparent reason, to bursts of short-tempered strictness, described his behavior as "rebelliousness" and said that he would come to a "bad end." He said this with rage and pain and sometimes he would even hit the door or the table furiously as he did so, since the hopes he cherished for his son were prodigious, although they never took on any definite shape in his mind.

Since he wanted to be independent and was attracted to the idea of doing things with his hands, Chaim Baruch abandoned his studies and went to learn carpentry with a German Meister, both in the face of his father's disapproval. His progress in the craft of carpentry was slow and paved with difficulties, but he stuck to it nevertheless. The activities of sawing, planing, and joining gave him a thrill of happiness and he loved the smell of the wood and the sawdust. At the age of eighteen he joined the *Bund*[1] which he did after becoming convinced that theirs was the correct path. With this act he brought down the wrath of a number of his friends and all his family on his head, and his father announced that he was going to sit *shiva* for him and mourn him as if he were dead.

When his sister Leah asked him, in their father's name, to at least go to synagogue on Yom Kippur, he replied that he had no wish to cause anyone sorrow by any of his actions, but that since he did not believe in God he would not go.

To the German Meister, who would sometimes break into abusive tirades against the Jews and call them money grubbers, he replied in the same spirit, saying that money grubbing in itself was not a sin in a world of money grubbers and anti-Semites, and that in a certain sense it showed, perhaps, that for all their religious beliefs, the Jews were an eminently rational people.

At the same time he felt great admiration for his Meister. The latter was a big man with a pair of hard hands, who performed his craft with absolute confidence, while at the same time speaking to the tools and the wood both gently and harshly.

"You have to feel it," the Meister would scold him.

Sometimes the Meister would hold forth in a sermonizing vein. He would contend that "this world is mixed-up and foolish, and only suffering, which is from God, introduces a little logic into it," and that "a little sin saves a man from drying up," and that "Satan, too, who was created by God, has to be fed once in a while, in order to enable us to feel suffering and repentance."

To these statements Chaim Baruch made no reply, although he dismissed them in his heart.

2

When he was about twenty-four Chaim Baruch made the acquaintance of a girl from the village of R. She was not remarkable in any respect, apart, perhaps, from the fact that she was a large woman with something soft about her. A few months later he married her, and since she was her parents' only child, he decided to go and live with her in the village of her birth. His father said nothing, but when Chaim Baruch came to say good-bye he turned his back on him.

In the village of R. Chaim Baruch set up a carpentry shop. Despite his effort he was obliged to close it down after a year, and he opened a liquor store. Most of the day he was busy in the store, but nevertheless he kept up his activities on behalf of the *Bund*, and also found time to read books by socialist authors. The knowledge he gained from them gave him confidence and inspired him with enthusiasm. The world seemed to him like a kind of rather simple machine, which operated according to fixed laws and which, if only its parts were put together according to the right plan, would work smoothly for the good of all concerned.

His political activities gave rise to grave reservations on the part of his father-in-law, who had taken up the Zionist cause, and from time to time arguments broke out between them. In his wife they gave rise to anxiety. She accused him repeatedly of neglecting their livelihood for the sake of politics, and said that one of these days he was liable to find himself in jail. But her arguments fell on deaf ears. Although the possibility of being arrested deterred him, it also attracted him to such an extent that he sometimes actually wished it would happen. This was because suffering was essential in his opinion, and even desirable, as the price to be paid for his beliefs and deeds and the incontrovertible proof of their rightness.

After the great fire, which consumed a large number of the village houses, Chaim Baruch joined the fire brigade, and became the only Jew in it.

An old photograph shows him sitting in a group of four firemen. All four are young and sturdy, and they are wearing dark uniforms with silver buttons and epaulettes, with broad leather straps crossing their chests from shoulder to waist. Their feet are shod in gleaming boots and their heads crowned by helmets like those worn by the heroes of the *Iliad*.

On Sundays and holidays Chaim Baruch would march with the firemen in a parade that proceeded through the streets of the village to the strains of a brass band until it reached the Hospital Park. In the park the firemen would demonstrate breathtaking fire-fighting exercises for the benefit of the assembled crowd.

Only silences gave rise in him to a certain uneasiness and a wish to hide. These were the sudden silences, during the day or the night, which seemed to him to be welling up from afar, but at the same time to be taking place inside him; and the same was true of things which reminded him of these silences, such as the lid of the white china teapot, a bit of fabric, a puddle of water, falling snow.

3

When his daughter was four years old, about six months after the birth of his son, the financial crisis broke out. In general outlines the socialists had predicted it long before, and from this point of view he was happy. He was also made happy by the awareness that the crisis with its suffering was bringing the final defeat of evil closer, and he impatiently awaited the changes that were surely about to take place soon. But the impoverishment, the chaos, and the feeling of helplessness that accompanied the crisis filled him with confusion and misery. He was forced to shut down the store and set up a stall in the marketplace. His wife began to implore him to emigrate to America, but he refused adamantly.

In spite of the demonstrations and meetings in which he took part, the impoverishment increased from day to day. "Capitalism is worse than the Devil," he wrote to his sister, and for lack of any alternative he packed his things and moved to Danzig, where he hoped, with the assistance of his brother-in-law, to find employment.

4

The first days in Danzig were hard. The strange landscape of the big city, too, shrouded in fog, oppressed him. In the stone streets, between the gloomy buildings, Chaim Baruch felt, for the first time in his life, rootless and lost. Walking through the streets he would lower his head slightly, his eyes groping in front of his feet like a blind man's stick.

He did not complain, since from the outset he had not intended setting up home in Danzig, and in any case he had intended returning to the village of R. as soon as everything settled down again. But time and routine did their work: his daughter went to school, his son grew up, Chaim Baruch made friends and adjusted himself to the local customs, and after a few years he opened a store selling electrical appliances, moved into a spacious apartment and fitted it out with new furniture. He put off the return to R. from year to year.

In Danzig he dreamt for the first time of his mother. He saw her from the back, wearing his sister's brown shawl, whose hairy wool had pricked him when she carried him in her arms.

This happened soon after they arrived, and when he woke up from his dream he felt a sense of oppression.

5

The war hit him eight years later. The turmoil and violence that preceded it filled him with anxiety, but the anxiety was swallowed up in anger and activity. He took part in debates and demonstrations, and one day he came home with his jacket torn and his body bruised after being involved in a fight. His wife implored him again to take them to America while it was still possible, and he promised her that he would think about it. One day the shop was broken into and looted, and then his daughter was beaten up in the street by a gang of children, after which he wife gave him no peace. Sometimes she would wake up in a panic in the middle of the night. He tried to reassure her and calm her down, and in the meantime he forbade the children to leave the house.

Privately, he thought that the storm would soon pass, and later he tried to believe that the worse it grew the better it would be, and he even tried to persuade his friends and acquaintances of the truth of this theory. To his brother-in-law, who repeated anxiously that the earth was trembling and the Black Plague was coming and they should pray to God, he retorted angrily that the earth was not trembling under his feet and that one plague could only be destroyed by another, more terrible than the first, and so it would be.

During the same time he received, after a delay of several months, the news of his father's death. His last request was to be buried standing up; but this request was not fulfilled.

His father's death did not grieve him. He tried to carry on with his affairs as far as possible, and at the same time he began hoarding a little food. From time to time his father's last request disturbed his thoughts. For some reason it seemed to Chaim Baruch that the request was aimed against him. He tried to push this thought away and dismiss it from his mind, but it kept coming back, together with the memory of the Yom Kippur when he refused his father's request to go to the synagogue. This memory oppressed him now together with the fact that he had not been at his bedside when he was dying. On several occasions he made up his mind to assemble a prayer quorum to pray for the elevation of his father's soul, but a few hours later the decision would be abandoned, leaving a sediment of bitterness and anger behind it. At this time his brother-in-law was arrested with his family, people were snatched from their houses or beaten up in the street, and fear filled his heart. One night, after the children had fallen asleep, he took his beautiful dog October and killed it in a neighbor's yard with a few cruel hammer blows. Then he shut himself up in the house, took the clock down from the wall, and listened tensely to the voices coming from outside, or peered morosely through the slits in the shutter, and waited.

6

In the summer of that year a group of hundreds of Jews was organized by means of the Jewish community for the purpose of emigration. These Jews were foreign subjects whom the authorities had decided to expel from the country. On the eve of their departure Chaim Baruch packed whatever he could, wrote a short letter to his sister, from whom they had heard nothing for a long time, and waited for the morning. But the departure was postponed from day to day, and in the meantime they sat on their bundles and ate the provisions they had prepared for the journey.

At the end of August the sign was suddenly given and they were all hurriedly packed into a freight train, and while they were still panicking and looking for somewhere to sit, the engine hooted and the train set off under a heavy guard.

The train journey took three days. Through the high window of the freight car patches of sky were visible during the day and sometimes green branches or a pole, which immediately disappeared. Chaim Baruch squatted on the floor and never took his eyes off his wife and children. He looked at them intently and occasionally passed his hand over them. He was tense and full of worries. But above all he was depressed by the sense of isolation and remoteness. Again and again he clutched at fleeting images of Danzig and the village of R. and at the same time he tried to guess at their route by means of the light, the sky, and the snatches of passing views glimpsed for a moment through the cracks in the side of the car. But gradually he was overcome by torpor and a feeling of helplessness. In the end he abandoned himself to the noise and the swaying of the train and felt as if he had been uprooted from the ground and was traveling alone, awake but in a trance, through an empty labyrinth in the air. At night he had a dream, but in the morning he remembered only his sister's face looking at him with an aggrieved and hostile expression.

They arrived in Bratislava after dark. A fine rain was falling and there were only a few yellow lights flickering here and there. A radio was blaring marches and a few port workers huddled in overcoats were smoking cigarettes and watching the guards in their white stockings hitting the Jews and shoving them like cattle onto the three old river steamers waiting next to the quay.

"To the middle," cried his wife and hugged her son to her with the last of her strength, "to the middle!"

Everyone was trying furiously and savagely to push their way to the middle of the deck. A man was thrust overboard and fell into the Danube with the two suitcases in his hands, and they sailed through Slovakia, Austria, Hungary, Yugoslavia, and Romania.

The weather was fine, with something soft and caressing in the air. The banks were dotted with sleepy villages with church steeples, and gardens and fields with peasants working in them. The passengers stood on the decks and from a distance you might have taken them for a group of vacationers on a pleasure excursion.

The mood of the passengers was one of panic and gloom. They guarded their luggage and spoke to each other of the things they had been forced to leave behind, of the chances of war, of the journey ahead of them, and of Eretz Yisrael. In addition to clothes and bed linen and photographs and precious objects some of them had taken account books and contracts and promissory notes. A young student had brought along his text books, and he sat in the stern trying to learn passages of *Essential Roman Law* by heart, so that he would be able to take his exams as soon as things had settled down again.

Chaim Baruch got into a conversation with Mr. Tanz, who, like his wife, was as elegantly dressed as if he were going to a party. They exchanged views on the war, at first hesitantly and then with passion. Chaim Baruch spoke of it with hostility, but at the same time tried to explain that it and all its sufferings were neither accidental nor in vain, since it was inevitble for it to break out and inevitable that things would change for the better in its wake, and he even tried to persuade Mr. Tanz that man had it in his power to create a world ruled by justice, logic, and brotherly love.

Mr. Tanz derided the war and everything else too. He contended that the world was chaos and man was a dog even though he walked on two legs. That's how it always was and always would be. In fact, he added, ideas like good and evil, happiness and suffering, sin and grace were completely meaningless, since everything was equally senseless and any attempt to prove otherwise was like trying to dig a hole in water.

The young student, who was listening to the argument, finally intervened and compared the war to a kind of inexplicable eruption of the elements of nature. After that he softened his words somewhat and spoke of it as a tragic misunderstanding that would pass. But after further thought he said that war was apparently a human phenomenon with causes and reasons of its own, but that the latter were complex and as yet beyond our comprehension, and they had to be studied.

Occasionally, especially in the early morning, Chaim Baruch enjoyed the voyage. Suddenly he would sense the beauty of the open air and the continuous motion and he would abandon himself to this sensation. Then he would forget the war, the worries of the present and the future, and his anxious longings for his sister, which grew more intense the farther he travelled from Danzig.

After three days they reached Tulcea. In Tulcea they were loaded onto three Greek freight ships, and they sailed into the Black Sea under the Panamanian flag bearing visas for Paraguay and making for Eretz Yisrael.

7

For seventy days the black ship made its way between the Bosporus and the Dardanelles and the Greek islands. Like a blind ant it bobbed up and down on the waves, approaching the shore and beating a panic-stricken retreat.

On the Captain's orders they all remained in the hold. Like shadows in the bowels of the earth they lay side-by-side, crowded and sweating, or took a few groping steps in the heavy darkness, which was alleviated only by the faint rays of light coming, as from a great distance, from the air vents. But for the sudden lurching of the ship the passengers might have imagined that they were incarcerated in a cellar surrounded by darkness. There was a heavy smell in the air, a smell of cattle and dankness and later of human vomit and urine and sweat as well.

"We've turned into pigs," the man in the adjacent bunk muttered without stopping, "We've turned into pigs," and he sniggered to himself.

Their voices died down too. But a ghostly murmur hung permanently in the air like a low cloud. Sometimes the Greek Captain would appear at the head of the stairs. He would stand there for a moment and disappear.

Chaim Baruch spoke a little to his neighbors, but his wife

remained silent most of the time. At first she would keep asking him where they were and when they would reach Eretz Yisrael. With regard to these two questions the man in the next bunk would also conduct frequent arguments both with his wife and with another man with a deep voice, and the arguments would generally be concluded by the man with the deep voice pronouncing bitterly that they would never reach Eretz Yisrael, since they weren't sailing anywhere but were buried in one place, perhaps Tulcea. Afterwards Chaim Baruch's wife desisted, and she would only ask him occasionally what day of the week it was. But to this question too he had no answer, and in the end she stopped asking it. The children were silent too. They aroused his pity, but more than pity he felt oppressed by his impotence to do anything for them.

For hours he would stare wordlessly into the darkness, which swirled around before his eyes in ring after ring of blackness, in the midst of which he would occasionally see a fitful gleam of silver-gray. Sometimes the shadows of the people, the pillars and walls of the ship would suddenly vanish and he would see an endless void, full of mist, making him wonder if he wasn't looking inward instead of outward. His head emptied of thoughts, except for fragmentary views of Danzig and the village of R., or fitful reflections on the war. It seemed to him very far away now. So far away that it sometimes seemed to him that it must have ended long ago and that somewhere up above, in the light, the world was at peace; and sometimes he had the feeling that the war had never really taken place at all, that it was only a kind of hallucination, or a bad dream, just as this whole voyage was only a bad dream that existed within a larger dream, and that in any case had nothing to do with the war but with something else, whose nature was not clear.

From time to time he would conjure up his sister and talk to her. In spite of all his efforts her face and figure would quickly crumble before his eyes and he would not be able to hang onto them. His conversations with her too would somehow be cut off and fade away. Once he felt the urge to try to understand the nature of the bird seen by his father, but he soon gave up the attempt.

The man in the next bunk asked him questions about Eretz Yisrael. He spoke of it dismissively at first, and afterward with hostility and dread. The heat and the Hebrew frightened him, and he didn't know how he was going to make a living there either. Once he said sullenly that rather than landing in Eretz Yisrael he would prefer to go on sailing like this to the end of time.

8

The murmur in the belly of the ship continued unabated, with sudden, momentary interruptions. Then the dull roar of the sea and the engines would be heard, the sailors' footsteps, unexplained thuds, and the dragging of chains. Sometimes these sounds would be joined by the sound of mumbled prayers.

The sound came from below, from the darkness of one of the lower bunks. But sometimes it seemed to be coming from above as well, or even to be breaking out and seeping in through the sides of the ship.

At first these prayers would come at more or less regular intervals, and Chaim Baruch would listen to them indifferently and take in words and sentences here and there. But gradually the sequence was broken and the prayers came completely unexpectedly, as if on a sudden impulse.

Once Chaim Baruch asked the man why he was praying, and the man replied that he had a lot of time on his hands here, being exempt from the cares of earning a living. Although Chaim Baruch could not see the man's face, but only the dim shadow on the wall to which he addressed himself, it seemed to him that the man was smiling. He asked again, more insistently, and the man replied, this time seriously, that he was fulfilling his obligations, just as God was fulfilling his. Here someone interrupted, apparently the man on the next bunk, and asked in what way God was fulfilling his obligations, and what these obligations were, anyway, "apart from sitting in the sky and basking in the sun while we suffer." To this the praying man replied impatiently that the suffering was not in vain and that the obligations of God were known only to God.

"Then I spit on it," said the man who had intervened in the conversation, "On all of it."

"No. You mustn't say that," said a frightened woman's voice.

"I haven't got any children," said the man who had intervened angrily, and fell silent.

9

The man on the next bunk was taken ill, and his illness grew worse from day to day. He lay like a dark lump under a pile of blankets and tortured his wife with questions. Suddenly he imagined that he had forgotten to lock the door of their house when they departed. His wife tried to reassure him, repeating over and over in a gentle, imploring voice, "It's locked, Franzi, it's locked," but her efforts were in vain. The suspicion grew into a certainty that drove him out of his mind. He commanded her to hang the key of their house, which was in his pocket, around his neck, and placed his hand firmly on top of it. By day and by night he never stopped talking about the furniture and the other things and the piano they had left behind, at the same time threatening his wife and entreating her by turn.

On the last night he stopped. He began to talk about death with bitter animosity. He cursed it and called for the establishment of an anti-death league to present memos, protest, and declare a strike.

Chaim Baruch tried to hide him from the children and to distract their attention from him. He himself looked at him with open, inquiring eyes, and as he did so he began to feel that the whole thing was taking place somewhere else, beyond many veils, as if in a trace.

At dawn the man said suddenly that he heard flutes, and later on he asked for a green leaf. He repeated this request insistently, several times, and Chaim Baruch looked around and even groped with his hands, frantically seeking a green leaf, even though he knew that no green leaf was to be found there. The man's voice was now beseeching.

At noon he died, and his death made everyone very afraid. Then they carried him up the narrow stairs to the deck in order to cast him into the sea. His wife walked behind him, swaying between the railing and the wall, and moaning quietly, "Franzi."

After that the ship reached Lesbos.

10

They anchored in Lesbos for a few days and Chaim Baruch stole ashore to buy some fruit. When he emerged from the depths of the ship onto the deck the early evening light dazzled him and the touch of the air and the sight of the wide sky, uniting in the distance with the sea, made him feel dizzy, so that he was obliged to lean against the wall with his eyes shut. Afterward he started walking, and as he walked he felt an immense weakness: trees and houses swayed around him, the ground slipped away from his feet, and the sky spinning above his head yawned like an abyss trying to sweep him into it.

On his way back to the ship he suddenly noticed among the passersby a young woman who reminded him of his sister.

Although he knew that it wasn't his sister, he became very excited. Above all he was astonished by her gait and the movements of her hands. He followed her for a while, until she disappeared into one of the houses, whose lintel was painted blue. He lingered there and for a moment he was filled with a feeling that he had once seen this house before, and even been inside it. Then a child came out of the house, holding a live piglet in his hands. The child looked at him, and he turned around and walked away.

That night the ship cast off and set sail, and he dreamt that his sister Leah asked him to keep an eye on their mother in the early evening, when she was subject to fits of terror. His mother appeared and sat down splendidly dressed on a splendid chair holding a green branch in her hands. She looked like a grand lady, with a hefty body and a spiteful expression on her face. He sat at her feet, but suddenly she stood up and began hitting him on the back with the branch, until he ran away. And he was astonished and depressed because he knew that she was kindhearted and that she loved him very much.

11

A few days later they arrived at Heraklion, where they cast anchor for several hours, and then put to sea again, and sailed for a few days until they ran out of coal and the ship stopped. They dismantled the walls of the cabins on the upper deck and threw them into the furnaces. Afterward they threw in doors and railings and benches and partitions and the black piano that stood in the saloon too, and the ship sailed, consuming its own flesh, until it stopped again.

The British towed it to Cyprus and from there to Haifa, and in Haifa it was already autumn.

The passengers stood huddled on the decks and looked with burning eyes at the land and the green mountain coming closer. A wave of enthusiasm and thanksgiving gripped them, together with a kind of pleasant lassitude. They knew that the British would not abandon them to their fate. When they drew closer to the quay they waved at the crowds of people waiting for them behind the fences, and afterward they sang "Hatikva." Chaim Baruch sang along with the rest. A great longing now flooded him for the land stretching out beyond the quays and the fences, to tread on it and find peace in it. If only he knew what had happened to his sister.

"That's Mount Carmel," said Chaim Baruch to his son and daughter standing among the passengers.

"That's Mount Carmel," he heard the young student saying behind his back.

"So it's over?" asked Franzi's wife anxiously. "So it's over?"

"No," said someone calmly, and Chaim Baruch turned his head to see who had said it.

12

The British loaded them onto two Dutch freighters. They resisted to the best of their ability: they lay on the ground, kicked, screamed, clung to poles and fences. But the British soldiers tore them away and they sailed south, following the summer.

For three weeks they sailed and everything grew bright and wide. Chaim Baruch's eyes hurt, apparently because of the empty spaces and the glare of the harsh light. But he stayed on the deck, standing and staring with stubborn indifference at the infinite azure spaces that reminded him of nothing at all, or at the water that kept changing its clear colors, and from which brilliant fish occasionally suddenly leapt, flying for a moment in the air and then diving back again with a slight splash.

His son couldn't understand how it was possible for summer to last the whole year long, and he explained to him that somewhere else in the world it was now winter. But even as he did so, even as he drew the sun and the earth on a piece of paper for him, he wondered if it was really so. And the wondering took hold of him and turned into a feeling that filled him completely, that the sun and the sea and all the countries with their towns and rivers and forests that he had pictured in his imagination only a moment before were only an illusion, just as it was only an illusion that connected him to the boy and the girl and the woman standing next to him like figures in a dream, and that it was not him, but someone emanating from him like a delicate vapor, who was traveling on this ship, sailing around in circles on a ball of empty water.

The feeling was obscure but absolutely palpable, and he smiled. For beyond the bewilderment, it held the sweetness of falling asleep and it filled him with tranquillity.

13

None of the passengers knew their destination, and nobody told them when they crossed the equator either, because they were prisoners-of-war of the crown.

But on a fine morning at the end of December an azure island appeared in the middle of the horizon, veiled in a light mist, rising slowly as a whale from the bottom of the sea.

"Treasure island!" cried his son.

It was Mauritius.

Most of the passengers had never heard of Mauritius in their lives. They clung to the deck railings without taking their eyes off it. Because of the refraction of the sun rays, the light mist and the movement of the waves and the ship, there were moments when the island itself seemed to be bobbing and floating on the sea, like a ship turned upside down.

14

They anchored in Port Louis. The sun beat down on them from the north and the temperature reached forty degrees. The radiant blue of the sea hit them in the eyes together with the brilliant green of the leaves of the tropical trees and the giddy colors of the flowers shooting wildly out of the black volcanic soil. The colors seemed to be bursting out of their own accord and splashing like a whirlpool into the humid air, which was charged with a kind of tension and full of sharp movement and a hard silvery glare and a ceaseless twittering sound. Everything made Chaim Baruch feel lethargic and uneasy, except for the ground.

Buses took them to Beau Bassin, a little town on the west coast. Chinese and Indians and mulattos with jutting cheekbones looked at them slowly as they passed, and English ladies in modest suits and elegant, broad-brimmed hats were waiting to meet them, holding two trays of sandwiches in their slender hands. They were waiting at the entrance to the camp the crown had allocated for their domicile: a bleak stone building with barred windows, which had once served as a French prison. In this building the crown had decreed that the men would reside, while the women and children would be domiciled apart, in a camp of Nissen huts.

"What will we do here?" asked his wife anxiously.

"Live," said Chaim Baruch and loaded their luggage onto his back.

15

Within two months his son and his wife died. They died of typhus, which the voyagers had brought with them from the voyage. His son lay for a few days with half-closed eyes, and his dry lips swelled and expanded until they filled almost his whole face. Behind these lips he faded away, sunk in delirium, occasionally asking for water and for "the little morning deer."

16

During the first year Chaim Baruch went to visit the gravestones often. He lived with the rest of the men in the bleak stone building and worked as a tailor. But after work he would take his daughter and go to the graves. On one of the stones the word "Yaakov" was engraved, and on the other, "Rivka Leah." On every visit he would take fresh flowers, since they wilted fast. He would stay there for a long time, passing his hand gropingly over the names and feeling the chill of the stone.

During these early evening hours he would be vividly aware of the separate presence growing ever stronger inside him. It seemed to him like a big, smooth stone made of thick smoke, floating in his chest and hanging onto him with soft fingernails and spreading inside him and penetrating all the cracks and hollows, feeding on him and thinking his thoughts. Thoughts clung to him like little barnacles and however hard he tried to push them away he couldn't. Again and again this presence unrolled his life and acts before him and urged him to discover the fault in them, or, at least, the act which, if he had refrained from committing it, everything would have been different, or which would have made sense of everything that had happened.

All around stood heavy trees and all kinds of tangled tropical bushes, and the black volcanic soil clouded and exuded dense vapors like incense smoke, which mingled with the translucent air and dissolved the quiet moths and the birds and the leaves and the branches and the sea, and his daughter held his hand without speaking and waited for him to take her back to the camp.

More and more he came to believe that he could see a resemblance between her and his sister, although he could on no account say where it lay. Sometimes he imagined that it lay in the neck and chin, sometimes in the eyes or the slight inclination of the head; but there were moments when he knew that there was really no resemblance between them at all.

In any case, his concern for his daughter grew until it took him over completely. She seemed to him like a butterfly. Like his daughter, they too gave rise in him to anxiety and compassion in their silence, their purity and the feeling that the slightest touch could make them melt like snowflakes. He shrank from laying his hand on her, but he never took his eyes off her, as if he wanted to wrap her in a web of looks. A terrible fear began to obsess him—the minute he took his eyes off her she was liable to disappear.

At night he could not fall asleep. He would lie with his eyes closed, tired out by the light, and hear the chorus of harsh twittering voices filling the darkness and continuing into infinity with a kind of dull obstinacy, until in the end it seemed to him that they were coming out of his own head.

17

Now he began paying frequent visits to Beau Bassin. He found that at the sight of the colorful shops, among the crowds of Chinese and Indians, his thoughts and worries melted away and left him for a while. He made the acquaintance of a certain Indian, who kept a gray bird in a cage in his textile store. Since the bird made sounds which bore a faint resemblance to words, the Indian called it a "southern parrot," but since its language was unintelligible, he described it as a "blind language" or a "white language." At the same time, however, he claimed that if you listened in utter self-abnegation, the abnegation of will and knowledge, you could obtain a profound knowledge, which could not be expressed in words.

The Indian's words did not convince Chaim Baruch. He found them strange and even ridiculous. But nevertheless, he began to save and to bring the bird sugar cubes, seeds, and bits of bread, and to sit in front of it and listen in eager expectation.

The understanding he hoped to acquire eluded him. On the other hand, at certain moments he would be filled with a feeling that it was not really him sitting there, but only a kind of memory of himself inside the shell of his body, whereas he himself was somewhere else, but there too only as a kind of memory, just like his sister, who existed in him as a memory within a memory.

But when he was on his way back to the camp, still full of the same feeling, as he passed the graveyard, which he hardly ever visited any more, and saw the gravestones and the heavy trees and the vast expanse of the sea, which would splash strips of hard silver into his eyes, and the air was full of the movement of butterflies and birds and warm scents of water and flowers, he would be assailed by the almost opposite feeling again, the feeling that he had already been here before. More than that: he had been born here and spent all his life here, and all the other items of knowledge and memories were only the vestiges of dreams and stories he had once heard, like the war, which was going on somewhere, beyond an infinite barrier of empty air, and of which his neighbors would speak passionately every day. They listened a lot to the radio and learned about the movements of the armies and the state of the fronts and tried to assess the chances of the opposing forces.

18

By this time the volcanic soil was already in his blood. It seeped into him slowly, through his eyes and pores, like light and the air are absorbed by the leaves of plants. At first he paid no attention, and later on he did not resist, but neither did he yield himself. As if something had not yet ripened inside him. He still hung back. He went on contemplating the soil, especially the hard, solid lumps of black rock, and he did not take his eyes off them. They frightened him, and at the same time something in him was drawn to them as if by magic. The more he contemplated these stones, the more he felt as if some dark, primeval force was stored up in them, and that this force was taking him over.

One day Chaim Baruch bent down to pick up a large stone. He hugged it to his chest and sensed in all his body its heaviness and hardness and something else that he could not define, a kind of living fullness that existed in the stone like a special essence and that emanated from it and filled him with serenity and the wish to devote himself.

A few days later Chaim Baruch asked to be allocated a plot of land off the beaten track, so that he could clear it of stones and plant it with sisal, and his request was granted.

The work was back-breaking. He would arrive in the morning, while it was still cool, take off his shirt, and go into the field. One by one or two together he would carry the stones, which would scratch his chest and hands with their sharp protuberances, to the edges of the plot, where he heaped them into piles. The big lumps of rock he would have to push and roll, and sometimes it would take him the whole day to get rid of one rock. But he liked the big lumps of rock better than the small ones, and the slowness of the pace did not bother him at all. He wasn't even aware of it. The pleasant morning sun would spread through his limbs and time melted away. His movements were deliberate and relaxed, even when his heart was full of growing anticipation of noon, when the sun would beat down on the stones, which would reflect a black glare into his eyes, and all the heat of his body would suddenly be concentrated in his chest like a dense ball of fire. Then he would stand erect, slowly spread his arms out sideways, close his eyes and open his mouth wide to the sun shining radiantly in the middle of an arid, ashen, silver sky.

After sunset he would return to the camp and stretch out on his bed. His body was still giving off heat and in his eyes were two burning flames. He would acknowledge any of the inmates he met on his way with a wordless nod. Except for Franzi's wife. Whenever he encountered her he would stop and greet her meaningfully.

His daughter would be waiting for him in the room, and she would sit on a chair opposite his bed. She had grown taller. They did not speak much. She would tell him the latest news about the war, and he would watch the movement of her lips and listen distantly. Franzi's wife began dropping in to see him too. She would stay a while and tell him about life in the camp. Inconceivable though it seemed, people's lives had settled down into a routine: a few had married, a few had died, they had set up a school, factories for the manufacture of brushes and ornaments and cardboard, and Zionist political parties. Someone had organized an orchestra and someone else had founded a dramatic society. Sometimes people would visit the cinema in Beau Bassin, and recently, Franzi's wife told him, the charitable English ladies had organized the children into the 13th troop of the local Scouts movement. As she spoke she would introduce broken little stories about Cologne and other towns and about her parents and her sister and about Franzi. Sometimes she even showed him old snapshots, which she kept in an envelope. Chaim Baruch would listen attentively, but her words gave rise in him to nothing but bewilderment. In his mind's eye he saw only a small piece of land surrounded by endless salt water.

Sleep came slowly and sweetly. Before he fell asleep he would feel the whole island floating with him and rocking gently on the ocean waves.

He slept well. Occasionally he dreamt about his mother, who appeared for a moment in the brown shawl before vanishing from view. It was only rarely that he woke in a fright and sat up in bed, something that happened when it seemed to him in his sleep that the island had cracked in a sudden buffeting and its pieces were being swept away on the ocean currents, farther and farther away from each other. This vision frightened but never surprised him, since it was as if he had always, even in his sleep, been expecting it and known somewhere at the bottom of his heart that it was going to happen.

19

Chaim Baruch loved the sudden showers of rain. The big, heavy drops held something of the heat of the sun and the clarity of the air in them, and also the colors of the flowers. As they approached the ground they would take on the dark color of the soil and sink into it, or collect in shining black marble puddles, trapping the sky. He would stop working and stand in the rain, until it passed with the same suddenness as it had begun.

One day, after the rain, he saw a small child.

At first, taking the figure in at a casual glance, he was astonished. He thought it was a large stone, which had not been there before. This mistake was due to the fact that the child was sitting at the edge of the plot without moving. Only afterward he noticed the thin arms hugging the legs to the chest, and the big head resting heavily on the knees.

"A little shepherd boy," said Chaim Baruch tenderly to himself and went on working without turning his head around.

But he was no longer at ease. Even behind his back he could feel the child's eyes on him and his image stayed before his eyes.

After a few days of this Chaim Baruch could no longer restrain himself. He went up to the child and asked him what he was doing there. There was no sternness in his tone, and he even smiled slightly, and the child replied: "Looking." This reply did not satisfy him, since he had hoped that the child would get up and go away, but he went on sitting there as before. Chaim Baruch waited a moment and in an attempt to overcome his embarrassment he asked him what his name was and if his mother and father weren't worried about him. The child made no reply, but went on looking at him indifferently, licking the leaf between his lips. Chaim Baruch waited a little longer, after which he turned around and began retracing his steps. Then the child asked him what he was doing there. Chaim Baruch turned to face him and said he was clearing the plot of stones. To this the child said with an elderly gravity, that in the end every stone would return to its place. He asked the child where he got that from, and the child replied: "From the water and the birds."

On his way back from work Chaim Baruch thought about what the child had said. At first he dismissed his words, but they went on disturbing him and would not leave him be, even when he got into bed and tried to fall asleep. His thoughts grew more and more confused. In the end he decided that the shape of the stones could not possibly be insignificant, and with this he fell asleep.

In the following days this thought went on nagging at him, and the more he turned it over in his mind the more convinced he became that all the stones were parts of some pattern that had come apart, and that it might, perhaps, be possible to put together again.

20

He set to work carefully and with a kind of solemn intensity. At first he walked around the field and for a few days he examined the lumps of stone, trying to imagine what the form of the original shape could have been. Afterward he stopped this and turned to the stones themselves, in the conviction that the whole would become clear to him by means of the separate parts.

He bent down and lifted stone after stone, turning each over and over and examining it slowly and scrupulously, running his hand and his eyes over every hollow and protuberance, and trying to discover the significance of its shape by comparing it to the shapes of other stones he had engraved in his memory, and seeking the hidden connections between them. After a few weeks he began dismantling the piles of stones on the borders of the plot. From day to day the piles decreased, and the exalted calm that filled him faded a little, and something like impatience began to interfere with his work, obliging him to stop every now and then in order to compose himself and get back his concentration.

At the same time it occurred to him that he had to find "the first stone." He was sure that such a stone existed and that he would certainly recognize it as soon as he saw it. True, he knew that this meant he would have to re-examine all the stones he had already examined, but his certainty of finding "the first stone" inspired him with energy and new hope.

He addressed himself to this new task, but as he bent day after day over the black stones, which were now scattered over the plot again like the remnants of ancient altars and temples, and as he looked at them for hours with his strained, tired eyes, he felt his previous impatience turning into panic.

Now he had to stop working for hours on end, and even for whole days. He would stand as if turned to stone and gaze with empty eyes at the trees and the sky and the sea, or he would sit on the ground and unthinkingly throw bits of stone into the air, or watch the swift flight of small birds impinging for a moment on his field of vision. Gradually he abandoned the idea of "the first stone" and went back to trying to picture the pattern in its entirety to himself. But the possibilities were countless, and all of them were possible and impossible to the same extent, and this gave rise to such baffled anger and despair in him that he began to doubt the very existence of that original shape.

At night he would pace to and fro in his room, sunk in thought. At the beginning of the evening he would feel sure that he was very close to the revelation, and that all he had to do to see it was put out his hand and draw aside one more flimsy veil. But his thoughts grew more and more confused, always following the same direction, and in the end he would press himself to the window bars, or flop down exhausted on the bed, and resolve to stop it. In the morning he would get up and drag himself to the plot like the day before. He now worked without exaltation, and especially without one spark of hope, but in a kind of gloomy rebelliousness, gritting his teeth and sometimes on the verge of tears.

From time to time he regretted not having tried to get something more specific out of the child.

21

Suddenly he began to go blind. At first it was only a dull pain in his temples and between his eyebrows. Then the trees and stones and sky and sun began to disintegrate into thin threads of mist swaying before his eyes, in which the graying rays of light were trapped as they broke up into fleeting splinters of radiance. And the fog grew thicker. The doctors in Beau Bassin could do nothing for him. Nor could those in Port Louis. They recommended rest, and someone else told him to go see an Indian woman. He laughed to himself and he went to see her. She laid her hands on his eyes, whispered something, and gave him a sweetish brew to drink; plant juices diluted in rain water. But this did not help either. He grew blinder and blinder, as if his vision was gradually being absorbed in the black earth until it united with it completely and everything was swallowed up in darkness: the trees, the prison, the butterflies, the graveyard, his daughter, his plot, the stones, the sky above the empty expanse of the sea, and the yellow southern sun.

He stopped working. But even through the soles of his shoes he could sense the hard volcanic soil and smell its special smell. This smell would thicken and take on forms inside his eyes that would shift and change like clouds or mushrooms of smoke.

His daughter would tidy his room and sometimes read aloud to him from a book. He now felt no special closeness to her, but he tried to listen to her voice, resting his thick hand gently on her shoulders or her knees. But his ears were full of the twittering, whispering sounds of the island and inside his head he kept trying to examine his life.

However hard he tried he could not find anything to take hold of in it in the sense he sought. It seemed to him that to the extent to which his life depended on him and his actions, it was generally speaking simple, right, and logical, and alongside the suffering he had also known occasional joys. In this he found reassurance and even a little satisfaction, but only for a short while. Because he was bothered by the feeling that this was not the thing that he had to know and that the truth was that he had never succeeded in examining it properly, link by link, and getting to the bottom of things. He put the blame on the shifting shapes, and especially on the many ghostly figures—his father, Franzi, the German Meister, and others—which kept surfacing in his darkness and distracting him from the main thing, and he would follow them until he felt that he himself was one of them too, a misty figure existing in his own memory and merging with all the other figures that subsisted in it like mist within mist. Only the figure of his sister, whose face and features he could now conjure up only with an effort, vaguely and fleetingly in his mind's eye, only she would suddenly restore the feeling of the reality of his existence to him, and then, for a moment, he would be filled with a calm confidence that some day, somewhere, he would still meet her again, because it was inevitable and necessary. And then he would go back to examining his life, without pain, but with a feeling of dull expectation.

22

In the winter of the fifth year the cyclone came. Chaim Baruch heard it coming close like a muffled thunderbolt rising from the depths. It seemed to him that he heard someone calling him from behind, but he knelt down and clung to a tree trunk. Afterward he felt a wave of heavy heat, and after that a mass of air whirling around itself, and after that his ears were deafened by the sounds of the cyclone tearing off roofs and tumbling walls and breaking rocks and snapping the branches of trees. And suddenly the air cleared and stood still, and there was an unbearable silence, a chasm of silence, as if the world had been torn out of itself, and he saw her coming toward him like a figure of emptiness filling everything to overflowing, bluish-white, dim and radiant as the light before dawn, and he wanted to call out, but his voice was inaudible and his lips did not move. Afterward he fell face down on the volcanic ground and the storm passed over him with a loud roar.

23

And in the summer of the same year a French freighter came and took them back to Eretz Yisrael. Chaim Baruch walked slowly down the ramp, with his daughter at his side. He was wearing a blue suit and his broad, lined face was tanned as the face of someone coming back from an ocean cruise. With his heavy gray mustache he might have been taken for a retired Greek sea captain. He turned to one of the officials and asked him in Yiddish to tell him how to get to his relations in Tel Aviv.

NOTE

1. Bund: abbreviation of "General Jewish Workers Union in Lithuania, Poland, and Russia," an anti-Zionist, socialist Jewish party.

A Private and Very Awesome Leopard

Whoever aspires and does not give up—
is worthy of redemption.

—GOETHE

I HAVE AN UNCLE in Monaco, but recently rumors have abounded that he's gone to Lisbon, and that there or close by he's established a farm for the rearing of fighting cocks. The last clear information about him was received three years ago. Aunt Idel from Buffalo, my grandmother's vague sister, told us in one of her letters that Philip. her son, who owns a large jewelry shop in Beverly Hills, imagined he saw my uncle hurrying by into one of the streets of San Francisco.

This information didn't elicit any reaction from us. It was buried in cold silence and erased from memory just as my uncle had been ever since he last departed the country. He left behind him a residuum of shame and hatred in addition to two fair children, four women, a despondent group of creditors, a heap of moth-eaten suits, official hats, a sad Great Dane, and one visiting card, which he gave to his childhood friend, the artist Edmund Rubin, on which all his names and titles were printed uncompromisingly in fancy gold letters:

ALBERT, ALBERT ABRAHAM JOIACHIM IMMANUEL WEISS—DOCTOR OF LAW, DOCTOR OF ECONOMICS—SPECIALIST. This was seven years ago, one winter's day.

When he first arrived in the country, four years after the end of the war, all the members of the family donned their holiday attire and went by taxi with a bouquet of gladioli to Uncle Noah's house. Already relatives, acquaintances, and a few people from his home town were assembled there. Aunt Shoshannah, Uncle Noah's wife, clad in the most flowery silk dress served tea and poppy-seed biscuits. The company drank, had snatched conversations, and glanced into the street. They were all waiting for the fugitive. The door-bell rang at seven o'clock exactly.

"It's Fink," called Uncle Noah and everyone hurried to the entrance.

"I'm here," Fink announced and stood in the doorway. He stretched out his arms sideways, bowed his head slightly, and his smooth brown hair came down on his pleasing brow. Thereafter he pushed his way inside and with shrieks of delight he embraced the men, slapped them on the back, kissed the ladies' hands, wiped away tears. A sweet and inno-cent smile ensconced itself in the middle of his round face and remained fixed all evening, like a fatty stain floating on milk.

The scent of citrus blossom in the courtyard wafted into the rooms with a fluttering coolness that came from the sea across the sand dunes. The vases were filled with fresh flow-ers. The crockery and the silver, which were specially taken out of the bottom of the sideboard, shone in the lamplight. The floor glistened. Fink sat at the head of the table, under the picture of Berl Katznelson, his cuffs and tie were fastened with gold pins, and he was surrounded by affectionate and tearful looks, and burst of happiness.

"Tomorrow I'm dining with your Finance Minister," he pronounced in Yiddish, while eating his fish. He lightly smacked his ruddy, effeminate lips. They adjourned to the big veranda for coffee.

There was a calm in the air. No chirping birds, only nearby and distant dogs barked at one another, on this transparent Canaanite night. Azriel, Aunt Shoshannah's brother, sang old songs with a cantorial voice and Fink reminisced about happy childhood days and the terrible wartime. At one A.M. they all got up to go home. The leave-taking at the open door took another hour; eventually Fink handed out small gifts and visiting cards on rough parchment on which were printed in English and German: ALBERT A. JOIACHIM WEISS ENGINEER, CONSTRUCTOR—INVESTOR. THE BIG FRANKONIA COMPANY FOR BUILDING AND INVESTMENT LTD.

For a whole week Fink didn't appear. And when he did return he was excited, sunburned, and trembling. He was dressed in a new suit and wore mustard-colored suede shoes, which were also new. Uncle Noah had just returned from his job at *Tnuvah*.[1] He sat in the kitchen and ate. In one hand he held a chicken leg and in the other a piece of radish. His eyes were fixed on *Davar*.[2] Fink entered with a hearty hello. He kissed Aunt Shoshannah on her perspiring cheeks, slapped Uncle Noah on the back, and like a magician, pulled out a bouquet of flowers and a bottle of Madeira wine from his suit. After the storm of entry had subsided, Fink sat himself down next to his uncle and over tea gave him a lecture on all his business affairs and projects.

And so Tzirel and the children remained in Frankfurt for the time being. Up to five months ago he had been a partner in a big company, which dealt in the providing of holy objects to churches, such as statues of the crucifixion and saints, candlesticks, incense burners, bowls, chalices, crosses, chandeliers, and pews. He had also engaged in the import of tea and coffee, and he was a member of the society whose aim it was to encourage the custom of riding in horse-drawn carriages.

For a variety of reasons he had given all these up and had come here as a partner and agent of the Frankonia Company Ltd. This company had interests throughout the world. He proffered the information that this company sought to set up a combine in the country for the production of prefabricated houses, partially for local use and partially for export.

"Where will you export?" asked Uncle Noah disbelieving, as he proceeded to crack the chicken bones and suck out the marrow.

"To the whole world," Fink answered, and his dovelike eyes were filled with moisture. "Even to France, perhaps to Indonesia. It has tremendous potential."

"Really?" Uncle Noah spluttered without looking at Fink. "We're also going to set up factories for glass, cement, and iron."

"There's no iron here."

"Then there will be," Fink announced. "It's Okay."

After the meal in the large room, Uncle Noah listened to Fink's meanderings, at first with reserve and scepticism, but then with steadily growing interest. While picking his teeth, he perused the prospectuses, charts and colored programs, which Fink casually spread out before him. Uncle Noah followed his finger, which shifted with the agility of a grasshopper, over the map of the world. All the while he sketched circles here and there, complexes that expanded in the thickening grayness of the evening into giant imperial cities, until Aunt Shoshannah lit the four-branched chandelier and again served tea with slices of honey cake.

Fink gathered up the papers and Uncle Noah rested his head on the back of the armchair. He was tired but excited, like someone just returned from a wondrous voyage to the ocean bed.

Two weeks later Fink departed the country and left behind Elsa Neidoroff, who presented herself as his secretary.

For half a year no sign of life from him, besides a New Year's card with a Viennese postmark, in which a kissing pair of doves, dotted profusely with silver tinsel, featured. But one day there was a phone call at *Tnuvah* and the hotel reception asked that Uncle Noah be informed that his brother was staying there and would be very happy to see both him and his wife.

Fink himself opened the door for them. A glorious smile was poured over his face. He wore a purple silk gown covered with a garden of golden Persian flowers and a thread-like Latin mustache was stretched out at the edge of his lip. Elsa Neidoroff, looking like one of Solomon's yellow raffia camels, stood at his side and at the end of the leather strap she held was a giant dog, whose quivering tongue was hanging out of his mouth.

"This is Leon," said Fink proudly and cast a frightened yet admiring look at the dog, "a real Great Dane."

Fink ordered fruit and wine to be brought into his room and they sat around a low table on which a goldish visiting-card lay: DR. ALBERT IMMANUEL WEISS. UNIVERSAL CIRCUS LTD. BRAZIL-HELSINKI-MILAN. PRESIDENT."

Aunt Shoshanna asked after Tzirel and the children and Uncle Noah inquired about the housing business. Fink poured out the wine and started holding forth.

In a short time, he said, he would establish a circus of universal proportions in the country, and in the not-so-distant future perhaps even a farm for the training of animals. All the plans and calculations, which were arranged and examined by the best specialists, were already in his possession.

"This country needs a circus," he shouted emotionally, and the ash of his cigar fell on the table and was smeared all over.

Fink didn't pay attention to this. He also didn't allow Uncle Noah to say a word. The muse was upon him, and smitten with joy he ran about like a somnambulistic Archimedes in another world. And the words gushed from him like a waterfall of confetti: Lions, leopards, an American bear, clowns, loans, tight-rope walkers, investors, a top hat, the force of gravity, a march, someone standing on his head, a notary, a parrot, and a singing saw.

Elsa Neidoroff accompanied him with an acquiescent expression, and Aunt Shoshannah nodded her head with habitual benignity. But Uncle Noah's face expressed great concern. He buttoned up his coat and felt about in his pocket for his bus fare home. Then Fink grabbed him under his arm, apologized to the assembled company, and led him to the window. There, in the presence of the expanse of sea enveloped by a dreamlike mist he offered him a partnership in an investment scheme of fifty thousand pounds. He would get back six percent of the gross amount. Uncle Noah gave him a look and pulled his hand away without saying a word. Fink hastened to raise his share to 6.4 percent.

It appears that other investors were found. A week later, Fink arranged a press conference. He arrived there in golf trousers and in a green, Robin Hood hat. Leon crouched at his feet.

The conference was successful and in the coming months Fink was very busy.

He shook hands, smiled, held meetings in cafes, had secret talks in the foyers of hotels, phoned abroad, consulted lawyers, sent flowers, presented calculations, was astonished at himself, swore with hand on heart, ran backwards and forwards to government and municipal offices, conferred with bank managers, made copies of contracts, signed his initials, sighed, made toasts, until one day at the end of summer the laying of the foundation stone was arranged.

It was a great day. The heavens were a dry abyss in whose void fiery thorns wandered continuously, glistening in the silvery luster. The heavy air swallowed the earth, trees, and shrubs with its desertlike dryness. Nothing remained of them but silent ghostly shades hovering without movement in the emptiness. No grasshopper chirped and not even an ox lowed, only dry blasts of wind moved the thorns, which hissed like lizards slipping away.

Fink stood in the center of the universe in front of the open pit in a black suit, black hat, and black glasses. His pale face was wreathed in a crablike blush. Leon stood next to him breathing like a grampus, and around them a small group gathered—members of the family, workers, officials of institutions, agents, and potential investors. In the front a limp placard was hanging between the two national flags: BLOW THE HORN IN ZION—UNIVERSAL CIRCUS LTD. appeared on it.

A trumpet was sounded, a man fainted and Fink spoke.

He spoke about our country, the beautiful country, the land of bands of prophets, about Bar Kochbah, who rode on a lion, about Jews and tightrope walkers, who make a mockery of the earth's force of gravity. Finally he extolled the awesome spotted Leopard, the embodiment of strength, flexibility, and nobility, the symbol of the circus.

The assembled company stood with bowed head, and silently wiped their faces with handkerchiefs.

Someone recited a blessing and someone else read from the scriptures, after which they took down the scroll and covered up the hole. The owner of the hotel, The Gardens of Solomon, placed a bunch of roses he had brought with him on the covering, and the rest followed his example until there was a heap of flowers, which shortly before had been fresh. As a finale the company sang "Hatikvah" and the circus began.

Two weeks after the ceremony, Fink signed contracts with two well-known troupes and with a magician who also happened to be an acrobat, and handed out generous advancements of pay. But other groups with whom he had negotiated backed out, for the time being at least, or demanded impossible conditions. However, the main difficulties were presented by the banks and institutions, who lacked vision and continued obstinately to demand guarantees for their loans. All this was happening while the owner of The Gardens of Solomon and Mr. Ehrenfreiz from Vienna began to display worrisome hesitations, and the butcher Chernowilski suddenly announced that he was withdrawing his thick hands from the affairs of the circus and demanded that the money be returned to him, failing which he would sue Fink.

"It's only natural," Fink said to Uncle Noah and flew to Paris and from there to Vienna, where he bought equipment, flew to London, returned, and came to supervise the laying of the foundations. Then he flew with Elsa and Leon to Greece and returned to receive the equipment at the port. This he placed in storage. He tried to convince the contractor, flew to Copenhagen, returned, and the work was curtailed through lack of funds. The heavy winter rains fell on the foundations, scaffolding, the sacks of cement and piles of iron and wood.

Between flights, Fink would visit Uncle Noah. He was always accompanied by Leon and would bring a bunch of flowers, a bottle of choice wine, or a box of china tea, despite the protestations of his uncle and aunt. On his aunt's forgotten birthday, he brought her a gold watch.

He was as elated as usual. He informed them that shortly he'd be finishing the designing of the circus officials' uniforms. It would be a cinnamon suit after the style of an Austro-Hungarian marshal's with something a little reminiscent of a drummer's outfit from the Napoleonic period, together with a sombrero-like hat decorated with golden braid.

Afterward he passed on in his inimitable way to speak about the circus and the animals, all the while smoking the best quality cigarettes in an ivory holder. He spoke of them with pride and intimacy, as if they were distinguished members of the family with highly developed sensitivities. In the same manner he exaggerated and talked about tightrope walkers, Onassis, European kings, and opera prima donnas. All this he said in a way that his uncle and aunt were never to grasp fully, but nevertheless it aroused his uncle's suppressed anger. All these personalities were happily flying around in one big flowering globe, in another sphere, led by Fink.

"Back to the Jungle," Uncle Noah exploded bitterly and gathered up a few crumbs with his finger. Outside, the last winter rains caressed the shutters.

Fink drew out his Parker pen and wrote out rows of small numbers energetically on a paper serviette. He called them out as he committed them to paper. These included the sum of Mr. Chermowilski's participation in the expenses and the anticipated money to be given by the owner of The Gardens of Solomon, Mr. Ehrenfreiz, the asphalt company, and other investors. He also jotted down the expected loans from the government and banks and the income from the sale of tickets. Opposite this he listed the expenses: one-time expenses, operational expenses, interest, and tax rebates. He easily added and subtracted as a familial smile illuminated his face, and eventually he was left with two hundred thousand legitimate pounds.

"Examine this," Fink said and handed his uncle the serviette.

"Back to the Jungle," Uncle Noah repeated, crumpling up the serviette and throwing it into the ashtray. At this juncture Aunt Shoshannah served oranges.

"What's the problem?" Fink asked and drew Leon close to him. Uncle Noah withdrew into himself. Fink was also silent. He patted the dog's head and said that in fact it wasn't the money that attracted him but that nobility and greatness which are fast disappearing from the world, the tightrope walkers on the trapeze, and the awesome spotted leopard.

With genuine delight Fink described the beauty of his colors, the smoothness of his shiny skin, the splendor of his flexible body, and majestic grace of his awe-inspiring pounce.

Uncle Noah continued to be gloomily silent, while he cut up an orange skin into strips and squares.

Spring arrived and Fink, dressed in a light sport suit, went out to the circus building with Leon.

A festive silence pervaded the surface of the wide pit, which overnight had become overgrown with tall green vegetation. For a long while they wandered through the moist grass, knocking themselves on stones and falling over potholes, until they came upon the circus. All of it from the piles of gravel and sand to the wood and iron, was sunk as it were in the bed of a green pool, and only rusty pieces of iron rose up from the foundation holes in which a little rainwater still stood.

Fink filled his lungs with the scent of the fields and the smell of the wet slabs, felt the iron, lifted his eyes to the wonderful heavens, and in that very place he decided to erect the highest circus top in all the world.

The contractor agreed to start building again on condition that the debt be paid. But the owner of The Gardens of Solomon and Mr. Ehrenfreiz finally abandoned the project. Others who had promised loans slipped away like water through a sieve and the butcher became rude and threatening. Fink was in possession of a contract, but he preferred to give in. Hastily he sought new investors so that he could resume the building and have money in hand to give to the butcher, whose investment had been eaten up by cement, bricks, flights, and banquets. Temporarily Fink was able to fob him off with logical arguments and conjured up for him a golden future. He did the same with the owner of the storage company, who politely claimed the money for storing the equipment, which had already accumulated into a sizeable sum.

The butcher's patience gave out. Eventually he made a legal claim and also took the law into his own hands. He appeared in the cafe one splendid, sunny day.

A pleasant breeze blew from the sea and moved the flaps of the umbrella. Fink noticed the butcher approaching like an angry bull. Time was against him. He smiled in a melancholy way, put out his cigarette, put down his coffee cup, and fainted.

Elsa Neidoroff paled, and the gentleman who was sitting with them withdrew in disgust. Only the butcher didn't lose himself. He flung Fink aside wildly and slapped his face twice.

Fink opened his eyes and then in an attack of unruly confusion pushed Mr. Chernowilski aside and snatched his hat. He jumped over the fence and ran down the street to the accompaniment of curses and threats in Yiddish and Polish on the part of the butcher, who also waved his fist fiercely.

The next morning Fink returned to the hotel. He was washed and sparkling. There was no discernible difference in him except that he was sunk in thoughtful tranquility. He poured a Martini for himself, stood next to the window, and held forth on the beauty of the world, which was spoiled by butchers and Socialists with their popular and democratic crudeness. He also spoke of the spotted leopard. Possibly he'd acquire one shortly from Malaya or Tasmania, from one of the Maharajahs.

Elsa Neidoroff patted one of her plaits and in German offered him all her savings and inheritance on condition that he marry her. Tears welled up in Fink's eyes. He rejected the money and proposed unconditional marriage as he showered her with moist kisses on her forehead and on the palm of her hand.

In the evening, when they returned from the cinema, he insisted on writing out the "pledge of a decent man." From then on he started making use of her money and postponed the marriage from day to day.

He was right, and for two overriding reasons. Firstly, he was still married to Tzirel, and secondly, at the very beginning of the winter he had promised to marry Diana Procter, the owner of a hair-dressing salon. Oh, Diana! Oh land of cream and honey! Oh a corner of happy purgatory!

She had such clearly defined lips and her black hair dyed ash-blond was arranged occasionally like snakes, sometimes like flowers and even like a mushroom patch. Near her body, which exuded the mingled scent of perfume and perspiration, Fink felt romantic, like an errant youth who was beyond redemption.

"If you don't marry me Lulu, I'll murder you with my scissors," Diana naughtily tormented him and pinched the lobe of his ear until it hurt.

"Very soon my doe, shortly." And he really meant it.

Floating away on his emotions and stifled by the holy spirit of magazines, Fink used to overwhelm her with waves of beautiful love avowals, which brought a dreamy devoted expression to Diana's face and Fink himself close to tears. More than anything else Fink loved the stories of their shared future. In the long hours, when he was stretched on his back and his moist gaze saw towers in the dark, he described the house in which they'd live, the French furniture, the hearth, the thick carpets, the piano, orchids in the garden, race horses in the stable, and an eternal and fresh spring standing and waiting like a servant on the threshold, both in summer and in winter.

They'd honeymoon in the Greek islands, Spain, and in a place called Martinique, whose location neither knew and whose existence they weren't sure of.

Diana asked if she could ski in the snow. She made this request in a lisping voice. It was a very innocent, coy, and spoiled voice. And Fink hastened to promise her St. Moritz and all the pine forests. Oh, he was so profligate in his love.

Elsa waited around patiently on her low-heeled shoes. She, unlike Diana, didn't investigate or ask him about his activities. But occasionally she'd fix one of her dry looks on him, which aroused discomfort and a kind of hunger pang in him. With her money Fink paid back half his debt to the butcher and also half to the hotelier. He put down a deposit on the uniforms, so that the tailor would go ahead with the work. He pushed aside his other debts—to restaurant, barbers, florists, outfitters, taxi drivers, and notaries, together with money owed to the contractor and to the owner of the storage company. And without saying a word to anyone he flew off to Europe.

He returned for the High Holy Days, complacent and full of hope, like a picture postcard. Elsa and Leon waited for him at the hotel and Diana expected him at her home. The creditors awaited him in the streets and cafes and the summons to appear before the court in connection with a demand made by the owner of the storage company to confiscate the equipment, attended him at Uncle Noah's.

Fink was humiliated.

"Be a man," Uncle Noah tried to coax him. "Leave it alone. Find yourself something proper to do." He was ready to arrange work for him at *Tnuvah*.

Fink mopped his brow with a perfumed handkerchief, lit a cigarette, jotted down a few small figures on the border of a newspaper, and the world became pleasant again. He assessed the situation of his business—it was good, and the prospects for the future really bright. He had held meetings with a few investors abroad and they were most enthusiastic. At the moment he was just short of a small sum that would enable him to pay off current debts and would facilitate the completion of the building. As far as the confiscation went, he still had time. And it seemed to him that it was just as well to pretend the thing didn't exist. It would right itself. The case would not go to court. He had connections and he was *au fait* with all sorts of procedures, and moreover the owner of the storage company seemed a decent and rational man. He would come to an arrangement. There was nothing to worry about. When he was in Holland he had bought a booklet of photos of leopards. It was a pity it was in Dutch.

When stretched out in a deep armchair in a well-cut suit, with nicely manicured nails, Fink used to smile softly, grunt, and make promises, which helped him fob off his pestering creditors. He manoeuvred Elsa and Diana, and sought funds still outstanding. He tore up the letters that kept coming back from the court without even glancing at them.

But suddenly a writ of confiscation was taken out.

The day of the auction sale burst from the rainy season like a new-born spring day. Fink woke up early. A vague anxiety disturbed his sleep. He wore a checked coat and Panama hat and went to the storage depot. Leon dragged after him like a calf.

A yellow sun hung at the edge of the blue sky and the air was full of cool scents of earth, grass, and rain. He felt buoyed up. After all the evil was still far off, and to some extent it seemed to him even unreal. But as soon as he saw the giant boxes of equipment, which were brought into the yard, he was overcome by feebleness. Something weakened inside him and he grew faint. Momentarily he considered retracing his steps and disappearing from the scene, but he walked around the yard and groped among the boxes. His head was empty. Not a single idea of how to get out of the messy situation crossed his mind. Everything was dust and ashes. His fate had been decreed.

A pleasant warmth percolated from the sun, but his hands and feet were cold and damp. He leaned on the fence and waited, devoid of any desire. It was as if he were far away from the reality of the situation and had become one with something that seemed like a desert of thick water. But as time passed and no one appeared something began to crack inside him. Suddenly he believed that everything was just a figment of his imagination or just a misunderstanding, which could be explained away in two or three simple sentences. He straightened his hat, lit a cigarette, and began to wait for a miracle—perhaps a war would break out or the owner of the storage depot would die of a sudden heart attack.

The storage depot owner arrived, followed by the merchants. The boxes were broken open. The auction finished at noon. One merchant bought the big projectors and electrical equipment, others bought nets, canvas sheets, metal poles, rope ladders, fireworks, drums, and bugles. Fink shook hands and even smiled. After a few hours had elapsed and the yard was empty, only piles of wood shavings remained, which were borne like chaff in the wind.

Fink arrived at Uncle Noah's home toward evening. He was excited and active like a dizzy tin frog. His eyes sparkled and loud laughs escaped from his lips. Uncle Noah put his newspaper aside and asked for an explanation of the mirth.

"The circus," cried Fink in glee and placed a bottle of wine, cheese, and salami on the table. He poured the wine, emptied his glass, and spoke in a bellowing tone about the circus, which was eighty meters high, about the wall of death with its four motorcycles. He talked of Tzirel, white orchids like wedding-gowns, shrouds, and eternal spring, and of his awesome, spotted leopard, a native of Malaysia or Tasmania.

"I'll be a Communist!" he suddenly yelled and waved his pudgy fist threateningly. "I like Stalin! I like Molotov! I like mustaches!" and in wrath he poured the contents of the wine glass in his hand over Leon, who was dozing next to the table. But he immediately bent down on his hands and stroked Leon's head compassionately as he mumbled "Doggy, Doggy, Doggy," and with the fading of the day his face froze and became ashen.

"Oh Mamma, the world . . . ," Fink burst out in Yiddish and slumped into an armchair; he sank into a state of dulled senselessness, and heavy tears, like those of an insulted baby, rolled from his eyes and made faint stains on his jacket and trousers. Aunt Shoshannah hurried in a confused state to bring him Valerium and a slice of lemon.

Despite this, the situation wasn't desperate. The foundations of the circus stood, and when the requisite sum of money was found it would be possible to establish the whole structure on the existing base.

At this point Fink happened upon the widow Mrs. Michaela Bronfmann, the wife of the deceased entomologist, Dr. Levi Bronfmann. He became acquainted with her through the dog's veterinary surgeon, who ceaselessly praised this woman for her family connections, her personality, and her property. Upon which Fink realized that he had at some time met her brother or her brother-in-law, but he couldn't remember if it had been in Brazil or Trieste, but they had even become friends.

"Madame," Fink said, and doffed his hat with a ceremonious but sad flourish, "Albert Joiachim Weiss." He had firmly decided that this time he would put up a good fight.

A vague smile appeared on the pale lips of Madame Michaela in her black mourning dress, as she led him to the drawing room. The room was shrouded in a pleasant dimness, saturated with the scent of flowers, books, and oil-colors. He ensconced himself in an armchair and Michaela served shortcake biscuits and tea in Chinese porcelain cups, which were decorated with blue mountains, waterfalls, and

Chinamen. Fink intended to convince her it was worth her while to sell part of her plots and orchards and invest the money in the circus business. Instead of this they spoke about thoroughbred dogs and belief in God. And Madame Michaela lectured him in a disembodied and distant tone on the spiritual possessions of the East and its beliefs— Buddhism, Taoism—with a quotation from the sayings of Lao Tsu.

He didn't understand a word of all this. And moreover he wanted to discuss the matter in hand. Nevertheless he followed her every word, feeling that a wonderful world was being opened up before him. The obscurity and the mystery in these things and the quiet nobility in her long face and slow fingers captivated him and aroused exalted feelings in him.

One visit followed another and Fink became absorbed, like the sound of his steps on the carpets. Whole evenings, while Elsa and Diana vainly waited for him, he sat in a state of purity and ease in the Bronfmann house, listening to ancient words of wisdom and Bach partitas, which Mrs. Bronfmann strummed on the piano in a Buddhistic way.

Unintentionally he became a reformed character, as if he were reborn in one of the silent monasteries on the Himalayan mountains. For him it took on the form of a blue-tinted Nirvana, which became embodied in a person, and the whole world faded away with him gently in the orange, purplish-gray emptiness of everlasting twilight.

Tzirel's letter, in which she announced that in two months' time she would be sailing to Israel accompanied by the children, arrived on the same day Fink received an additional warning concerning Mr. Chernowilski's claim, and he suddenly awoke, as if from a sweet afternoon sleep that is broken by a banging on the door.

He placed the two letters on the table and turned his face

to the wall. But again he didn't find any peace of mind. Tzirel's letter disturbed him.

The whole letter only consisted of a few thin words, written in large letters; but it had a genuine note of devotion and submissiveness about it, sending a wave of regret over him. If only Tzirel were here, he would cover her face and small head with kisses and tears.

Fink tossed and turned in bed all day. And only in the evening did he go out to wander in the town after a day of fatigue and torment. He walked about the streets aimlessly, went on to the promenade and stood facing the black, turbulent sea. Blobs of foam landed on his face and disappeared again. Life now seemed to him complex and without solution, in short, desperate.

He loved Tzirel, Elsa, Diana, and Michaela. But on the opposite side the creditors and the rest of the world, which was set on entrapping him, was poised.

He would commit suicide.

This was the first time in his life that this thought had crossed his mind. It spread through his cold limbs like a comforting cognac and aroused in him something akin to a feeling of exaltation and also self-respect. This was an entirely new emotion, which was extremely pleasant. He'd commit suicide.

Again and again he described to himself how he would die. Perhaps he'd be thrown up from the sea covered in seaweed, or maybe he'd be stretched out on a bed of dry leaves. Another possibility would be his sitting in an armchair with Leon crouching at his feet. If only he were able to commit suicide and at the same time to remain alive to witness the shocked and depressed faces of the world, which was filled with deep regret, his happiness would have been complete.

The heavens divided from the water and a gray light filled in the space. A feeling of deep exhaustion took hold of him. He again took account of his love. There was no comfort for him. And suddenly, just like Venus rising from the sea, an idea came to him—to live with the four women in one spacious house, or at least divide his time between them.

From the first he was infatuated with this notion. Despite the difficulties, which he didn't ignore, he saw it as a just and rational solution. In this euphoric state he imagined this to have become a concrete reality and the great relief filled him with fervent gratitude for this wonderful world, in which everything was possible in unending measure. If he hadn't been afraid of the sea, in his glee he'd have jumped into the water.

Toward morning Fink returned to the hotel. He was fresh and energetic. The reception clerk smiled at him and he saw in this a good omen. After he had showered and changed his clothes, he went out to find the requisite moneys to square his debts and complete the circus.

Again the day was fine and the people were beautiful, and even the manifold possibilities were promising. The almond tree across the way from the hotel was already blooming.

This spring lasted a whole month. A mixed-up spring, and at the end of it all doors were closed to him and the streets became dangerous.

Merchants and money lenders pushed him aside rudely. Creditors pursued him, they clamored for their money forcibly and pronounced threats and abuses. The hotel owner demanded that Fink pay his account and vacate the flat. Elsa pinched him with her looks and Diana caused scenes in the street. On one occasion the search for him led her to Uncle Noah's house. She was dressed in a gown and her hair was in rollers. Mrs. Michaela Bronfmann was the only one who didn't know anything.

Then Tzirel and the two children arrived.

The day was cold and hazy. The dying sun, resembling a ghostlike moon made of wax, floated in the empty space beyond the sooty sky.

Fink came to the harbor to meet them. He was adorned

in a blue suit. His eyes were red and his lips dry like chalk. He embraced the children and without saying anything caressed the birdlike face of Tzirel, who stood quietly. She wore a white hat with a feather and held a white leather bag and handkerchief. A scorching wind came up from the sea. Afterward they went to the flat, which Fink had rented with money he had borrowed from Madame Michaela.

The first week was happy. Fink walked about the flat in slippers, with dreamy eyes. He stroked the children, Tzirel, and the porcelain figurines he had bought to decorate the rooms. Sometimes he would take Tzirel by surprise and kiss her on the neck. On Shabbat he brought her tea in bed. He was at peace with the world. The demands of the creditors, the affairs of the circus, the three women—these all were unreal—they seemed to be nullified like young love that had come to an end.

But on Monday at dinnertime there was a ring at the door and Elsa Neidoroff in a greenish tweed suit burst into the kitchen like a thin bloodhound. Without any introduction she turned to Fink and demanded that he marry her or, alternatively, return her money. All this she said while waving the "pledge of a decent man" in his face. It resounded like the flapping of wings in the noisy silence.

Tzirel took the children out into another room. When she returned, she found Fink stretched out in a faint and Elsa standing over him and demanding her rights, threatening to take legal action. She was as hard as a clothes peg.

Tzirel groaned and Fink got up and ran out of the house with Leon at his heels. In a fit of calculated madness Elsa shattered all the porcelain figurines, as she said in Dutch:

"This is mine. All is mine."

At six in the morning Fink knocked on Uncle Noah's door and went in. His Uncle was drinking tea while reading *Davar*. Fink asked him for forty thousand pounds, in return for which he would give him fifty thousand within a year. His Uncle put on his coat and said that he didn't even have four hundred pounds, and his Aunt confirmed this with a nod. Fink went after him to the shower and suggested that he sell his house, courtyard, and gardens.

Uncle Noah fumbled around in his purse and took out twenty pounds, placed them on the table, and went out to work without saying a word and without closing the door.

The day was a cold dough of clumps of cloud. Strips of sky and a little gloomy light, and rain borne on the East wind poured hour after hour on the damp streets and on the fallow field, in which the scattered foundations of the circus lay in the midst of the waste. The sterile bundles of iron protruded heavenward from the rubble.

The sky was already heavy with twilight sliced by a moon peeping out and disappearing. Fink sat on a pile of dry grass. In the morass of his stunned dizziness he realized that he was betrayed and abandoned by the world. He felt insulted and humiliated. If he could only find one warm lap, he would bury his head in it and cry.

Leon urinated on an iron peg and came and stood in front of him. A fine needlelike rain mingled with grains of gravel was carried by the wind. Fink picked up stones and threw them at Leon. The dog went off and came back as if he were attached to Fink by a rubber band. Again thoughts of suicide crossed his mind.

Fink returned home late. He was cold and dirty. Tzirel didn't ask any questions. She offered him a cup of tea, took off his shoes, and made the bed for him. All night he nestled against her and wept "My sister, my sister," and in the morning he awoke a new man.

For almost a year my Uncle Fink punished the world. He fulfilled his mission with piety and zeal, like a cannibal turned vegetarian. He didn't make friends with anyone, nor did he permit anyone to become friendly with him. He was silent, became submissive, stopped drinking coffee, sweetening tea, smoking, and going to the cinema. He ate little and worked as the mate of a thin decorator. Occasionally he would groan, and he hoped that he'd have a fatal heart attack. His face was impenetrable, and he bore it on his shoulders like a saint bearing a halo.

Only very occasionally, perhaps because of his hunger pangs, he had short bouts of hatred with the accompanying desire for revenge. In their wake he used to have psychedelic hallucinations, in which he imagined the circus and the tight-rope walkers dressed in white climbing up and down the ladders with their heads disappearing somewhere in a heaven illuminated with fireworks. And he stood in the center of the highly polished parquet floor in a wig and top hat, next to him was his own private leopard, both of them seen again and again amid the thousand spectacles.

This time the world wasn't at one with his desires. The court declared him bankrupt. All his property, including the remnants of the circus, was confiscated and sold. Fink accepted the verdict with a benign and understanding smile; and even weathered the abuse with which his creditors assailed him. Worst of all was Mr. Chernowilski, the butcher, who secretly and cruelly gave him a pinch.

He was forced to vacate the flat. He found an old flat with high bluish walls, colored glass panes, a balcony with rusty plaited railings, the smell of cabbage, and refuse in the air and street cats in the yard.

He was now at ease, and a cellarlike silence enveloped his life. It was disturbed momentarily only once.

Two months after he went bankrupt a commercial van stopped outside his house, and the tailor who had made the circus uniforms emerged. He shook Fink's hand affably and apologized for not having been able to find his new address.

The uniforms had been ready for some months and he'd been worried that no one would claim them. "Genuine regal uniforms," he said proudly. "Uniforms for the aristocracy," he added and asked where to put them.

"On the balcony," Fink said.

"On the balcony?"

"Rain," Tzirel burst out and looked at the sky.

"On the balcony," Fink repeated with a voice as straight as a stock and closed the door after him.

Then suddenly a son was born to the Prince and Princess of Monaco and everything changed. On the same day, moved by one of his uncontrollable moments of undefined insight, Fink, inebriated, sent an emotional greetings telegram to the Prince and Princess. After a month of excited expectation he received a polite reply, signed by the Prince's private secretary.

He hid the letter in a drawer, and from time to time he would examine it. The very paper wrought a magic effect on him, and the complex curls and flourishes of the secretary's signature sent a delicate intoxication through him. Oh Monaco! Oh graceful gazelle! The blue sea laps the soles of your pure feet. The fast speedboats that spread a train of foam in their wake. Onassis. Oh paradise on earth! There's no direct taxation, and a whole sun like a golden coin is always in the center of the sky above. The streets are clean and genuine princes drink coffee and say "Bonjour Monsieur."

Again he was unable to rest. And in the cellarlike silence under the monk's toga a spring storm was brewing. Tortuous ideas sprung up and budded in his round head, like the ferns in the virgin forests of the equatorial lands. They hurled him from messianic ecstasy to a desertlike inertia, and Tzirel approached him on tip-toe to ask whether he wanted tea or an aspirin.

"No, no," Fink answered her impatiently and looked at her strangely.

Soon the program became clear to him, and one day he went to see his friend the painter Edmund Rubin. After a careful opening and a vague introduction, Edmund closed the door and swore to preserve secrecy. Fink then unfolded the program in detail.

When he had concluded, a perplexed silence prevailed. Edmund didn't cry "Oh!" He removed the pipe from his mouth and tapped it lightly on the edge of the ashtray, and with great caution he tried to evade the issue and even to hint at the weaker points in the program. But Fink didn't wish to listen.

At one in the morning Edmund gave in. He agreed to help compose the memorandum, but only insofar as polishing the French was concerned and on condition that his name would not appear.

The work lasted ten wearisome days. For hours and hours they sat at Edmund's table, and with the help of dictionaries, encyclopedias, and history books they tried to spin a spider's web with which to ensnare an elephant. Another four days elapsed before Fink chose the right paper. He handled dozens of various kinds of paper and eventually chose a rare type of silk paper, on which, according to his instructions, a special watermark was impressed.

He now devoted himself to the task of copying. There were another three nerve-racking days when Fink changed every word, even altered the shape of the letters, the color of the ink, the space between the lines and the width of the margins.

The memorandum occupied two full pages. It opened with: "His Majesty Prince Rainier the Second of the House of Grimaldi, the Prince of Monaco and its Surrounds" and concluded with "Your faithful servant, Albert, Albert Abraham, Joiachim, Immanuel Weiss, Doctor of Law—Doctor of Economics—Specialist."

Between the introduction and the end there were the usual courtesies and praise, which related to the Prince himself and to the whole Grimaldi dynasty, from Otto Canala, who was the Genoese consul in 1133. Between the lines very gently and circuitously a suggestion of an honest partnership between His Majesty the Prince and my uncle, was made. The aim of which was to establish a worldwide lottery, which would be based in Monaco. According to all calculations this project was bound to bring in millions of pounds from Europe, not to mention India, Pakistan, Madagascar, Brazil, the Seychelles Islands, Ethiopia, North America, Canada, including Alaska, and the Straits of Bering. In short: a flood of gold.

After a night of coffee and biscuits the copying was complete. Edmund felt sick as a result of too much smoking. He was yellow and his fingers were cold and damp. But Fink was as wide awake as a robber. He combed his hair, washed his hands, perfumed the memorandum, put it into an envelope, and sealed it with three separate wax seals.

On his way back from the post office he gave a pound to a poor man and another pound he slipped into a charity box of Rabbi Meir, the miracle maker. Now all he had to do was await a reply.

Fink didn't wait. Toward evening he started making preparations for the journey. This time he knew no bounds. He was energetic, sly, and full of cunning plans.

He made promises, swore on the life his father and mother, presented himself under assumed names, handed over forged documents and recommendations, smiled, rolled his eyes, and even brought on tears to extract money from relatives and strangers. With the aid of a marriage date, kisses and tickling, he managed to get all Diana's savings and sold his brother-in-law part of an orchard that belonged to Madame Michaela.

He saw nothing disreputable in any of this. He decided for himself that these were loans he would repay with the first sum of money he'd earn and add a fair share of the interest. He jotted all this down in his notebook.

In the few enforced hours of idleness, as during the late night hours, he would lie next to Tzirel and, accompanied by the sound of her tranquil breathing, he'd silently conduct friendly chats with the Prince and Princess. Or he would assiduously revise in his head the rates of exchange, rules of etiquette, names of streets of Monaco-Ville and Monte Carlo, the words of the National Anthem, "Pricipaoute Monaco ma patrie."

He also went over important historical details of the principality, for example, one of the descendants of Otto Canala was an ambassador at the Court of Frederick Barbarossa, or that Francois Grimaldi disguised himself as a monk and in this way some of his men penetrated the fortress of Monaco, captured it, and established the princedom there.

Within three weeks the preparations were complete. After a depressing lunch of fried carp and barley soup, Fink announced to Tzirel that he was going out to buy a hat. Taking a roundabout route he hastened to Edmund's house, changed his clothes, took his suitcases, and went to the airport.

It was a rainy day. Fink wore a black English cloth suit, above which his face floated like a delicate half-moon. His soft fingers were adorned with two gold rings. One of them had an imitation diamond inserted in the middle.

He had very little ready cash. But instead of this his suitcases carried six suits, six pairs of shoes, a dozen shirts, two pairs of golf trousers, bow-ties, kerchiefs, gloves, cuff links, white silk dressing gowns, a complete *Who's Who of the Aristocracy*, by the Marquis Martin De Vigo, an illustrated pocket edition of the *Book of Etiquette*, a map of the world, documents, memos, and a bundle of visiting cards.

A few visiting cards were ready to hand in his suit pockets. Next to his full name and the full blaze of his titles, a symbol was impressed like a watermark: a laurel wreath around a globe, in the center of which was a leopard. Above the globe was a pair of crossed swords, and under it one word stood out: L'HONORITE.

Fink arranged his affairs quietly. When he had concluded official matters and before embarking, it occurred to him that he should use the few moments available to send a postcard to Tzirel and the children.

He leaned over the counter and his face took on a grave expression. He searched around in the expanses of his head to find a few special words to express the love, regret, and comfort that now filled his heart and would erase all that he had ruined. In the meantime, his name was called over the microphone, and so he hurriedly wrote: "My love. I'm alive. It will be OK. Be well for me. Yours as ever, Fink."

A gray curtain of rain was spread over the airport and over the whole world. Contentedly the rain blurred the planes, the runways, the earth and trees. It all looked like scenes from a very old silent film.

Fink donned his hat and with bent head hurried onto the tarmac. When he reached the top stair, he stopped a moment, turned around, stood erect, removed his hat, and waved good-bye to the empty balcony with a flourish and sent one of his most enchanting smiles into the splitting void. It remained hovering between the raindrops even after the doors were shut and the plane had taken off with a great noise and disappeared like a phoenix.

Now I have an Uncle in Monaco, but recently rumors have been rife that he has moved to Lisbon, and that there or close by, he has established a farm for the rearing of fighting cocks. The last clear information of his whereabouts was received three years ago.

NOTES

1. Large dairy firm.
2. Labour Party daily newspaper.

Uncle Peretz Takes Off

UNCLE PERETZ WASN'T really an uncle. He was a Communist, and apart from my grandmother everyone predicted that he would come to a bad end. His father turned his back on him in indignation and disappointment, and the rest of the family too wanted nothing to do with him. If only they could have shut him up in a dark room and forgotten that he existed.

Uncle Peretz took no notice of them. He wanted to redeem the world. His brother, Akiva, tried on a number of occasions to talk him out of it, but to no avail. He was firm as a rock in his faith, and all the discussions ended in quarrels.

For the sake of the salvation of the world he sacrificed himself with exalted ruthlessness. From the day of his conversion his warm voice, tenderly singing "Over the ocean and far away, Tell me, birds, do you know the way?" was silenced. He no longer danced, barefoot and bathed in sweat, at the meetings of the Working Youth, and he stopped going down to the beach and wandering at his pleasure amid the sand dunes and vineyards. He became gloomy and severe, sunk in mysterious activity and arguments full of anger. With   fanatical zeal and hostility he frequently held forth on the revolution and the freedom of mankind. Only his broad stride and the look of boyish innocence in his blue eyes remained the same, and in the early evening he would still stand on the roof of the shack, gazing far into the distance.

He was tall and gaunt, and his hair, which was prematurely gray at the temples, would stand up straight in the wind like a hoopoe's crest. His face was tanned and his fingers brown with nicotine.

As he stood there, intent and defiant and exuding an ineffable air of superiority, it seemed as if he was about to take off and soar over the roofs of the shacks and the Persian lilac and the tops of the sycamore trees, into the blue of the sky, where he would perform some great deed.

He remained standing, casting a thin lizard's shadow on the roof tiles while his decapitated head rested on the sand of the yard, not far from the dovecote, over whose dwindling doves my cool-cheeked grandmother watched. She did this without enjoyment, filling in for my dead grandfather until he came back, even though, for all her pure-hearted faith, she knew very well that he would not come back.

When darkness fell Uncle Peretz would climb down from the roof and go inside. The light of the kerosene lamp would fill the little entrance and the room with a shifting, wintry shadow. The shadow stretched over the floor, clung to the furniture and corners, and climbed the wooden walls, from which the faces of Marx, Engels, and Lenin looked down severely. Their writings filled the shelves of the bookcase to overflowing, together with other socialist tracts and various propaganda pamphlets published by the Party. They were shrouded in a yellowish-brown gloom and looked like tomes written by rabbis or sorcerers. Books and pamphlets lay on the square table too, in the wavering circle of light, and sometimes also on the wide iron bed, heaped with two pillows and a thick feather quilt and covered with a blue velvet bedspread.

And in the middle of all this, surrounded by the smell of books and bed linen and the hot smell of the lamp, was his wife, Aunt Yona, and she wasn't really an aunt either, but a small, fragile woman put together from slender bones and a melancholy moon face.

At first her future seemed promising. She knew English and worked as an accountant with good chances of promotion at the exclusive Spinney's food store where the Mandatory officials did their shopping. Her cheeks were rosy and her soft, black eyes hiding behind their long lashes concealed a lively, intelligent smile, which only rarely spread and lit up her whole face. She was tender and pure. But from the moment Uncle Peretz decided to redeem the world her future collapsed, and she became a seamstress. All day long she sat bowed over the old Singer sewing machine standing in the corner of the room, a bit of thread between her teeth and the tape measure hanging around her neck.

When he walked in, the shack would fill with a subdued commotion, as of angels and seraphs racing behind an invisible screen. All her muffled hopes revived, and she was full of fear. To and fro she rushed, handing him a clean towel, a pair of socks, or an ironed shirt, putting away his heavy boots, preparing supper. She did everything with exaggerated caution, fearful of every step, as if one reckless movement or jarring sound might destroy everything on the brink of coming into being again.

Actually, her behavior aroused Uncle Peretz's resentment, but he suffered it in silence and resigned himself to his fate. He did not want to hurt her feelings.

They ate supper in the white kitchen. They sat facing each

other with the oil lamp between them. On the table, on plates and in bowls, were fruits and vegetables, various leaves, nuts, raisins, and seeds, as well as marmalade or strawberry jam, which Aunt Yona made herself. She was a vegetarian, and he had adapted himself in order to make things easier for her and also to make her happy.

After supper Uncle Peretz usually went to committee meetings. When he had no meeting to go to, he would sit at the table and immerse himself in one of the Party pamphlets or in a work by some socialist philosopher. His face and his calloused hands were illuminated, but his back and the rest of his body were in darkness and the shadow of his head hung high above him, floating somewhere in the corner of the ceiling.

Aunt Yona sat in her usual place on the end of the bed. She would embroider or do the finishing off on her sewing, looking at him out of the corner of her eye with silent expectation. If only she had tied a pretty scarf around her neck, she thought to herself, or worn a necklace like Geula, maybe he would have favored her with a glance. But once upon a time he would have taken her head in his hands and kissed her on the eyes without any incentive at all.

Afterward, when the lamplight began to dim, they would drink a glass of cold milk and go to bed.

Friday night and Saturday morning were devoted to the Party. Uncle Peretz would go to public meetings and demonstrations and come home exhausted and excited. Sometimes a few of his friends would come around on Saturday mornings for consultations. For hours they would sit debating with each other in a dense cloud of cigarette smoke: they would denounce evil, calculate the time-table of redemption, and search for ways and means of expediting the end and ushering in the brave new world. Yona would bring them tea in big china cups and biscuits, close the door carefully, and go and sit in the kitchen.

Outside, on the other side of the flimsy veil separating her from the world like a white mist, the days passed by like a caravan of camels. Only the castor-oil plant would bloom before her eyes with bright, purple flowers, produce its fruit, and let it drop to the ground. And the Persian lilac in Friedman's yard, too, whose scent would give rise in her to secret longings, and in whose shade she wished that she could lie down, imagining the pleasant cool, the freshness and delight this shade would bestow upon her. If only she had once said something beautiful, she thought, perhaps everything would have gone back to what it was before and been good again. And when she thought this, she had in mind the third day of Passover, which had been a mild day full of dry scents of blossoming, and she and Peretz had strolled through the vineyards and the virgin fields to Sharona and beyond. Everything was so alive and benign, and afterward they had climbed a sycamore tree, and as she was climbing down again she had been seized by fear, and Peretz had held her in his strong hands, swept her up and put her down in front of him, and laughed.

"Like a crocodile's skin," said Peretz and stroked the bark of the sycamore tree with his hand. Behind his head, through the green foliage, she saw little scraps of sky-blue and trembling yellow sunspots which slowly misted and dissolved, and she closed her eyes.

That was a long time ago, even before their marriage, but she remembered everything: the good smell of his sweat, the hard stubble of his beard, the little patch on the blue shirt he was wearing, the Arab who rode past on a donkey, the embarrassment.

On their way home they met David Roizman. He called them from a distance and afterward he embraced Peretz and invited them to go down to the beach with him. She didn't say anything, but Peretz agreed gladly, and she was annoyed.

"And where's Raya?" asked Peretz.

"The parcel's come undone," Roizman replied with a shrug. "The wine's been drunk and the bottle's empty," he added with a wink, and he slapped Peretz on the back and laughed.

Peretz laughed too, but he sounded embarrassed, and she could feel how he was avoiding her eyes. Afterward there was a silence and suddenly Peretz began to sing in Polish and David Roizman joined in, but her mood was already spoiled. When they approached her parents' house she stopped and said that she was tired and she was going home. She expected Peretz to accompany her, or at least coax her to come with them. But he only touched her shoulder and said "Be seeing you," and the two of them turned away and walked down Bograshov street, singing in Polish.

This episode, together with the feeling of insult and despair that overcame her when she was left alone, she tried to efface from her memory, but they kept on coming back of their own accord, when she was sitting like this in the kitchen, for example, listening to Peretz's voice mixed up with the other voices behind the closed door. She was sorry, as sorry as she had been immediately after the incident occurred, for not having gone with them, and she reproached herself bitterly for trying to force him to choose between her and David Roizman. That had been a big mistake.

At midday the door would finally open, and they would emerge from the room looking tired and serious, leaving crumbs, pamphlets, pieces of paper and cups full of ash and cigarette stubs behind them. Uncle Peretz would accompany them into the yard, where he would sometimes linger with them a while before going back inside.

But early in the evening, after a heavy afternoon sleep, a

great calm would descend on Uncle Peretz and he would seem like a different person. What he liked best then was to go out for an aimless walk. Taking broad strides, he would lope through the sand with his hands clasped behind his back. Aunt Yona would follow a few steps behind him, dressed in a black pinafore. Sometimes Uncle Peretz would break into a whistle as he walked, as in bygone days. His whistle was as clear and fluting as the warbling of the birds in the woods, and Aunt Yona would look at his straight back and listen proudly and gratefully.

At regular intervals they would visit Grandmother. Uncle Peretz loved her, and so did Aunt Yona. And on the Saturday after she turned seventy they came early.

Grandmother's room, which was shrouded in perpetual gloom, had an air of melancholy and smelled of velvet, mothballs, and featherbeds. The Sabbath was departing, and its departure left an oppressive feeling of emptiness behind it. Grandfather's dark picture hung in the center of the wall, which was painted a ghostly white.

"Good Sabbath and Mazel Tov," Uncle Peretz proclaimed in his warm voice and smiled.

"Good Sabbath," Aunt Yona chimed in like a hasty echo and placed her home-baked cake on the oval table. Uncle Peretz set a bottle of wine down beside it.

"Good Sabbath," responded Grandmother and her eyes shone. She thanked them for the wine and cake, but only after expressing disapproval at the unnecessary and exaggerated expense.

They drank a toast of Grandmother's raisin wine, and Aunt Yona exclaimed "May you live to a hundred and twenty!" to which Grandmother replied, "Amen, and the same to you," and added, "In good health and with a sound mind and strong heart."

The raisin wine made Uncle Peretz jolly. He poured himself a glass and another glass and began to sing, "Purify Our

Hearts to Worship Thee Truly," drumming his fingers on the table as he did so. Afterwards Aunt Yona asked Grandmother how she was feeling and what the news from her son in America was, and after Grandmother had replied she sat still and silent as a snail in its shell listening to the conversation between her and Uncle Peretz.

The conversation flowed quietly and calmly. They spoke of health matters and money matters and current affairs in the *Yishuv*.[1] Grandmother served tea and cut slices of cake. She listened quietly and gave her opinion quietly, smoothing out invisible wrinkles in the table cloth with her thick, brown, carpenter's hand as she did so. One thing led to another and in the end Uncle Peretz got on to the subject of the British rulers and the corrupt leaders of the *Yishuv* and the proletarian revolution that was going to save the world. Grandmother tried to change the subject, but he would not let her. Flooded by a wave of fanaticism, he gripped his glass of tea in one hand while the other waved up and down, one finger pointed threateningly at her.

"Leave off. Leave all that to the goyim," Grandmother interrupted him in Yiddish. "Better you should enjoy yourself in your life. Go to the cinema."

"The revolution is my life," replied Uncle Peretz sternly, and a vein throbbed in his temple.

Grandmother made a despairing gesture with her hand and shook her head with a smile. She was a shrewd woman, sceptical about all forms of extremism. Suffering and poverty had taught her good and bad, and in her own attitudes she kept deliberately to the golden mean. Even in her attitude to God, in whom she believed unquestioningly and whose precepts she observed, there was a healthy dose of moderation and consideration for herself.

"Why are you killing yourself, Peretz? All this isn't for you."

"I'm not killing myself. I know what I want and I know what I'm doing. I'm a free man."

"Then do what's good for you," said Grandmother quietly and almost compassionately, "Why do you have to climb up the walls?"

"This is what's good for me," said Peretz angrily. "The world's rotten. It has to be changed!"

"Are you responsible for the world? Leave it alone. God will take care of it."

"There is no God!" retorted Uncle Peretz nastily. "There is no God!"

"Good, good," said Grandmother, who wanted to put an end to the argument, a faint blush covering her cheeks, "Leave Him alone. At least on the Sabbath let Him rest."

But Uncle Peretz would not agree to "leave Him alone." He stuck to his guns and angrily listed all the evils that religion and its priests had brought upon the world—stupidity, hypocrisy, decadence, and subjugation—and announced that religion was the root of all evil and nothing but the "opium of the masses" and an instrument that served the interests of the ruling classes. In the end he referred her, with more than a hint of arrogance, to the works of Marx, Lenin, and Plekhanov.

"Good, good," Grandmother repeated almost soundlessly, smiling and overlooking the insult until he calmed down.

Grandmother did not consult the works of Marx and Lenin. She felt no need at all to change her views, even if they seemed old-fashioned to some. She was a free woman in her own world. Besides, she was far too busy. Her legs were heavy now and her movements slow. Her days were full. She cooked for herself, went out to do her shopping and visit her friends, cleaned the shack, fed the doves with birdseed and breadcrumbs soaked in milk, and prayed.

Aunt Yona, too, was not conversant with the works of Lenin. She, however, tried. On a number of occasions, when Uncle Peretz was not at home, she took one or another of his works from the bookcase and tried to read them, anxiety and breathless hope fluttering in her bosom. She soon despaired of the attempt. The strangeness and boredom seemed to petrify her brain and she could not take anything in. Marx, Engels, Lenin, Plekhanov—more than arousing her hostility they filled her with fear and a feeling of miserable inadequacy. She was fading away, dying for a single token of affection.

Uncle Peretz calmed down. He ran his fingers through his mane of hair and smiled a winsome, boyish smile. As usual, he swore that he would never get into an argument about these matters with Grandmother again. Grandmother asked him not to swear, since he was unable to control himself in any case. But Uncle Peretz insisted on swearing again, and gave Grandmother a hug. A spirit of reconciliation descended on everybody and he began to sing "The Temple Will Be Rebuilt."

Outside it was already dark. And inside the room too. The Sabbath had departed, but its memory remained like a pale square on the wall where a picture had previously hung. Grandmother waited a while and then lit the lamp. Uncle Peretz lit a cigarette and smoked it with enjoyment, after which he stood up and took his leave, and Aunt Yona made haste to stand up with him.

And on their way home, in this empty hour between the Sabbath and the working week, he was seized, as usual, by a feeling of depression as heavy as remorse, a feeling of suffocation, as if he had wearied of all his battles and wanted to rest and be consoled. Now everything seemed exhausting and futile, and for a moment he longed to lay his hand on Aunt Yona's neck and draw her lovingly closer. If only she would incline her head slightly toward him. But she walked next to him wordlessly, afraid of spoiling the mood.

Slowly they approached the dark shack. When they passed the mulberry tree he felt an urge to turn around and go on walking for a while. But he did not do so. He went on stepping beside her sunk in thought, and by the time they arrived and opened the door his heart was already locked up again.

For fourteen years Uncle Peretz devoted himself to redeeming the world, but the world remained as sinful as ever. Only the lines on his face deepened and the books and pamphlets cramming the bookcase multiplied. And then Geula Apter[2] arrived on the scene.

Geula was over ten years younger than he was. After graduating from the Teachers Training College, she spent one year teaching. In the middle of the second year she left her job and went to work as a tile layer and as a packer, and after that as a waitress in the Workers' Canteen. For four years she was married to David Roizman, and then they suddenly separated. He went to Alexandria and she stayed behind. Uncle Peretz was attracted to her and intrigued by her. Occasionally he tried to approach her or get into conversation with her, but he never succeeded in exchanging more than a few clumsy sentences with her, and once she appeared to him in a dream.

In his dream they had gone together to see his mother, who was living in a shack on Dizengoff Street. It was a fine, warm winter day with a blue sky and a yellow sun, and they were in high spirits. When they drew closer they saw that the shack was gone. On the plot, which was covered with fresh weeds after the rain, all that remained was a concrete platform and a bit of yellow-painted wall. Under the window, which was set in the wall, hung a tin mug. This was the mug used by his father for the ritual washing of hands, and it filled him with aversion. On the platform itself stood a rusty iron bed. He stepped onto the platform and approached the bed, while Geula remained standing behind him. She was playing with a gold coin and waiting. To his amazement it wasn't his mother lying on the bed but another old woman. She was wearing an eggshell-colored dressing gown made of a coarse fabric and something that looked like a surgeon's cap on her head. Her eyes were closed, with the lids like two big shells. He wanted to run away, but his heart wouldn't let him. He stood looking at her impatiently, and it seemed to him that she had something she wanted to say to him. He bent down, but she only held his hand with her thin fingers and mumbled his name. When he turned his face away Geula was gone.

This was in the summer, when she was still married to David Roizman. But the affair itself began later, by accident, one day in winter.

All night long it rained, and the rain went on falling at intervals throughout the day. A heavy cloud covered the sky, squatting on the roofs and the high treetops, and a cold gray light filled the low space. In the early evening, returning from Shaul Kramer's funeral, Uncle Peretz found himself walking next to her. He walked with his hands in his coat pockets and stared at the sky and the bushes and didn't know how to begin. At the same time they left the others and walked by themselves on the muddy loam path. The ground and the grass gave off an unpleasant chill and the air was full of drops of water. In the end he said something about Shaul Kramer and how death had snatched him unexpectedly, before his time.

"Nonsense," said Geula abruptly, "everyone dies at his time," and she pulled up a green stalk of grass and stuck it between her teeth.

"Yes," Uncle Peretz agreed, and suddenly he realized that he didn't really understand what she meant.

"And he's been dead for a long time already," Geula continued. "In his whole life he didn't have a single thing to regret or reproach himself for or long for, not even at night, before falling asleep."

"You knew him well?"

"Yes. A nice guy," she said scornfully and fell silent.

It started raining again, a fine, irritating drizzle.

"It's raining," she remarked, as if to herself, and then she suddenly asked: "Why did you hit David Roizman?"

"What?"

"He told me that you hit him."

"Yes. It was a long time ago. I was drunk."

"But why him?"

"God knows," replied Uncle Peretz and wrapped his scarf around his throat.

They walked on in silence, and suddenly he added:

"We were friends. I liked him better than anyone else, and I still do. No, I really don't know. And I've never raised a hand to anyone in my life. The next day I apologized. It was quite horrible."

The rain came down harder.

"Should we take shelter?"

"Don't you like walking in the rain?" said Geula and fixed her tired eyes on him, amber-colored eyes with a tiger slumbering in them.

Uncle Peretz smiled with his lips, but inside him something tensed fearfully. He looked at her and wanted to say something, but he was tongue-tied. Again he saw her, the woman who was now walking beside him, with her thick lips and hard chin, tall and shapely, sufficient unto herself and wide open to the world, in her brown leather coat trimmed with black fur on the collar and cuffs and hem, and the Russian hat, it too made of black fur, set jauntily on her head. In her coarse, broad face there was a kind of combination of youth and overblown maturity, and something fierce and desperate that defied definition.

Afterward his tongue was loosened and he spoke, feeling all the time like someone delivering a dull, stilted sermon, but however hard he tried he could not stop, and the words rose trembling from somewhere in his chest and tumbled out of his mouth like chaotic columns of refugees. And it went on until they reached the limestone hills.

Down below, at their feet, stretched the sea—gray and brown with fraying ribbons of murky white. It raged and hurled its waves noisily at the deserted shore. The horizon dissolved in the thick fog coming closer and closer. The rain poured down in silent sheets. It fell on the water and the sand and the eroded hills and the black huts and the Muslim gravestones and veiled the distant houses, which receded even further. Everything came closer and receded into the distance. Uncle Peretz wanted to run away, but he went on standing there, rooted to the spot, and the heavy drops of rain came down and bathed his brown face and a slight shiver ran down his spine.

"Look how beautiful the sea is," he said.

"There's no need," said Geula quietly and pressed her body lightly to his. Her face now looked pure and sad. The fair hair escaping from her hat was soaked with water, and it fell onto her forehead and her shoulders in a tangle of snakes, like the hair of a mermaid rising from the sea.

"Come," she said.

"Where to?" Uncle Peretz wanted to ask.

Geula went down first and Uncle Peretz followed on her heels. The path was steep and dislodged stones rolled down it. But Geula almost ran, and when she reached the end she leaped onto the strip of sand, where the waves suddenly sprang up and pounced with a roar. A gray cloud of spray floated in the air.

"Where to?" Uncle Peretz wanted to ask and put his hands back in his pockets.

They set off side by side, but a little apart, their shoes in the wet sand and the water of the sudden waves and the piles of heaped-up shells. From time to time Geula would bend down, pick up a pebble, and fling it gaily into the sea.

Uncle Peretz turned his head and looked back. The world had vanished into a vague endless void. There wasn't a soul to be seen and it seemed that nothing existed anymore in this murky emptiness, but for the eroded hills, the gray sky, the sea, and the unremitting roar.

"It's getting late," thought Uncle Peretz and stole a glance at Geula.

The chill grew sharper and sank into his skin.

They approached the harbor fence. Geula walked up to the sea and stood at the waterline. Her face hardened and grew ugly. There was something panic-stricken in it. Uncle Peretz stopped a few paces behind her and looked at her. He was tense and his eyes were burning, and the severe chill in the air and the wetness in his shoes and clothes made him feel uncomfortable and sullen. Cold shivers ran down his spine and something tightened and fluttered in his chest and choked him.

"We should start back," said Uncle Peretz to himself. "It's getting late."

"Are you afraid of it?"

"No," he blurted out and took a step toward her. His face was burning.

"It's frightening," said Geula and came and stood next to him. "It's cold."

It seemed to him that the sea was running toward him, and then that the shore was sliding into the sea, when he placed his lips fearfully on hers and kissed her. He gasped for breath, and only his arms were strong and hard in their embrace, as if he wanted to crush her to him in a vice.

"Be blind," murmured Geula and kissed him passionately on his eyes and on his forehead and his temples and his throat, and pressed herself to him as if she wanted to enter into him and find shelter in him, "Be blind and old," and her face grew blurred.

The wind blowing from the sea slapped their skin like wet sheets. Slowly and languidly Uncle Peretz stroked her damp hair, but the chill and the grains of sand sticking to his fingers made him feel sullen again. He opened his eyes and looked at the darkness and thought that it must be late already.

The way home lasted forever.

"To sleep," mumbled Uncle Peretz to himself after parting from Geula, "to sleep," and he made his feet go faster, treading stealthily as a thief. It seemed to him that he had parted from her too abruptly, and the thought upset him.

He entered the shack on tip-toe. In the kitchen the lamp burned with a low flame and his supper was waiting for him on the table. He drank the cold milk and went to take a shower. The jet of water took his breath away. It was cold as the blade of a knife. But nevertheless he went on standing in the dark cubicle and let it wash over him again and again.

Aunt Yona was invisible. She had merged into the darkness. But her feathery breathing, innocent as a baby's, hovered in the room.

"She's sleeping," thought Uncle Peretz in relief.

A warm feeling flooded him. Now he wanted to be as good as he possibly could to her.

"It's late."

"Yes. I was at a meeting."

And as he stretched out carefully on the bed he placed his hand with great compassion on the quilt covering her shoulders, and lay down beside her, his heart full of good will and his eyes wide open, but his spirit insisted obstinately on roving back to Geula and the sea.

"No," Uncle Peretz swore to himself, and moved closer to Aunt Yona.

"Is anything the matter?"

"No. Go to sleep," he said and turned over onto his side.

The next day he went to the Party. He was apprehensive, but the comrades greeted him as usual. Accordingly, his apprehensions were dispelled and he felt full of happiness and gratitude. But the meeting dragged on and on, and his mind kept clouding over and his thoughts wandered far from what was being said there and attached themselves to the figure of Geula rising up before him in his memory, and he followed her.

"I'm tired," thought Uncle Peretz to himself, and he tried to imagine what she was doing now. "She's probably sleeping," he said to himself and felt a certain sense of relief, "It's already late," and he tried to rouse himself and shake her off.

In the following days Uncle Peretz resumed his normal way of life. He went on studying Plekhanov's essay "On the Role of the Individual in History," but from day to day he felt himself sinking deeper into a foggy absent-mindedness. He was obliged to read clear, simple sentences over and over again, word by word, sometimes aloud, before he was able to take them in. And then he would discover that they were dull and flat, and awoke no echoes in his mind. But he kept on reading stubbornly, grim and haggard, even though by the time he reached the end of the page he had already forgotten what was at the top of it. If not for Aunt Yona, sitting on the edge of the bed in front of him, he would have closed the book and left the house.

Five days later Uncle Peretz saw Geula in the street. She walked past in her brown leather coat and Russian hat, crossed Ahad-Ha-am Street, and turned into Nahalat-Benyamin. He wanted to hurry after her, but he stayed where he was and watched her until she disappeared. The next day he went to her house.

When Uncle Peretz climbed the stairs he was overcome with anxiety, and he felt like turning round and going home again. He knocked gingerly on the door and waited. There was no answer and he hoped that she was out. After a moment he knocked again.

"Why did you come?" said Geula and got out of bed.

Uncle Peretz smiled in embarrassment and mumbled something and fell silent.

"I knew you'd come," Geula softened and took the hat off his head, saying "What a funny hat," and put it on her own, and said "No?", and put it back again. "I was afraid you wouldn't come," she said suddenly, in a different, serious tone, and seized his hand and held it tight, "I dreamt about you," and she leant her head on his chest as if she were afraid.

"This is a nice room," said Uncle Peretz and let his hand rest on her neck for a minute.

The room was small and nothing to write home about. It had four high, yellow walls and a tall, barred window. Nearly half the space was taken up by a double bed made of iron, which was in a state of total disarray. On the pillow lay an open book, upside down. Opposite the bed stood two plain chairs and a square table pushed against the wall. In the corner stood a water jar.

"Sit down," said Geula and went to tidy the bed.

"Who's this?" asked Uncle Peretz, pointing to the photograph lying under the glass covering the table-top.

"My father."

"He looks young."

"Yes. He died young," said Geula with a smile and glanced at the photograph and at him. "Don't run away," and she went out of the room.

Uncle Peretz sat down on the edge of the bed and picked up the book. Geula came in and stood combing her hair in front of a little mirror. She saw his head bowed over the book in the mirror and she said with a sad, mocking smile:

"Once upon a midnight dreary, while I pondered weak and weary,
Over many a quaint and curious volume of forgotten lore,
While I nodded, nearly napping, suddenly there came a tapping,
As of some one gently rapping, rapping at my chamber door.
''Tis some visitor,' I muttered, 'tapping at my chamber door—
Only this, and nothing more.'"

"Go on," said Uncle Peretz.

"I don't remember any more," said Geula, pulling the book out of his hands and throwing it onto the bed.

"What a pity."

"Never mind. Come on, let's get out of here," and she took her coat off the peg.

Uncle Peretz glanced at the window and saw that everything was already dark.

They went outside and entered a little restaurant. A yellow light illuminated the walls, which were painted halfway up in green oil paint and hung with portraits of the leaders of the *Yishuv*. Uncle Peretz chose a corner table and sat down with his back to the street. He ordered two salads and two portions of fried fish.

"If you love me eat your egg," said the woman sitting at the counter close to the little boy. He refused and burst into tears.

Geula laughed. She ate with relish and with slow movements of her hands. She had slender wrists and long fingers. Uncle Peretz looked at them and glanced occasionally at the owner of the restaurant, who was leaning on the counter and reading a book. From the bulb hanging right over his head dangled a brown ribbon of sticky paper, covered with the flies that had fallen into the trap.

"Atrocious," said Uncle Peretz.

"They're flies," said Geula argumentatively. "Why shouldn't we kill them?"

"Let's go," said Uncle Peretz after they finished drinking their tea, and they stood up and put on their coats.

It was a clear, cold evening. They walked up Sheinkin Street, turned into Rothschild Boulevard, and went out into the vineyards and virgin fields. Uncle Peretz really wanted to say goodnight and go home.

"Oh, what a night," said Geula and opened her arms, with a kind of reckless, desperate gaiety in her tired eyes.

The white, metallic light of the moon filled the landscape. Everything was still, with a delicate, misty radiance in the air. Sounds receded into the distance, as if they were happening somewhere else, behind transparent barriers. Here and there trees loomed up, like frozen puffs of smoke spangled with a harsh, silvery glitter.

The ground gave off a chill and sharp smells that mingled with the warm smell of her coat.

"Slowly," Geula implored, "slowly," and the expression on her face, which was wild and distraught, gradually gave way to a trancelike concentration, very still and dreamy and relaxed, which spread through her entire body.

"Don't leave me," begged Geula, "don't leave me."

"I won't," whispered Uncle Peretz firmly and tightened his embrace, and as he did so he felt everything focusing and thrusting inside him, and afterward he went limp and felt nothing but emptiness and weakness. And after that he grew calm, and he wrapped her in his coat and she rested her head on his chest.

The gray light of morning came in at the window. Aunt Yona lay in bed without moving. She lay on her back and slept, and only her head, which was sunk in the pillow, peeped out of the quilt. Her eyes were hidden beneath her big, closed lids. For a moment it seemed to Uncle Peretz that she wasn't breathing and he bent over her. Her eggshell-pale face seemed very tired to him and also old.

He took off his clothes and threw his shoes into a corner. His perspiration dried and the chilly air in the room made him shiver. He longed to lie down and sink immediately into a deep sleep. The room made him angry. And Aunt Yona. And Geula.

Aunt Yona opened her eyes and turned to face him. A feeling of hostility overwhelmed him. He was seized with a desire to tell her, to smash everything in one harsh sentence, and to go away.

"Your food's on the table," said Aunt Yona quietly, closed her eyes, and pulled the quilt over her shoulders.

He paused for a moment, and then went up to the window, stepped into the kitchen, came back into the room, turned over Plekhanov's book, and went back to the window. Then he sat down carefully on the edge of the bed and took Aunt Yona's feet, which were always cold, between his hands in order to warm them, and all the time the sentence went around and around in his head and trembled on the tip of his tongue.

The light outside grew a little brighter, and Grandmother's doves cooed. Strange birds flew past his tired eyes, and dark lumps floated in seas shrouded in a cold mist.

"It has to be done," Uncle Peretz exhorted himself, an immense weariness, like that of a hangover, making his body heavy and stupefying his senses. In the end everything was swallowed up in this weariness, except for one word that kept going around and around in his head without stopping, "Geula, Geula."

Genia's baby began to cry, and Uncle Peretz opened his eyes and glanced at his watch, and got up and went into the kitchen, and made himself a cup of tea, and put on his white housepainter's overalls, and went to work, closing the door quietly behind him.

Winter departed and spring arrived. Next to the kitchen window the castor-oil plant bloomed and in the Friedmans' yard the Persian lilac bloomed and gave off an overpowering scent. Aunt Yona put the thick feather-quilt and the winter clothes out to air, and Uncle Peretz was beside himself.

Immediately after work he would change his clothes, grab a bite to eat, and go out. Aunt Yona would watch him until he disappeared between the shacks. Only then she would turn back to face the empty room and examine it for a moment with a puzzled look. The table was littered with the socialist books and pamphlets he had not looked at for weeks, and which she did not dare return to the bookcase or even move aside to make room on the table.

With a hurried or perhaps a frantic air, Uncle Peretz would trudge through the sand, walk up King George Street to Allenby, go down Nahalat-Benyamin, turn into Herzl, and then wander aimlessly up and down streets and alleys with his hands in his pockets and his eyes straying over the pavement and the walls and the passersby without coming to rest on anything. From time to time he would glance at his watch, which Aunt Yona had once bought him for his birthday.

The time passed tortuously between desires full of anxiety, thrilling fantasies, and reluctance. He longed for Geula and at the same time he hoped that she would not be there, until he heard her voice behind the door and he saw her, and she was afraid and abandoned herself without any reservations, like a solitary ship with all its sails unfurled, borne along unknown currents, buffeted by strong winds, seeking shelter. Her sensuousness, her sensitivity and painful, bitter despair together with her sudden bursts of joy captured his heart like deserted courtyards, old stone houses, ancient palm trees and places that lay beyond the sea. There was something touching about her, and everything held a mystery and the flavor of a different freedom.

They sat in little restaurants and wandered in narrow, deserted streets. Geula would link her arm in his, rest her head on his shoulder, and keep step with him. Sometimes she pulled him toward the boulevards, but Uncle Peretz preferred her room and the fields and dunes and orange groves. There he would sing and warble and whistle and hug Geula and kiss her. Once he gave her a lecture on the differences between the idealist and materialist approach, and the importance of human praxis, and freedom that was the recognition of necessity. She made an effort to pay attention to what he was saying, like a little girl at school, and he asked her if history and the future of the world and the *Yishuv* in Eretz Yisrael interested her.

"No," said Geula and snuggled up to him.

"Never mind," said Uncle Peretz and smiled.

"Mayakovsky committed suicide," she suddenly remarked gaily. "Would you commit suicide with me?" she added provocatively, and when he remained silent she continued to insist, "Well, would you?" and her face grew very grave, "Would you?"

Uncle Peretz laughed lightly and placed his hand on her head.

"Why?" he said gently, "Life is good, isn't it? Don't think about such things."

"You're wonderful," said Geula and laughed. "In any case we're dead already. Just twitching a little."

Uncle Peretz kept quiet.

"Will you marry me?"

"Yes."

"Then now. Not tomorrow. Today," said Geula and looked at him expectantly. After a moment she added: "Oh, if only you were old. Very, very old."

When they were in the fields she liked to gather white snails and try to coax them out of their shells. She would go on urging them until they poked their transparent horns into the air of the world. Usually she would lie on the grass, with a stalk between her teeth, and she could lie there like that for hours without moving. But most of all she was drawn to the sea, especially when it was dark. The darkness of the sea and the noise of the waves held her spellbound, calm, and full of awe.

Sometimes they would go to the Eden or the Gan Rina cinema, and Uncle Peretz would maneuver so that they went in after the lights went out.

"Are you afraid?" Geula once asked him.

"No. Why?"

"You are afraid," she said and gave him a hostile look. "But you're a free man, aren't you?" she added mockingly.

"Let's go inside."

"No," she said and crushed the tickets furiously in her hand, "You can go in by yourself," and she threw them onto the ground.

Without a word, Uncle Peretz bent down and picked the tickets up.

"Love me. Love me," pleaded Geula as if she were pleading for her life, and she buried her head in his chest and wrapped her arms tightly around his neck, as if hanging on to him so as not to be swept away into the abyss. "Love me. However you can. But love me."

Summer came. Geula took off her coat and sweater. Her long arms grew tanned, and her hair bleached in the sun. They spoke of marriage.

Uncle Peretz knew what he had to do, he did not doubt it for a moment. In actual fact, he felt that he was no longer the master of his fate, and apparently had not been so ever since meeting Geula, and this feeling made him happy and gave him the authority to do what had to be done. He was only waiting for the right moment, and at the same time he was also hoping for a miracle, of whose nature he himself was ignorant, which would let him off the hook.

The days went by and the miracle tarried.

Aunt Yona asked no questions and dropped no hints. She pickled cucumbers in big glass jars and made strawberry jam and pined away with an air of nobility and reserve, busy and harassed, sewing and cooking and cleaning the house. Her slightest movements and actions filled Uncle Peretz with resentment and irritation, but he bottled them up inside him. In her presence he was gloomy and taciturn, and also perpetually restless and ill at ease. He seemed sunk in thought, as if he was not there but somewhere else. But at the same time, in sudden outbursts, he would bring home flowers for the Sabbath, take her to the movies, help her a little with the housework, and once he bought her a purple silk scarf. Aunt Yona's eyes shone with joy, but she hardly thanked him, and only stammered a word or two, even though she was so grateful to him. All that evening Uncle Peretz felt benevolent and relaxed, and after supper he sat and read "Marxism and Empirio-Criticism." The text itself did not awaken any interest in him, but the mere fact of reading it gave him pleasure.

The heat increased. The fields and empty lots were covered with yellow grass and dusty thorns. Lizards scuttled between them. There was a smell of figs in the air. Geula reproached him and upbraided him, with pleas and scorn and love. She would give way to despair and rise again, be glad and miserable, passionately abandoned and estranged. Sometimes she would braid her hair and put on a new dress in his honor, and sometimes she would go about as dishevelled as if she had just gotten out of bed.

"Soon," Uncle Peretz promised, "in the winter."

"Why the winter?"

Uncle Peretz explained and promised. He spoke constantly of his love. With all his heart he desired Geula. But the words lost their vitality. Suddenly they sounded forced and brittle. A depressing atmosphere of parting began to dominate their meetings and conversations, together with a feeling of barrenness and hopelessness. They grew sullen, heavy, and tortuous, like all things in which people no longer believe, but only in the power of a blatant lie. Again and again they went to the places where they had first been together, and to new places too, but everything remained arid and became indecent too.

Only sometimes, unexpectedly, brief, dreamlike interludes occurred. Thanks to the power of desire and illusion the world would fill out around them again for an hour, and Uncle Peretz would give his imagination free reign and create the lives which would be theirs before long, after they were married.

"And we'll go to Ireland," said Geula.

Her long fingers played with his hair and stroked his neck.

"Yes," Uncle Peretz agreed, feeling joy and longing.

"You'll never do it," Geula would suddenly burst out and her eyes would grow very tired.

"I will," promised Uncle Peretz imploringly and clasped her to him.

"Never. You're so careful not to come to any harm," she said painfully, "and you want so badly to be a good man and you haven't got the strength to hurt anyone or the ability to give anything up. When will you be a little bad?" And her face grew hard and ugly. He wanted to say something, but he felt that it was all useless, and slowly he took his hands off her and turned his eyes to the ceiling.

"Give us a chance," begged Geula the next minute, snuggling up to him and kissing his face and his lips passionately and desperately, as if she wanted to suck his soul out or breathe a new one into him.

Uncle Peretz recoiled.

"Come on. Let's run away."

"No. I'll do it. Soon. It will be all right. I'll leave her."

"If I wait for you I'll have to wait until kingdom come. Oh, if only you were old."

And when he got home he would see Aunt Yona. He hated her, but on no account did he want to hurt her. On the contrary. He wished that she would die.

The first rains fell, and again the air was fresh and the sand gave off a good smell. Geula waited, but in her sleep. For days on end she lay in bed, huddled under the thick winter quilt, and slept. Even when she got up in the afternoon and went to work, or when she let him in and gave herself to him, she seemed to be fast asleep. As if everything was happening without her.

And Uncle Peretz came and went. He felt that the deed was ripe and that he could do it easily. All he had to do was lift his hand and tear the web of delicate threads in which he was trapped. At the same time, however, he recognized, however unwillingly, that something, a kind of big ball of cotton wool, was restraining him, and that somewhere, in the center of the circle, a bubble of impotence was spreading and the hour of grace was gone.

"I'll do it," Uncle Peretz would swear frantically to himself, and for a while he would believe it too. He simply could not resign himself.

Now he began feeling hostile toward his comrades in the Party, whom he would frequently meet and with whom he would exchange a few tortuous remarks, and also toward the members of his family, especially his mother and his brother Akiva. He did not hide this hostility, which was only strengthened by his occasional moments of contrition. Every now and then he would drop in on Grandmother, exchange a few words with her, and go away again. He hoped for a sign from her, but was careful not to disclose his predicament to her, except in obscure hints.

"Some people jump into the sea and try to swim, whatever the consequences," he said to her once, in the middle of a conversation.

"The ones who want to," she replied seriously, "but not everyone wants to."

"No. You need courage."

"You need to want to," said Grandmother in Yiddish and looked at him with eyes full of sympathy, "but you don't have to want to." And after a moment she added: "Courage sometimes means standing still and doing nothing."

"No," said Uncle Peretz, disappointed. "You need courage."

Grandmother gathered the breadcrumbs scattered over the table and pressed them with her finger and kneaded them into a little ball.

"You don't love her anymore," she said suddenly, "only the memories and what you think that you could have been."

"No," said Uncle Peretz vehemently and sank into a silence, which Grandmother made no attempt to break.

That night he dreamt that he was walking down Lillienblum Street by himself. He wanted to pee and looked for a convenient place. Suddenly he heard someone calling him from a big building in the process of construction. It was David Roizman, who was standing there and peeing. He went and stood next to him, but as soon as he began the head of his penis tore and fell off. It didn't hurt, or give rise in him to any surprise or fear. As if he had always known that it was going to happen one day. All he felt was discomfort. David Roizman offered him a handkerchief to mop up the blood and said jokingly, "He who spills his seed on the ground," and laughed.

Geula took a bag and traveled to Tiberias and from there to Jerusalem. This was at the beginning of spring. On the door of her room he found a hastily scribbled note, "To my beloved, a good, honest man." For a moment he stood there in front of the locked door, and then he tore the note to pieces and went out to wander the streets. As he walked he made up his mind never to see Geula again, and after an hour or so he went home and stretched out on the bed. Aunt Yona gave him a glance, and without saying a word she went into the kitchen and sat down to supper alone.

When Geula returned Uncle Peretz was waiting for her at the railway station. He was unsmiling, full of tension and gloom. Geula waved at him from the window, and when she dismounted they stood on the crowded platform and embraced. Then she linked her arm in his and he led her away.

Evening was falling. The streets were filling with shade and people, and there was a feeling of relief in the air. Uncle Peretz asked her how she was, and Geula told him about her trip. Aimlessly they wandered from street to street: Jaffa Tel-Aviv, Herzl, the Commercial Center. Spicy smells wafted from the shops and the warehouses, cooking aromas and smoke. Geula's face was beautiful and her spirits were high. She seemed really happy to see him, but he was silent. He felt tired and remote.

"Did you miss me?" he wanted to ask.

A merry chiming of bells came closer, immediately followed by the appearance of a black horse-drawn carriage.

"Shall we go for a ride?" asked Geula.

"Where to?"

"It doesn't matter," she said and waved her hand.

"To Jaffa," she said to the Arab coachman after they had mounted and seated themselves on the soft velvet seats, under the black canopy that almost touched their heads. "Kings of the earth," laughed Geula to the sound of the bells, and snuggled up to him.

"Yes."

When they were close to the harbor the driver stopped the coach and asked them where to go from there.

"Go back," said Geula.

They got off at Nahalat-Benyamin and the bells chimed merrily again until they were swallowed up in the distance.

"Did you miss me?" Uncle Peretz wanted to ask.

Geula laid her head on his chest and nestled up to him. As they walked she played with his fingers and then she took his forefinger and middle finger and passed them over her lips. Something yielded and thawed and delicate webs were woven again in the agreeable dimness of the evening air.

"Are you tired?"

Geula shook her head. Again he sensed how lost she was and how much she needed his protection, and he was flooded by a warm, paternal feeling.

"Like this forever," he said to himself and kissed her on her head.

They turned into the market. The main street and the alleys were deserted and the stalls were bare as gravestones. Everything was dirty and squalid, with a pervasive stench of fish and rotting vegetables and puddles of stagnant water.

Uncle Peretz wanted to turn into Sheinkin Street, but Geula pulled him in the direction of the sea.

"Look at it," cried Geula and freed herself of his embrace.

The sea lay in front of them heavy and coagulated as a paste of lead. But for the lapping of the ripples as they reached the shore there wasn't a whisper to be heard. Uncle Peretz laid his hand on the nape of her neck, as if he wanted to hold her back.

They went down to the beach, took off their sandals, and started walking. The soft cool touch of the sand was pleasant to their feet. Geula's steps grew light and joyful. She paddled in the shallow water and laughed.

"Like a little girl," thought Uncle Peretz, and at the same time he felt that her laughter was strange and no longer belonged to him, and he was seized by an urgent desire to grab hold of her and hold her tight and stroke her head.

"Come here. Feel it."

He walked next to her, a few steps apart. Once or twice he wanted to stop and talk to her, make promises, vows, but he couldn't seem to open his mouth.

"You're old," teased Geula and splashed water with her feet," but I'm even older than you are."

After the Red House she stopped.

"Let's swim."

"It's cold."

"Never mind. Look at it. It's calm enough to walk on," she said and took off her dress. "Come on, Peretz, come in with me," and she entered the water.

"Wait."

"Come on," said Geula and waded in deeper, "The water's warm."

Uncle Peretz got undressed.

"There are rocks here."

"Come on!"

He walked into the sea and stood still. The water reached his knees and sent cold shivers up his spine. He dipped his hands in the water and ran them over his face and chest.

"Come on! It's good!" cried Geula, and she added: "There are stables of horses there!" and pointed, arm outflung, at the clouds resting on the horizon.

Uncle Peretz took a few more steps and stopped. More than that he did not dare, and perhaps he did not want to either. In any event, he was a poor swimmer and the sea was now completely dark.

"Come on, Peretz. Let's swim," her voice came from a distance.

"Come back! There are rocks there! Be careful!"

Geula laughed out loud, but her laughter was full of pain and desperation, and fear of the fathomless dark depths of the water. Then silence fell, and Uncle Peretz stood there looking, and it seemed to him that he could see the outline of her head floating farther and farther out to sea. He waited a little longer, and then he walked back to the beach and got dressed.

One month later Geula Apter picked up and sailed for Vienna. She sailed in the morning, and suddenly everything stopped.

Uncle Peretz came home from work and his face was gray and stony. He put his tools down and went out. Like a spider blinded in both eyes he stumbled lost through the streets, which were no longer his, treading with alien feet on the skin of an alien earth. The air did not touch him and the views and the people did not impinge on his eyes, only the dazzling mirror-glitter of the sea somewhere at the end of Yona Hanavi Street.

The following evening he went to see Grandmother. She was busy praying, ". . . by thine abundant mercy animating the dead; supporting those that fall, healing the sick, setting at liberty those that are in bonds and performeth thy faithful words unto those that sleep in the dust," she whispered. From the little shack rose Genia's voice, singing to her baby:

"Round and round the cranes will fly,

Above the gray fields in the sky . . ."

Uncle Peretz waited a while and went away. Friedman's stupid dog fell on him barking, but he didn't lift a hand to chase him away. Hairy feathers whirled around in front of his eyes and sank down, and a flock of startled crows flew out of the foliage of the sycamore tree. They glided through the air cawing loudly.

A week later, when he came home from work, he went up to the roof again. When darkness fell Aunt Yona came out. She waited a while and went back inside. An hour later she came out again. Up above her stood Uncle Peretz. She invited him to come in and eat his supper, but he did not answer her or give her so much as a glance.

The next morning he came down and went to work. In the afternoon he came home and went up to the roof and after that he hardly ever came down again.

The summer intensified and the days lengthened and grew heavy and incandescent. Lizards appeared and the scent of the sycamore trees filled the hot air, together with the smell of the smoke from the fires where cauldrons of laundry were boiling in the yards.

Uncle Peretz grew lean and his skin, burned by the sun, grew dry and hard as parchment. His blue eyes, which were wide and staring, grew increasingly clouded from the smoke and the dust and the bright, glaring light. His hair grew down on his forehead and neck like coarse sheep's wool, tangled with dry leaves and stalks of grass borne on the blazing wind. Sometimes he would suddenly break his silence with a few parched whistles, which sounded as if they were coming out of a cracked reed. Toward evening, in the slow twilight, he looked like a wicked tin bird.

Aunt Yona would emerge from the shack at regular intervals and invite him to come inside and eat. She would coax him gently, in a wheedling voice.

"I'm taking off," Uncle Peretz would finally snap in a dry, threatening voice, and Aunt Yona would say nothing and go dumbly back into the house.

If only she had said something, she thought to herself, or done something when he took her feet between his hands, perhaps everything would have been different. But she had been very tired, and besides, however much she racked her brains she could not think of anything she might have said or done then to please him.

"I'm taking off, I'm taking off," Uncle Peretz would repeat firmly and endlessly to himself, raising his eyes to the depths of the sky, "I'm taking off." And he still could not make up his mind if the sky was the firmament into which one flew or the abyss into which one fell.

He never saw Geula Apter any more. At the beginning he clung to obsessive hopes and her image would accompany him with a terrible pain from which he could find no escape. She accompanied him like an animal, until he could sense even the characteristic smell of her skin and her hair, and he would talk to her and tell her things that he had never told her when they were together. But gradually, as the days went by, her image was torn to pieces, and it grew blurred and disintegrated and disappeared. Now Geula remained to him only as a deed left undone. He despaired without giving in.

And as the summer drew to a close and he was scorched and short of breath, Aunt Yona emerged from the shack holding a bowl full of wholesome leaves and seeds. Her feet were as cold as ever, but her face was warm and there was something fresh and tender in it.

It was their wedding anniversary, forgotten and ignored for years, and from the minute she woke up she was enveloped by a feeling of freedom and festivity, like the feeling of a Sabbath morning at the beginning of spring. She opened the shutters, tidied the room, returned the books to the bookcase, spread a floral cloth on the table, put on her white dress with the red spots, and tied the purple silk scarf around her neck.

"Come down to eat," she invited him in a voice that was gentle without being meek, and looked at him standing there stiff and bitter, surrounded by silver vapors, "Come on, Peretz, come down to eat," and she held out the bowl, and even tapped it with her finger. "Look what I've got for you. Nice seeds. Come down to eat."

Uncle Peretz said nothing, but he lowered his head a little and looked at her in bewilderment, and something in his face seemed to be thawing and acquiescing in great agony.

"Come on, come down to eat, Peretz."

His Adam's apple rose and fell.

"I'm taking off," responded Uncle Peretz stubbornly, but there was a note of supplication in his voice.

Silence fell, broken only by the sound of Aunt Yona tapping twice on the tin bowl without thinking.

"All right, take off," she suddenly blurted out quickly in a frightened but firm voice.

Again there was a silence, in which even the movement of the warm air between the leaves on the mulberry tree was audible. The smell of the sycamores hung heavy and suffocating.

"I'm taking off," repeated Uncle Peretz and raised his head.

"No. Don't take off," Aunt Yona wanted to shout. But she didn't say a word. She just stood looking at him with compassionate, wide-open eyes, eyes that saw the end.

If only she closed them for a moment, perhaps everything would go away like a bad dream.

Uncle Peretz appeared to be hesitating. Something seemed to have slackened inside him. Maybe he was still making up his mind. Only his Adam's apple pointed, sharp as an arrowhead.

Aunt Yona took a step toward him.

"Come. Let's sit down to eat together, Peretz," she wanted to say, "It's our wedding anniversary today," but at that moment Uncle Peretz stretched and quivered slightly. Then he spread out his arms and opened his mouth wide.

The chill crept up from Aunt Yona's feet to her thighs and her back. And more than fear she felt sorrow, sorrow at the waste and sorrow at the ending. But also a kind of relief, like the relief that had filled her on that third day in the week of Passover, when, on their way home, before meeting David Roizman, he had sung for her, "Over the Ocean and Far Away." If only he had said one frank word, the thought crossed her mind, or if he had done one true deed, however cruel and hard and painful, then perhaps he might have been redeemed, even if his redemption lay in sin and suffering.

But Uncle Peretz neither said nor did anything. He refused everything. Stubbornly he raised his head and fixed his eyes, in which there was no more innocence but only dust and ashes, on the empty summer sky, and his face was frantic and haggard and mean. He flapped his arms limply and suddenly, as if pushed by a rude hand, his shadow moved and dived into the yard, which was lower than the firmament and the sycamores and the Persian lilac and the roofs of the shacks and the castor-oil plant, and disappeared into the fine golden sand, which was mixed with dry leaves and dove feathers and pieces of coal left over from the fires.

This happened before the dovecote was pulled down, when a heavy *hamsin* lay over the land.

NOTES

1. The Jewish population of Palestine before the establishment of the State of Israel.

2. Geula, a common first name in Hebrew, means redemption, while Yona, the name of Uncle Peretz's wife, means dove.

The Visit

THE BOOKSELLER HELD OUT Maimonides' *A Guide to the Perplexed*. It was a used copy and he offered it to me for a very low price. But I preferred *Ahitophel's Complete Almanac of Signs and Portents*, which I had come across by chance after browsing at length among the second-hand homiletical and exegetical books and prayer books and other sacred books lying packed in cardboard boxes and piled up in stacks in the courtyard of the building. I had never heard of this book, but its title appealed to me and made me smile. I dipped into it and read a few sentences here and there, paid and emerged into Allenby Street.

It was a hot summer day. The street was full of blinding light and the motionless air was damp and stifling. I glanced at the introduction and found the following: "And if anyone has a question in his heart or a desire, of his own or another's, or if some evil thing has entered his mind, and he is troubled by frightening thoughts, and wishes to set his mind at rest, let him turn to these pages and he will find in them what he seeks. And if anyone wishes to consult this book, let him do so only with pious and serious intent, if he indeed desires to hear a right and true answer to his question."

I smiled to myself. The truth is that I had intended to buy a prayer cycle for the High Holy Days, not in order to pray from it, but to read and study it. At this time I was in the throes of a "return to the fold" of Judaism and it was in this connection that I had begun to dip into the prayer book and devotional literature, and especially to read various articles dealing with the explication of Judaism and the analysis of its revealed and hidden sides, and with endless attempts to get to the bottom of its essential meaning.

At the end of the Carmel Market crowds of perspiring people milled about in the blazing sunshine, filling the road and surrounding the various stalls. There was a smell of spices and pickled herring in the air. I crossed Allenby Street and walked down King George Street. Suddenly it occurred to me to pay a visit to Chaim Leib.

Chaim Leib lived with his family in the Nordiyah quarter, and of all my parents' relatives and *landsleit* he was the one I loved most. His hands were thick and heavy, and there was something wise and shining and full of life in him and everything he did. He loved eating and drinking, reading newspapers, strolling the streets, aimless chats, political arguments, parties in honor of briths and Bar Mitzvahs, weddings, and funerals. He lived in frank enjoyment of the world and at peace with God, in whom he believed, but gladly and without stern fanaticism. Often, when he went to the synagogue, or when he set off to deliver a load of washing in the rickety pram to one of his customers, he would dawdle on the way and only come home after half the day had passed. His wife, Mrs. Dvora, cooked and cleaned the shack and brought up the children with pleas and screams and terrible aggravation, and she also did her husband's work at the mangle while he dallied on his way. And every now and then she would poke her head out of the window and yell without any hope and with the last of her strength into the empty air of the street:

"Chaim Leib!"

I stood in the shade of the sycamore trees opposite "Fort Ze'ev," the Revisionist Party Headquarters, and leafed through the book. I read that: "These are the days on which it is sure and certain and also tried and tested that Moses our master, may he rest in peace, laid down that any man who travels the roads, or who moves goods from place to place, or from house to house, will not profit by it. And if he takes to his bed—he will not rise from it, God forbid. And if he goes to war on them—he will be slain. Even if he is a great warrior. . . ." And a detailed list followed of all the ill-omened days in every month according to the Hebrew calendar. I glanced at the newspaper and saw that today was not one of them.

I knocked on the door of the shack and waited. A feeling of happiness spread through me, mingled with anticipation and longing. I thought of how surprised Chaim Leib would be when he opened the door and of how glad he would be to see me. It was many years since I last visited him at home, and the last time I saw him was two years ago, at Grandmother's funeral. He marched ahead with Mrs. Dvora floating behind him like a still feather, a little beige felt hat on her head. When he passed me he smiled his warm smile and said:

"Don't worry. God doesn't forget anybody."

"My brother, have no fear of those who persecute you without your knowledge, they are full of wiles but fortune smiles on you," caught my eye. I closed the book and knocked again.

The huge sycamore cast a greenish shade. Its trampled fruit lay scattered about, staining the pavement and the street. It gave off a strong scent, recalling sand lots and virgin fields, vineyards and melon patches and Arabs driving donkeys. Once I used to spend a lot of time in this place. Grandmother used to live in a shack not far from here. I used to stand quietly in a corner of the room, which was full of a good smell of starched laundry, and stare at Chaim Leib and the huge wooden mangle moving steadily to and fro. It fascinated me and frightened me with its great rollers and its mysterious power. At any moment I expected a brown devil to jump out of it. Chaim Leib fascinated me. He set the rollers in motion and operated the machine and laughed with his eyes and all the wrinkles of his sunburned face. I knocked a third time and wiped the sweat from my face and neck.

The tarpaper covering the walls of the shack had torn here and there, and the watchmaker from next door had died. His shop had been taken over by a hatter, whom I did not know. In the seedy little display window stood two painted wooden heads. They both wore hats and looked like a pair of dusty English gentlemen. The tinker, Mr. Feldman, had moved, and his shop was locked up. He had a flat nose like a boxer's and he was never properly shaved. His daughter was called Rucha. Like everyone else, the tinker supported the *Hagana*, whereas Chaim Leib supported the right-wing, nationalist *Irgun Zvai Leumi* and denounced the *Hagana* and the *Histadrut* Labor Federation. This used to upset me, and I would tell myself that he was only joking.

The door opened and Chaim Leib stood on the threshold. His brown eyes were sunk deep in their hard sockets and the skin was stretched taut as dry parchment over the cheekbones of his shrunken face. His black beard had gone gray.

"Shalom," I said happily and smiled at him.

He looked at me with dull, lifeless eyes, like the eyes of an old American Indian.

His body gave off an overpowering smell of old age. His stomach had caved in, and his trousers were gathered in pleats around his waist by means of a belt whose end dangled negligently.

"Shalom, Chaim Leib."

He gazed at me blankly, and I saw that he was straining to remember me, but to no avail. I waited for a minute and then I told him my name and my mother's and father's names.

"Ah."

A smile, the shadow of a different smile, appeared on his face for a moment, and he took my outstretched hand in his. His grip was limp and cold. Nothing was left of the old strength and gladness.

"Dvora, a guest," he announced soundlessly when we stepped inside and mentioned my father's name.

I was on the point of correcting him, but refrained from doing so.

The room, which was once big and high and dim, had grown small and light, and the old furniture now seemed disappointingly ordinary. In the corner stood a white, electric mangle.

Mrs. Dvora came in from the kitchen. As always when visitors came she was flustered and she shuffled her slippered feet in agitation. Her wet hands were holding the skin of a chicken's neck, a needle and white thread. When she saw me she shrieked with joy and her long, faded, whey-face lit up. She hurried into the kitchen and came back drying her hands on her apron.

Mrs. Dvora was a tall, long-limbed and slightly stooped woman. For some reason she made me think of a chicken's leg. The blue of her eyes had completely faded and her hair had turned white. She came from a wealthy family, and in her youth she had worn satins and silks and washed her face in lilac milk. Chaim Leib had dragged her to Eretz Yisrael, among the Arabs and the heat and the sand, and nothing was left of her former glory but for the little gold earrings in the lobes of her ears.

We went into the other room and sat at the table.

"How are things with the goyim?" asked Chaim Leib in a brittle voice and smoothed out a wrinkle in the tablecloth. "Your rabbi is the Marxist Meir Yaari if I'm not mistaken?" And he chuckled dryly.

I told him how things were with me.

"And did you lay *tefillin* this morning?" he said with a weak laugh and pulled *Ahitophel's Almanac* out of my hands.

Mrs. Dvora set the table with the bottle of brandy, little glasses of clouded red glass, pieces of pickled herring arranged on a china plate, and home-made onion crackers that she took out of an old Quaker oats tin, which bore the picture of a man with a sunburned face wearing a broad brimmed straw hat.

"Eat your oats," my mother would urge me, "it's good for you. Eat. Hundreds of thousands of children like you are dying of hunger right this minute in India."

We raised our glasses and drank.

"Take a piece of Jewish herring," said Chaim Leib and called me again by my father's name. He himself did not touch the herring, since the doctor had forbidden it.

The conversation proceeded heavily. It dragged along without interest, and all my attempts to arouse him were in vain. I felt disappointed. Even politics didn't interest him. Only once he remarked that everyone would come back to the fold in the end, even Meir Yaari. Behind his shoulders, and behind the net curtains lay King George Street with the sycamore tree and people and cars passing. I remembered that very many years ago I had once seen through this same window an Arab making two bears and a monkey dance in the sand.

"My brother, correct your heart and desist from your double heartedness and turn away from this question which is wicked, for if not—you will regret it," read Chaim Leib without interest from the Almanac.

"Eat, eat," urged Mrs. Dvora, and pushed the onion crackers toward me. "It's good."

"And what is your question?" asked Chaim Leib mockingly, placing his hand on mine.

I giggled and averted my face slightly. I could not bear the smell of his old age.

"Eat, eat," repeated Mrs. Dvora.

The warmth of my hand was draining into his, but it remained cold nevertheless.

"I saw your grandmother wrapped in a fox fur," said Chaim Leib suddenly, "she must have made money in the next world." And a smile crossed his face.

I withdrew my hand carefully and stood up to take my leave. Out of the corner of my eye I caught a glimpse of the picture of the Garden of Eden hanging in its usual place above the sideboard.

In the middle of the picture stood Adam and Eve, both of them young and beautiful, girdles of fig leaves around their waists, holding a pink baby in their hands, with a number of animals in the meadow around them: a lion, a tiger, a lamb, a horse, and a squirrel. On either side, on rising steps, one opposite the other, stood a boy-child and a girl-child, a boy and a girl, a youth and a maid, a man and a woman, and lastly, on top of the steps, an old man and an old woman leaning on their sticks, and above them a kind of flying scroll. I knew what was written on it: "This is the Torah— and this is its reward."

"Go and visit her," said Chaim Leib from where he sat and sniggered.

"Give regards to your mother and father," screeched Mrs. Dvora in her shrill voice as I opened the kitchen door on my way out.

"All right."

I went down two steps and trod in the sand. A sudden space stretched out in front of me, still and brightly lit. It was familiar and strange to my eyes at once. The ruins of a few shacks were scattered about, uprooted and lost and forlorn as refugees from a war. Here and there stood a gate without a fence, a Persian lilac casting its shade on the floor of a vanished room, a single wall, a tap, a collection of old boards and bricks, a tub, a sheet of tin, a cypress tree. And in the distance, suddenly rising into the summer sky, two blocks of high buildings, white as paper.

I took a few steps and turned my head and saw Mrs. Dvora, who was standing at the kitchen window and watching me walk away. I turned back toward the path along which we used to walk to go and visit my grandmother. I could still feel Chaim Leib's hand lying on top of my own.

The old path was still visible, although it had been blurred by sand and weeds and smothered beneath the tangled branches of a mulberry tree growing wild. Once I used to climb this tree with Rucha.

I walked around the mulberry tree and came to the place that had once been the front yard of Grandmother's shack. Here, in this yard, the dovecote built by my grandfather had once stood. He was a Zionist. Next to the dovecote he had laid out a few beds of vegetables.

The shack had disappeared, but by some miracle the blocks upon which the walls had rested had survived, so that the essence of its shape remained stamped in the sand.

I went up to the kitchen. This was a dark cubbyhole, stuck onto the facade of the shack, populated by enamel saucepans, brown walls, black iron frying pans, a salting board and a kneading board, assorted sieves, china plates, a blue teapot, a bronze mortar and pestle, a mincing machine, two kerosene burners, and one deafening primus stove. A large black lock hung on the creaking door, which was made of whitewashed wooden boards.

I stepped into the entrance to the front room. The glass panes in the high door were thick and grainy and they were colored orange and green and a dense honey gold. I stood in the place where the table had once stood, covered with a thick cloth decorated with large flowers. On the right stood the brown cupboard and on top of it two copper candlesticks. In this cupboard Grandmother had hidden during the Second World War when the Italians had dropped a bomb on her. On the eastern wall hung Grandfather's portrait, and next to it the portraits of some other man and woman. The golden sand, which had been hidden under the floorboards all those years, was revealed. It was mixed with broken glass and china, dry leaves and stalks and pieces of coal, which the wind had carried here from the yard.

I stepped through the entrance to the second room. It was smaller than the first and stifling. Its air was saturated with the smell of cushions and feather quilts and mattresses, as if it was never aired. Most of its space was taken up by a big bed and an old sideboard. The walls of the room and its ceiling were distempered a harsh white, but nevertheless it was perpetually dark and unbearably stuffy in there. Now everything was dazzlingly light and spacious. Overhead stretched the wide blue sky, and the castor-oil plant, which had once rested on the wall of the shack, sent its broad leaves into the room—a fresh purple-green. I looked around me for a moment, and then I stepped through the wall and walked away.

Departure

LITTLE BY LITTLE MY grandmother died. Like a strip of brown land, receding from the eyes of the travelers on a ship until it merges into the horizon and disappears into it, so she faded away. And during all that time we continued to keep kosher and separate the milk from the meat.

At the beginning came the fits of weakness, which were accompanied by pallor and shortness of breath and the valerian drops whose sharp smell clung to her and to her clothes and hung in the air of her room. She would put on her reading glasses and drip the brown drops with a trembling hand into a pale green wine glass, counting them in a low, tense voice, as if whispering an incantation to drive away the evil spirits.

Afterward came the coughing. At first it was a slight, insignificant cough, as if a crumb had lodged in her throat. But from day to day the cough grew deeper, more stubborn and troublesome, until in the end it conquered her entirely, with only an occasional and unexpected respite. She would shuffle around the house in her brown slippers, broad as a goose's feet, and cough and cough. She coughed at her prayers too, and also at night, in her sleep. The kindly, red-cheeked Dr Gottlieb would come, smile at her, pat her shoulder affectionately, and the medicines on her bedside table multiplied. And still she pursued her daily round without bitterness, punctiliously and serenely.

Because she slept so lightly, she would wake up even before the ringing of the alarm clock, which she would set every night and place on her bedside table. Slowly and wearily she would raise her gray head from the thick pillow, lift the vast down quilt, and rise from the depths of the mattress in her limp, white nightgown. All of them—the pillow, quilt, and mattress—had been brought from Poland in carts and trains and on board ship and had gone on serving her here as they had served her there, at the end of that distant century. With a careful movement of her hand she would take the clock, wind it, and return it to its regular place on the shelf in the kitchen.

Her son Aaron had given it to her many years ago. It was a tin clock with thin little legs, a ridiculous bell-hat and long hands with ornamental tips, like the tufted letters of an old bible. It was always slow and sometimes it stopped, and Grandmother would shake it like a bottle of medicine to bring it back to life. In addition to telling the time, it was fitted with a gadget that was supposed to switch off the light in her room on Friday nights. But if it failed to do so, she would throw me a rapid glance, and I would do it instead, quickly and as if without her complicity in the act.

The Sabbath prohibitions were of no consequence in my eyes, as they were of none in the eyes of my parents. Nevertheless, I was taken aback by her behavior, and I would wait curiously, with some anxiety and more than a little animosity, to see what God would do. It was clear to me that he did not exist, but at the same time I was still somewhat in awe of him, in the guise of my step-grandfather, my German grandfather who had died in the meantime, who was brown and irascible, who when he was alive had sat in the dim light of the entrance hall on his pharaonic throne, mumbling his prayers, or gulping watery, yellowish soup from an enormous silver spoon, keeping an eye on everything that went on in the house, and aware of the slightest transgression committed in each and every corner of its rooms.

After taking out the chamber pot and washing and praying and tidying her room, she would go out and come home flushed and panting with her shopping, which was barely enough for a bird to live on. The she would sit down at the kitchen table to do her accounts. Meticulously she would set down large figures on the margins of a newspaper, from time to time wetting the point of the indelible pencil with the tip of her tongue. This was invariably a miniscule stub of a pencil, which was kept in the drawer with the *paraveh* cutlery used for dishes that were neither milk nor meat, and which was so small that she could barely get a grip on it with her thick, carpenter's fingers. Concentrating intently she would add up the sums, whispering the numbers to herself in Yiddish as if she were praying, check the result, exclaim at the exorbitant prices, and copy the total into her black notebook. Life had taught her to calculate carefully, to darn old stockings, to peel potatoes with the thinnest parings possible, and to try not to be dependent on other people's favors.

In the early evening she would say her prayers from the brown prayer book, whose pages were the same color as her face. Afterward she would sit in the heavy armchair and read *Ze'enah u-Re'enah*, a pious work of popular biblical exegesis and homiletics in Yiddish, considered particularly suitable for women, or some other book. But sometimes she would still knit things for her grandchildren, patch worn garments, exchange views on politics, give cautious advice, or settle some dispute that had flared up in the house. She did this by means of snatched, whispered conversations that she would conduct, apparently casually, with the different sides in the bathroom, the little storeroom, or the corners of the rooms. In the same way she fought for my brother when he was going out with a divorced woman, causing a great commotion in the house, where divorcées were regarded as distant relatives of whores. Grandmother saw nothing wrong with it. In her own way she was a free woman in her world.

In the evenings she would entertain guests, read the Labor Party newspaper *Davar*, or brown copies of the Yiddish weekly the *Amerikaner*, or else she would write letters to her son and faceless sister, Idel, in America.

All her life, until the appearance of the ballpoint pen, she wrote with an old-fashioned wooden pen, dipping the long thin nib in an ink pot and blotting the ink with blotting paper. The pen lay in the table drawer next to the ink pot, the writing pad, the air-mail cards, the reading glasses, the calendar, the long hairpins, the mirror, the brown comb and the red chocolate box in which she kept her Sabbath wig.

She lived with her belongings in great economy and intimacy, reserving to each its proper place and time and use, like objects in the performance of a rite.

From day to day she faded. Like a chick inside an egg death grew inside her, while she herself shrank. A permanent flush bloomed palely on her sagging cheeks, whose flesh was the color of clay, and suddenly her coughing stopped. Now she passed through the rooms without a sound, the nostrils of her broad nose like the two halves of an empty walnut, and her clever eyes, which had sunk deep into their sockets, grew very wide and strained, with a strange, baffled stare. And still she went on salting the meat, cooking her meals in little enamel saucepans, doing her accounts, dragging herself to the Rabbi with her questions, lighting Sabbath candles, quoting old proverbs, spitting to the right and the left against the evil eye, trapping roaches in bits of newspaper, and hurrying, gritting her teeth in disgust, to throw them into the lavatory and pull the chain. Sometimes she would still even sing little songs in Yiddish and Polish in a dry, hollow voice, smiling a weary smile as she sang. It seemed that in spite of everything she was glad to be alive.

Her friends kept on coming. The wealthy Mrs. Abeles, her heavy face shadowed by elegant hats smothered in flowers or embellished with feathers and net veils, who filled the house with her loud, rough voice, hoarse as a cigar-smoker's. Old Leibshu Krupp with his tanned face, who wore a bowler hat, guffawed coarsely from time to time, and noisily slurped glasses of black, boiling tea, breaking the sugar cubes between his strong teeth. On every visit without fail he would repeat the tale of the two widows, one of whom he wished to marry, only he could not make up his mind between the one who owned the kiosk and the one who owned the orange grove.

Grandmother refused to give her opinion in this matter, just as she preferred to say nothing in response to the stories of Shmuel Zilberbaum, who would turn up at intervals like a fresh spring breeze, wearing an old striped suit with a spotless handkerchief in the breast pocket, a large ring on his finger, and milk-white shoes with holes punched in them on his feet. He would sit on the edge of his chair, drum on the table with a white finger, and hold forth to her on his business affairs and his chances of making a fortune from stocks and shares and land speculations and currency deals. Grandmother's reaction was reserved. She rejected such feats of financial wizardry, which bordered, she felt, on fraud. And she didn't believe in them either, just as she didn't believe in lotteries or miracles and suspected anything that smacked of the supernatural.

Among those who came to see her were also the synagogue treasurer, the gardener, the grocer, the *landsleit* from the old country, neighbors and members of the family. But the one who came most of all was Mrs. Chernbroda.

She was a busybody of a woman, skinny as a thorn and sprightly as a grasshopper, dressed in frocks of thin black silk. They would sit side by side, Grandmother with her broad face, and Mrs. Chernbroda with her sparrow's face, and conduct long, peaceful conversations.

Now Grandmother no longer went out, not even to the synagogue. But the calendar of significant days and the deeds appropriate to them—holy days, birthdays, anniversaries of the deaths of brothers and parents and grandparents—continued to be observed.

And on Fridays, after setting the table in her room with the two glass candlesticks, which were decorated with colored crystals, and after covering the plaited challah loaf with its pink silk cloth, she would get dressed in her Sabbath dress and sit down to put on her wig. She did this with serene concentration and a ceremonious air, repeatedly examining her face in the mirror. When she had finished, she would wind the clock, put it in its place, and bless the candles. And then it was Sabbath.

Afterwards they took her to the hospital, and she was already very small. From there she was transferred to the sanatorium. One day my mother came home carrying a bundle of clothes, brown slippers, a few copies of the *Amerikaner*, a pen, two air-mail cards, a calendar, a prayer book, reading glasses, hairpins, and a picture of the family.

When we came home from the cemetery we sat in the kitchen and my mother served tea. A number of friends and relations came and sat with us. There was a feeling of weariness and emptiness, but also of relief. It seemed as if we had all come back from the docks, after seeing off a departing member of the family. It was all over. The radio spoke, someone read the evening paper, my mother set the tea on the table, and people spoke quietly to each other. From time to time they mentioned Grandmother, but as if she were someone who had set off on a long voyage from which she would return. After all, she had left all her belongings here.

No rites of mourning took place and the days passed without being counted off from the day of her death. Grandmother's room remained open and we went in and out of it as when she was alive. All the furniture, clothes, and other things remained where they were. And so did the meat-salting board, the old china jug in which, and only in which, she made the Sabbath raisin wine, and the tin clock that stood perpetually at twenty to eleven, since nobody had bothered to wind it after she was taken to the hospital.

One day Mrs. Chernbroda appeared and took away Grandmother's clothes and bedclothes to distribute to the needy. Two floral silk dresses, a coat, a thick woollen scarf, and the knitted bag in which she used to carry her reading glasses and her prayer book to the synagogue, Mother gave to the Yemenite maid, who had been in the habit of leaving part of her wages with Grandmother in order to save something from her drunken husband. Her purse and towels she gave to a poor old man. He used to call on Grandmother at regular intervals and she used to give him milk soup, rusks, tea, and fruit. Now he announced that he would pray for the elevation of her soul. The candlesticks and the pink silk challah cover were taken by Mrs. Abeles.

A few months later the pillow and quilt, the bed and armchair and brown wardrobe were sold for a song. The account books, together with the old receipts, the certificates attesting to donations made to yeshivas and orphanages, the prayer book, the knitting needles, the balls of wool, the scraps of cloth and needles and thread in the old tin tea caddy with the picture of the sailing ship on its lid, were piled up untidily on the table standing in the middle of the room.

This was a heavy, dark brown, oval table with carved legs and an expression of stern antiquity. Worn carvings of tendrils and flowerets also embellished the two austere wooden chairs that stood beside it, like two loyal bodyguards, the dark, eroded remnants of a defeated army. There was something strange and foreign about them that belonged to another century, to the remote country towns whose peculiar names fell so naturally from Grandmother's lips, together with the names of vanished relatives and kinsmen, of rabbis, Emperors and lords. There she had been a child and there she had married her first, beloved husband, and her second husband too. There she had lifted heavy bolts of cloth, measured with a tape measure, felt with her fingers, traveled days and nights in carts and steaming trains, bargained humiliatingly in fairs to save a few zlotys, given birth to children, concealed bread baked from potato skins under her clothes when pogroms broke out against the Jews and wars raged about her unsuspecting head. There she saw squires and communists and preachers and the German soldiers of Kaiser Wilhelm, who treated her politely and gallantly, and even gave a big doll to her daughter, my mother.

Mr. Zinger came to take the table and chairs. He smoked a cigarette, stroked the table with a callused hand, and said with satisfaction: "Very nice. Very nice."

He meant the wood.

Two workmen carried it all downstairs, and my mother took the opportunity to get rid of all the worthless objects. In the room, which grew very big and full of light, all that was left was the bedside table, upon which reposed the prayer book and the red chocolate box, and the big portrait of Grandmother hanging on the wall in a dull gold frame, which was already peeling here and there.

In the portrait she appears seated in her dark Sabbath dress, one hand resting serenely on the arm of the chair and the other on her knee, the Sabbath wig on her head, and a serious, formal expression on her face. Thus she sat now and looked down from the heights of the wall on her empty, light-filled room.

That year we did not hold a Passover *seder*. This involved some doubts and a certain feeling of uneasiness, but the nuisance of making the house kosher and all the other preparations tipped the scale against it. We ate a big meal, and everyone went about his business. The special Passover dishes—all kinds of bowls and jugs and pots of clay and copper and iron, vast plates and cups of white china rimmed with blue and gold, old silver forks and knives and spoons, ladles, salting boards and pastry boards, blue kettles and black pans—all these remained stored away in the entresol, packed in sacks and big wicker chests, pirate chests locked with black locks.

But at the end of summer, when some modest renovations were made on the apartment, my father went up to the entresol and brought down the dishes. Most of them were sold, but a few were added to the everyday household stock. Among them were some pots and jars, the Prophet Elijah's goblet, and the basin for ritual hand washing, which was now used for soaking small items of laundry.

At the same time Grandmother's room was whitewashed and refurnished with light, pale furniture. Only her portrait remained hanging on the wall as before. On the opposite wall my brother hung photographs of horse races and car races, which he cut out of magazines.

In the meantime the milk and meat dishes were mixed up. The change took place as if of its own accord, and without anyone being able to stop it. In the period immediately following her death we were careful to observe all the dietary laws, just as we had done when she was alive, but gradually our meals became mixed, and we even began eating forbidden foods. At the same time, however, we were careful to eat meat from the meat dishes and milk from the milk dishes, but not for long. Convenience overcame the old customs, which no longer seemed to have any point. And besides, most of the old metal utensils were found in the course of time to be clumsy and impractical, while the china kept breaking. I myself dropped the splendid dish meant to hold herring. On its lid reposed a plump, amazingly lifelike herring, which never failed to arouse my admiration. It was Grandfather who had brought Grandmother this dish from Leipzig, which he had once visited on a business trip. In place of all these dishes now came utensils of glass and stainless steel and plastic, which had never been either milk or meat. They were light, handsome, and elegant as bridegrooms. Among them one could still come across the occasional old fork, big as a pitchfork, or tremendous soup spoon, the curve of its bowl reminiscent of the belly of a plump fish cast up on dry land. They put me in mind of rejected poor relations, and gave me an uneasy feeling, as if we had tricked Grandmother in her absence.

The first anniversary of her death passed unmarked. It passed like any other day of the week and like all the anniversaries of the deaths of vanished grandmothers and grandfathers and uncles whose names we bore and who, ever since Grandmother's death, had been torn from the calendar too and wiped out completely. And the same thing happened to Mrs. Abeles and Leibshu Krupp and the synagogue treasurer and a number of the *landsleit*, who stopped coming to our house and were forgotten. And the same thing happened to the unfortunate Aunt Idel. As soon as Grandmother stopped writing letters to her in Buffalo, her fate was sealed and she vanished into thin air without anyone taking any notice.

But my mother remembered the day and so did Mrs.

Chernbroda. She called on us early in the evening, sat in the kitchen, drank tea, and conversed calmly with my mother. The tin clock was still standing on the shelf, its hands pointing, as usual, to twenty to eleven of the day or night of some unknown date. As they spoke my mother remembered the Sabbath wig, which she had hidden at the bottom of the wardrobe.

Mrs. Chernbroda took the wig, together with the red chocolate box. My mother wished her "To a hundred and twenty," and she smiled, thanked her, and left.

And one day, a few years later, I was rummaging in the bookcase when my eye suddenly fell on a thick, brown book. I took it out and saw that it was the old prayer book. I turned the rough pages and felt the special smell, the smell of old books, which reminded me of the smell of my grandmother sitting on the stool in the kitchen, the brown woollen shawl around her shoulders and the faintest of smiles on her face. When I was about to close the prayer book I saw that there was something written in ink on the white page preceding the title page. And this is what was written there in Grand-mother's handwriting:

Yaarzeit fun Tatte z"l—16 tog in Tammuz
Yaarzeit fun die Mamme z"l—10 tog in Elul
Yaarzeit fun Aaron z"l—yom D" ba Hanukka

I strained my memory to remember the date of her death, but all I could remember was that it was a cold, cloudy day.

The Czech Tea Service

When the lodger informed us that he was about to leave, we were upset. At that time we lived in tight quarters, cramped and depressing, in a state of disarray and despair, despite my father's many talents and notwithstanding the enormous effort he invested in work that drained all his energy. The management's pettiness, short-sightedness and lack of decency, coupled with his own integrity and pride, prevented him (as he saw it) from achieving the position and material success he deserved, a fact which made him extremely bitter. Still, he kept expecting that this cycle would be broken, that the situation would improve. This change was slow in coming; for the time being my grandparents lived in one of the rooms, surrounded by ramparts of old brown furniture, while my parents and I lived in the other, surrounded by ramparts of green furniture wedged together in front of a heavy black buffet looking like an exile from some ruined mansion. My uncle had acquire the buffet through some special circumstance and passed it on to use when he emigrated to America. There was also another small room, which we rented out.

The lodger was a pleasant young man who kept his room clean and was prompt with the rent. He was rarely in and, even when he was, his room seemed empty. His door, which was usually kept shut, would then open briefly, unpredictably. Wearing a coarse blue sweater and work trousers streaked with tar, he would cross the hall cautiously, say a timid "goodbye" and leave for his job in the port.

On the last evening, after packing his sparse belongings, he came into the kitchen and, with a shy smile, handed my father a large parcel wrapped in brown paper, blurting out: "It's for you."

"For us?" Father asked, baffled and somewhat resistant.

My mother and grandmother seconded his response.

"I enjoyed staying here," the lodger explained, blushing. He fidgeted with the thick silver snake ring that adorned his finger.

"It wasn't necessary," Father protested. "It really wasn't necessary to spend so much money," he added, placing the package on the table, reluctantly. "Have a seat," he said. "Have a seat," a benign smile spreading over his face.

Though he didn't consider himself, or any other member of his household, worthy of a present and he backed away from the slightest trace of ingratiation or charity, this attention, which was straight and honest, seemed to please him.

Mother backed up his protestations; but at the same time, she offered the lodger a chair and put water on to boil.

"Won't you have some tea?"

"I'm in a hurry," the lodger said, meaning to conclude this transaction quickly, but, yielding to pressure, he settled uneasily on the edge of the stool.

Untying the string carefully, Father opened the package; Mother and Grandmother followed his every move as if he was a magician. When he lifted the top, we saw, poking out of the carton, the rims of teacups and saucers, the top of a china pot, deep in a bed of white fluff, wrapped like an etrog on Sukkot. What an amazing sight! All of us, except for the lodger, naturally, expressed wonder and admiration.

"You shouldn't have spent so much money," father said, his tanned face beaming as he carefully lifted one of the cups out of its wrapping. He himself never gave a thought to price when buying a gift, being generous, endowed with good taste and an instinct for quality.

"They gave me a good price," the lodger admitted, not knowing whether to join in the round of exclamations. He blushed again, his gaze moving back and forth restlessly, like a dog's tail.

Father picked up the cup, examined it, tapped it with mock expertise, turned it over and read from its underside.

"Made in Czechoslovakia," he announced respectfully, passing the cup to my mother who accepted it nervously, as if there were no choice.

"Czech china is even better than the German kind," Grandmother pronounced, as her thick fingers moved over the cup. "Remember the Rosenthal service Grandfather brought back from Danzig?"

"Yes," Mother answered, putting down the cup gingerly as if she were afraid it would melt in her hands.

"I thought a tea service would be useful," the lodger said, still apologetic.

"Of course," mother assured him. And to erase any lingering doubt, she added: "We really had nothing nice enough for company." She directed the words to herself as well, perhaps mainly to herself, for together with the pleasure was a note of worry, even dissatisfaction, resigned as she was to her fate.

Slowly, deliberately, as if in a ritual, Father took the

pieces of china out of the box and handed them, one by one, to Mother, who set them out on the table. They handled the service with awe, reverence and care, continuing to marvel at its beauty. It was truly lovely and exquisitely delicate. The china itself was pure white; the cups and saucers had a design in shades of brown, red and blue, depicting a rural scene with small cottages nestled amidst mountains and lakes. The teapot soared above the other pieces like a tower of ivory, its pure aristocratic lines topped by a blue knob made of rubber bristles with little red balls at their tip. The blue knob was attached to the lid of the teapot by a thin rubber thread.

"Use it well and break it in good health," Grandmother said cheerfully.

Mother cleared some books from the top shelf of the buffet and the tea service was put in their place. Everyone watched as father placed each piece. His fine sense of form expressed itself in a passion for perfection. There was a dark and menacing aspect to this passion—any random error, any accident, any imperfection could set him off, unleashing violent rage, as if the entire world was at stake. When he finished, he carefully closed the glass door of the buffet and everyone returned to the kitchen to drink tea in our everyday glasses.

We now had a Czech tea service in the house. From its position on a dinghy shelf in a room stuffed with clumsy furniture, it made its presence felt throughout the house, much like a king in some small village, creating a mood of festivity and drama. With the exception of my mother, who from time to time would dust the pieces with a soft towel, no one dared to touch the service. It was being kept for a special occasion which was sure to arise before long, surrounded by a special aura reserved for holy objects, crowns, the sort of royal regalia that is displayed in museums. Now and then some member of the household or some guest would have a look at it and come away enchanted, singing its praises.

I was especially enchanted by the teapot and, in particular, by the rubber ball on its lid. I was tempted to touch it, play with it. Now and then I did approach the greenish glass and look through it longingly, but didn't dare make a further move, being fully aware of the prohibitions attached to it.

But, one Friday, I could no longer contain myself. I came home from school and went to put away my satchel. As usual on Fridays, I felt free and relaxed and, as I peered into the dimness of the buffet, the tea service seemed to become a storybook village made of sugar, nestled in the shadow of an ivory tower with a tantalizing ball at its tip.

"I'll just touch it," I assured myself.

Grandma was busy tidying her room and Mother was making gefilte fish for Shabbat. The rhythmic beat of the chopper filled the house.

I agonized a bit longer and then, very nervously, inched toward the buffet, slid open the glass door that enclosed the holy of holies and reached for the blue knob, saying to myself over and over, that I would merely touch it. And, in fact, that is what I did. I stroked it carefully, touched it with my finger, pressed it lightly. I was not disappointed. The ball was pliant and pleasant to my touch. I pressed it again and again; then, as I pulled at it, the lid began to rise and, as I released it, it closed with a mellow tinkle that delighted me. I did this again and again so I could hear that delightful sound.

The door bell rang and my mother stopped chopping to go to the door. I quickly let go of the knob, the lid closed and, to my horror, shattered. Just like that . . . suddenly, lightly, with the same delicate tinkle.

For an instant I was paralyzed, unable to believe my eyes. Then I grasped the scale of the disaster, pictured the retribution that would surely follow and, feeling on the brink of an abyss, was overwhelmed with panic and weak with fear. I made an effort, though my hands faltered, to collect the fragments and stick them together. I hoped that if I hurried I would succeed. But it was no use. I put back the dangling knob, closed the glass, took out a book, paper, a pencil and quietly sat down at the table.

A neighbor had come in to ask Mother a question. They stood in the kitchen for a while, talking. Grandmother joined the conversation. I heard the shuffle of her slippers as she went back to her room. Then the neighbor left, closing the door and the chopper was back in action.

He'll kill me, I thought, and a bitter sob began to form in my throat as I pictured my father's face, distorted with rage. Beyond the small window I saw a blue strip of sky; the voices of children playing ball in our yard rose above the sound of the chopper. I picked up my pencil, opened my exercise book, but could do nothing. I sat, like a block of stone, wishing I was an orphan, motherless, fatherless, a street child; I began to consider running away, which brought tears of helplessness and impotence to my eyes. I knew I would never run away; I wanted to die.

The chopper was silent and my mother called. I went to the kitchen wishing she would notice that the light had gone out of my eyes, and that she would see how frightened and weak I was, abject and full of regret—even though I knew that all was lost and it was not in her power to save me. I felt alone, abandoned, wished for some dreadful disease, for that alone might be grounds for compassion. My mother handed me a list, a basket, and sent me to the store.

"He's such a good boy today," Grandmother remarked when I came back and put the basket on the table. "Come, help me close my shutters."

I did as she asked, then crept back into the other room. There had been no miracle. The lid of the teapot was as shattered as when I had left, and the storybook village looked pathetic.

"Come and eat," called my mother. I went to the kitchen and sat down.

Life went on as if no disaster had occurred.

"It's good," Mother said, offering her usual testimonial as she produced a dish filled with brown noodles that looked like seaweed floating in milk dark with brown sugar. It must have revolted her as much as it revolted me, but she repeated, with emphasis: "Eat, it's very good." Though her face and her voice expressed great enthusiasm, she was mobilized for a spoon by spoon battle.

I ate the foul brew without so much as a peep of protest.

"What's the matter with you?"

"Nothing."

"You're not well?" she asked, feeling my forehead.

"No." And after a brief silence I blurted out: "The teapot."

"What?"

"The teapot. From the Czech service."

She stared at me and, at first, did not understand. Then she wiped her hands on her apron and rushed to the other room. A second later she returned, her face pale and distraught.

"How did it happen?" she asked, not expecting an answer.

Grandmother appeared from her room. Like an old hunting dog she could always smell trouble. Now she was our only hope.

She asked what had happened. Mother led her to the other room. After a few minutes they were back in the kitchen. Mother and I fixed our eyes on her, hoping for salvation though, in our hearts, we both knew there could be none.

"It's not so terrible," Grandma finally offered. "After all," she added, tightening her kerchief on her head, "it is only the lid. Everything breaks sooner or later," she reasoned, reassuringly, though her face registered deep worry.

The silence was intense and absolute; a deadly silence filled with fear. Mother went back to her cooking and Grandma wrapped herself in her brown woollen shawl. Everyone withdrew into a corner to wait, passively and in terror, for justice to be done. From time to time the quiet would be broken by footsteps or a brief exchange between my mother and grandmother who spoke in lowered voices as if there had been a death in the house.

Father's heavy footsteps sounded in the stairwell. I was overcome by a paralyzing fear. I could barely move a limb. The door opened and he came in, his presence permeating the house. With his last ounce of strength he was carrying a bundle of wooden planks held together by a rusty tie.

"Hello," he muttered in a hollow voice, breathing heavily and heading for the bathroom.

I could hear him taking apart the bundle of wood, undoing his tie, breaking the planks with his powerful legs so they would fit in the stove.

"The kerosene."

I brought him the tin and stood by, hoping he would pat me on the head, favor me with at least a glance. He bent down to arrange the wood, poured some kerosene over it and lit the fire. The flame flared up, illuminating his sweaty face so that it glistened in the firelight, hardened by fatigue, inscrutable. He straightened up, handed me the kerosene tin, took off his heavy shoes, sat down at the kitchen table. The sounds of crackling wood and whispering fire filled the house.

"What's new?" he asked matter-of-factly as he began to slurp his soup, eyes fixed on the newspaper. I stared at him with terror and yearning. I thought I detected a gentle note in his voice.

"Nothing," Mother mumbled, hiding her head among the pots.

Grandma was scurrying about like a frightened goose. She still seemed to be trying to find grounds for a reprieve.

Father pushed away the empty bowl and mother brought him some chicken. With strong fingers he tore the joints apart; he bit into the meat, chewed it and when he was finished began gnawing at the bones with great concentration and vigor. He cracked the bones, sucked out the marrow and finally chewed them to a pulp.

"Did something happen?" he suddenly asked, spitting out the mush.

No one answered.

"What happened?" he asked again, this time pointedly, wiping his forehead with the dishcloth.

"Did something happen?" He directed the question to my mother, who was bringing him a bowl of fruit compote. Playing for time, hoping at least to delay the confrontation, she ignored his question and tried to behave in an ordinary manner. But he did not relent. He repeated his question, this time with annoyance.

"The teapot," Mother said timidly, looking like a trapped animal.

"The teapot?" Father cried, flinging the chicken bone on to the plate. "The one from the set?"

Mother nodded. She wanted to say something more, something comforting, but he shoved away the table, spilling the compote and, wiping his hands on his trousers, rushed into the other room.

Though I wanted to escape, I remained seated, paralyzed, as if in a nightmare. I knew there was no way out; that I would have to endure the punishment that was about to be meted out by a man who aroused such great terror in me, and for whom I felt only fierce enmity.

"How did it happen?" he shouted to my mother in a strangled voice when he came back from the other room, banging the door violently. His face was transformed beyond recognition.

Mother muttered something unintelligible.

"How did it happen?" He continued shouting at the top of his lungs, pounding the door and the table again and again. His face was pale and a hostile glare lit up his eyes.

I bowed my head while Mother looked on at a total loss.

Mother muttered something else and even made a faint, desperate gesture, as if to restrain him, her face ashen. "You keep out of it," he yelled, pulling me toward him savagely. "Why did you do it?" he shouted, and slapped my hand, his face turning white with fury. "You're wrecking my house!" he shrieked desperately, slapping me again. "You want me to die!" He seized me by the shirt and shook me, continuing with his torrent of rage. "Why did you do it? Tell me. Why?" Then he let go.

"I'll teach you to break things," he snarled with suppressed fury and all at once the chaos subsided and silence prevailed, absolute and ceremonial, broken only by his footsteps as he made his was to the closet in which he kept his belts.

Grandma peered out of her room. She was distraught and angry.

"I'll be off to the place where the black peppers grow," she intoned in Yiddish and shut her door. I didn't make a move. I was waiting for him to come and get me. Mother stood in a corner in the kitchen, her back to the doorway, her head between her hands.

He returned holding a heavy leather belt. His face was hard and foam flecked the corners of his mouth. He grabbed me by the arm and dragged me into the narrow hallway.

"I'll teach you to wreck the house," he whispered under

his breath as he swung the belt. I fell to the floor and he struck the first blow.

"Take this," he whispered with every blow. "And this . . ." His face was cruel and wild.

"Not on his head," Mother implored from the doorway. "Not on his head." He didn't hear her.

"Take this. And this." The black belt swung up and down in a regular rhythm, as if wielded by a man possessed.

Light from the stove in the bathroom flickered through the doorway. Yellowish-black flames shone on Father's face and on the hallway wall, filling the air with the warmth and scent of fire, the crackle of burning wood, an occasional sharp sputtering retort.

He stopped. Perhaps because his strength had ebbed. He dropped the belt and walked away, his footsteps heavy. Again there was total silence, inertia, dejection.

After a minute Mother came in. She didn't dare approach me. She stood at the end of the hall, looking at me without uttering a word, and left. My entire body ached. I crawled to the porch and curled up in a corner.

"Let him die," I muttered to myself. "Let him die."

I sat close to the wall crying softly, bitter sobs of injury, pain, insult, that brought a measure of relief: justice had been done and the crisis was over.

My mother sat down in the kitchen while Father, still in his work clothes, was stretched across the bed like the carcass of an animal. No one stirred, no one uttered a sound. From the yard came the sounds of children, the twitter of birds building their nests on trees and water gurgling in the pipes. The sun was setting and an evening gray began to swirl across the blue sky. The house was slowly enveloped in dusk.

"Let him die," I repeated, without a shred of compassion, the slight evening chill making me shudder.

I crossed my arms, bent my legs and drew them up to my

chest. A great cloud drifted over the house from the west. Slowly, a giant arm with no hand seemed to extend from the cloud, disconnect and vanish. I stopped crying and lowered my head on to my knees. Under me the floor became damp and warm, a warmth that gave me comfort. Father now seemed like a heap of blankets and Mother had turned black, disintegrated, blending discreetly with the spreading dusk. I lay in the warm wetness feeling desolate but, at the same time, cosy and comfortable. In my head, I heard a song Mother used to sing to me as she laced my shoes when I was a baby. Though it was a gay Polish song, she used to sing it sadly. The great cloud hovered over our roof, very close, hiding the sky, I closed my eyes and the song repeated itself, endlessly, in the total darkness. I thought about the words, but hard as I tried I couldn't understand them. Then they fell apart in my mind and became random syllables I could play with in a state of semi-sleep until, after a while, they organized themselves again into a single quiet murmur, with no end.

Grandmother's door suddenly opened, filling the entrance with yellow light. I opened my eyes and saw her in her best black dress, standing near the table which was covered with a white Shabbat cloth, her broad back facing the doorway. She was lighting the candles, swaying as she sang the blessing. When she was finished, she said, as usual, in a festive voice: "Shabbat shalom," and sat down.